MY PROBLEM HAD NOW BECOME THE WORLD'S PROBLEM

I pictured children everywhere waking up Christmas morning to trees with no presents underneath. Or broken presents at best. The devastation Rudy must have felt, was still feeling all these years later, when he lost Christmas—I multiplied that by a billion. The world would surely stop turning under the weight of all that sadness.

And yet I couldn't help flushing with warm memories of that night in his sturdy arms under the Northern Lights.

What was it she'd said? *You will come to know of my power in time.*

"I think I know who can help," I shouted. "You stay here."

If my instincts were right, the one person on Earth who could help me summon the very power that Christmas now needed was the boy who hated Christmas the most. Our only hope was for me to find Rudy and make him forgive me, so together we could bring back the Snow Angel.

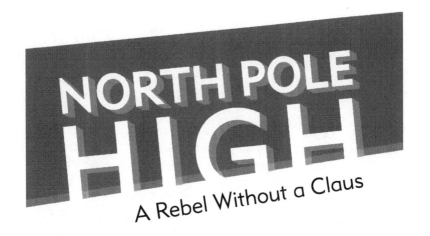

NORTH POLE HIGH

A Rebel Without a Claus

A memoir by

Candace Jane Kringle

elfpublished books

SANTA'S WORKSHOP ∗ THE VILLAGE OF THE NORTH POLE

elfpublished books
a division of Santa's Workshop
The Village of the North Pole

ISBN: 978-0615681917
First Printing, October 2012

Cover and interior designed by Jessica Weil
jayelleay.com

FOR KNUT

2006 - 2011

NORTH POLE HIGH

A Rebel Without a Claus

DAYLIGHT

"Thou and I will see him dine when we bear him thither."
- J.M. Neale

one

Don't get me wrong. I love my dad. Just not the way the rest of the world loves him.

He's not really all that holly-jolly the rest of the year. Someone once asked me if I get presents every day because of who my dad is. That's a laugh!

I'm not saying he's a bad guy. He just doesn't get me. I mean, he's great with kids and all. No question about it. But I'm *sixteen*. I'm becoming a woman. And Daddy's having a tough time with that. I imagine it's like that with most dads. Why should mine be any different?

So it's not like I blame him or anything. I'm just saying, if he would have let me be me, none of this would have happened.

But first, a couple things I have to get out of the way right from the start. I get a lot of letters asking all kinds of questions about how my dad slides down chimneys and stuff like that. Sorry, but that's *his* business. You'll have to wait for him to write his own book. This is *my* story. People don't understand what it's like growing up in this family. Sure, there's a lot of love and magic and joy. But I'm really just like everybody else.

The other thing I need to make clear up front is: If you're one of those people who thinks my dad doesn't exist, you might as well stop reading now. This isn't one of *those* stories. I've known the guy for sixteen years. Believe me, he exists.

Now back to how this whole catastrophe started. Or rather, how it could have been avoided. After all, I begged my father not to make me go to that stupid Welcoming Feast.

It was still Daylight time—the beginning of the school year,

3

before the setting of the midnight sun would plunge us into six months of darkness. Not dark darkness. Not Gothic vampire darkness or dystopian darkness. As a matter of fact, the Dark season up here is actually quite pretty, for obvious reasons. All the colorful lights, the sleigh bells ringing, the twinkling stars. It's kind of amazing.

Anticipating all the coming glad tidings, I skipped down Gingerbread Lane—yes, I literally skipped home that day. I know. Pretty dorky. But when you're sixteen, you still get to be a kid even when you're in that desperate rush to grow the heck up.

Anyway, I slipped in through the side door of the unassuming A-frame at the end of the quiet, snow-covered cul-de-sac and quickly pulled off my maroon moon boots. I hung my candy-cane-striped coat on my special candy-cane hook in the mudroom—candy canes are my namesake and style—then continued skipping merrily into the kitchen.

Chefy stood hunched over the twelve-burner cast-iron stove. He craned his thick neck, pointing his pencil-thin beak at me, the corners of his mouth curling into something close to a smile as he stirred something delectable in a five-gallon pot. "There's my little princess. Was your teacher duly impressed with your lovely little heart?"

Chefy gets me.

He was referring, of course, to the heart-shaped bauble I'd turned in for Ornaments class. Was it any wonder I sometimes felt more like Chefy's little princess than my dad's? I couldn't remember the last time Daddy had shown an interest in my homework, or even knew what classes I was taking. I doubted he even knew my friends' names.

Last year, I asked Daddy if Snowflake could come with us on the mall tour.

4

"This is a business trip, Candy. We can't have outsiders," he'd said.

Outsiders? You'd think he didn't know that Snowflake and I had been best friends since preschool. Sure, he knows if all of you have been bad or good, but he was sometimes pretty darn clueless when it came to his own daughter.

Come to think of it, that wasn't always such a bad thing. I got away with a lot. And it wasn't like he had to worry about me becoming some kind of 'toehead or something. I always got good grades.

"I got an A-super-plus," I answered Chefy.

The seven-foot-tall penguin frowned and said, "Shall I call that polar bear and demand he give you an A-super-*duper*-plus?"

LOL! He would do it too.

"Oh, Chefy. That won't be necessary. I'll just have to try harder next time."

Chefy laughed and patted me on the head with a flipper while his other flipper slid a plate of baked candy canes, fresh out of the oven, under my still-frosty nose. Yum.

Daddy had originally brought Chefy up from the bottom for his legendary culinary talents. But he'd become so much more than just a chef to us. He was Daddy's right hand. Not in the Workshop, mind you. Chefy would never have anything to do with that toy stuff, thank you very much. However, he did basically run our household. Even so, he never liked being thought of as anything other than the best chef in the North Pole.

And he truly was. Take this after-school treat melting in my mouth, for example. It wasn't just that Chefy had thought to take vine-ripened candy canes and wrap them in extra-virgin gingerbread dough. He had to wake up hours before the rest

5

of the family to handpick the juiciest canes from that garden he'd cultivated in the custom-built greenhouse he designed himself. He wouldn't have it any other way. There was simply no limit to the pride Chefy took in his creations.

As that warm, gooey goodness slid down my throat, I hungered for the many other wondrous delicacies whose indescribable aromas made my tummy rumble like a glacial avalanche. Then it hit me. White-chocolate truffles on the cob? Lollipops in taffy fondue? Marzipan-glazed turkey stuffed with bubblegum? There was way too much food here for just our family.

Chefy was preparing the Welcoming Feast—*for that new kid!*

two

"Now class, I am super happy to announce that I am giving you all As on your ornaments," Mr. Polar Bear had said a few hours earlier.

The eight-and-a-half-foot-tall shaggy white bear had to stoop to attach our homework to the naked, cardboard-cutout Christmas tree that stood on a tiny easel next to his desk. Some of my classmates turned red with embarrassment as they watched their ornament join the collection, perhaps feeling their work wasn't as good as the others. But one by one, our sparkly treasures beautified that silly facsimile until it suddenly shone as Christmassy as a real tree!

When finished, Mr. Polar Bear stepped aside and smiled with pride at his new charges as we applauded ourselves. But, as only two of us knew, one ornament was still missing.

"Class, this year there is one team I am giving an A-super-plus," Mr. PB said.

Johnny Toboggan, Silentnight, and Sugarcookie scanned their twenty classmates, trying to figure out whose ornament had yet to be presented. By then, the rest of the class had already guessed and turned directly toward me and my gloating boyfriend, Tinsel. I sent them back a grin that I hoped conveyed modest surprise and appreciation even though I had become accustomed to standing out in class ever since kindergarten, when I could recite the names of all eight of Daddy's reindeer backward and forward.

Tinsel, on the other hand, slapped high-fives with Elation and Cookiejar even before Mr. Polar Bear unveiled our shimmering dazzler.

I had come up with the idea to take two candy canes, natch, and join them into the shape of a heart. Then Tinsel and I added a few creative ingredients to make our shiny heart beat like a living, breathing instrument of love.

"This is the most magnificent Christmas tree ornament I have ever seen. Candycane, Tinsel, would you like to share your thoughts about your... I'm sorry, I can't seem to think of another word for it... *magnificent* work with the rest of the class?"

I'd never seen a polar bear cry before that moment. I bet no one ever had. Polar bears don't cry. But this one did. Just one little watery drop that formed in his dark brown eye. He wiped it away with the side of his paw before it could fall.

I'm not trying to brag when I say I've always had an easy time in school. But this whole eleventh-grade thing was beginning to look a lot like cake.

"We weren't even thinking about a grade, Mr. Polar Bear," I said. "Tinsel and I just thought about our love of Christmas. And then we wished upon a star. That was the most important part. And the heart just kind of shaped itself!"

The class let out a collective "Awwwww," and I blushed while Tinsel took a few exaggerated bows. But the praise from our peers screeched to a halt as a boy who could not have been more the opposite of my talented boyfriend appeared in the doorway of our happy little classroom.

His clothes were drab. He slouched when he walked. He looked like he didn't want to be there any more than he wanted any of us to be there, like he wished the whole world would end already because he thought he had better things to do.

Maybe I'm exaggerating. But he sure stood out in his dark gray overcoat, gray camouflage pants, and heavy black boots,

8

like he was ready to go to war or something. Where ever did he find such an ensemble? Abercrombie & Grinch? He met our gasps with an icy stare as he pulled off his knit cap—guess what color that was?—and all those poor, unkempt hairs scampered every which way across his scalp, screaming for a comb to save them.

As he breezed toward the head of the class—past Silentnight and his head of downy hair bright yellow like a baby chick, past Delicious in her neon-orange angora sweater and Clarence in his intense purple pullover—he looked like Dorothy's ugly stepbrother stepping into Technicolor for the first time. He handed the teacher a note and stood like an angry statue, daring the big bear to respond.

Mr. Polar Bear read the note, then looked up and said, cheerful as a cherry pie, "Class, we have a new student. Please give a North Pole welcome to Rudy Tutti."

Although initially put off by his appearance, we'd been raised to be pleasant at all times. This being one of those times, we showered the newcomer with pleasantries.

"Hi, Rudy!" Holly tooted.

"How's it going, buddy?" asked Doug Fir.

"Sit over here, Rudy!" Silentnight offered.

And so forth.

Rudy's whole body tensed, as if ready to punch somebody. I think he expected us to vomit on him at the mere mention of his name. But so far, his name was the only thing he had going for him. Rudy Tutti. I have to admit, it had a nice, normal ring to it.

"Rudy," the teacher continued, "would you like to tell us a little about yourself? Where you're from? Your favorite Christmas treats? That sort of thing."

"Not really," he grunted.

Mr. Polar Bear scrunched his nose, flummoxed by the boy's rudeness. And who could blame him?

Without uttering another syllable, Rudy moped to an isolated desk at the back of the classroom and slumped into the chair, bowing his knees out to either side and tilting his head back.

"Oh. I see," Mr. Polar Bear said, struggling to maintain the appearance of being in control. "Then just take a seat, I guess. Anywhere you'd like. Okay, boys and girls, let's move on to today's lesson plan, shall we?"

Stifled giggles choked their way out of several of us. If Rudy's clothes hadn't deemed him an irredeemable loser, the way he carried himself sure had. Anyone can make bad fashion choices—not me or my friends, of course, but regular people can. This new boy, however, had opened the door of our classroom and taken a long running jump right over the proverbial shark.

After that I tried not to think about Rudy Tutti. But in fifth period, a couple of my friends told me they'd seen him checking me out. *Please.* Then another friend said she'd heard him asking Silentnight about me at lunch. I finger-gagged. I hoped Silent had told him not to waste his time. What would I want with a boy like Rudy when I already had the best boyfriend in the whole North Pole?

I can't remember a time when Tinsel wasn't the most popular boy in class. In elementary school, we looked forward to his birthday parties most of all, because the elf side of his family was so much fun to hang around with when we were all still their size. By middle school, all the girls thought Tinsel was hot chocolate. The sole elfman in our grade, he had the height and handsome looks of his human dad, while the cute pointy ears, devilish grin, long skinny fingers, and stringy, shining tinsel hair came from his mother, a lead tester in Daddy's Workshop.

As Tinsel and Snowflake and I left the little red schoolhouse that day, we noticed Rudy sitting under a gumdrop tree, all by himself, poring over some book called *Zen and the Art of Motorcycle Maintenance*.

Snowflake spotted him first. "Look," she said. "There's the new guy. Let's go talk to him."

Tinsel and I glanced at each other and shared a giggle.

"Yeah. Right." I puffed out my chest and marched in a little circle in Rudy's angry slouch, deepening my voice to mimic him. "Look at me. I'm Rudy. I'm the new guy. You guys are so lame. I'm all that and a bag of marshmallows!"

I expected Snowflake to crack up with me, but instead she said, "I think he's hot chocolate."

That made Tinsel crack up. *"Him?"*

"Lords a-leaping, Snowflake!"

She frowned. "Well, what's wrong with him?"

"Nothing," Tinsel said, "if you're into bah humbug. Hahahaha. We really need to get you a boyfriend, Snowflake."

"Shut up, Tinsel!" Her shriek made Rudy glance in our direction. She quickly turned her pretty face to hide her reddening cheeks.

Tinsel and I both laughed at her.

Ever since we were little, everyone considered Snowflake the most outgoing girl in our class. But for some reason, she got real shy about boys once we reached that age where boys started to matter. Thank goodness she had me to guide her. Otherwise she might have actually gone and talked to that freak under the gumdrop tree.

The freak who had just caught me making fun of him.

The freak I was about to be forced to have dinner with—*at his freezing Welcoming Feast*.

11

three

You may have noticed my dad's a little on the hefty side. Well, he certainly didn't get that way by not taking his Welcoming Feasts seriously.

Any time a dignitary flies into town or a newcomer arrives. Any excuse for a really big feast. No worries about all the hard work Chefy and hundreds of innocent Poleans have to put into the extravagant affairs. Or how excruciating they are for me and my little brother to sit through while always on our best behavior because of who we are.

And who's he kidding anyway? No matter the guest of honor, these feasts are really all about Daddy.

I mean, I know he works hard too.

Okay, what he does is pretty darn impressive, I'll give him that. Who else sets out to make every boy and girl in the world happy all at once and succeeds at it year after year? He does kind of deserve to be treated like he owns this town.

But all that work—*his* work—it's only one night a year. And not to give away any secrets but, *duh,* he uses magic. Then he sits back and plays the Santa card about a dozen jillion times the rest of the year. Is that fair?

I don't mean to pout. But sitting through a feast to welcome Rudy Tutti? If my friends found out, they'd tease me all the way to Valentine's Day, calling it a date or something.

So I went and found Daddy sipping his cherry-chocolate root beer in front of a crackling fire and threw my arms around him, declaring him the greatest daddy in the whole wide world. He crinkled his brow, carefully considering my unorthodox request to skip this delicious feast—with all my favorite dishes—then reached the only conclusion he could. "Go ask your mother," he said.

Teachers tell us what to do in school. Then we have laws, presidents, kings, and fathers, roughly in that order. And then there are *mothers*. They use that tone and you know you have to go along with whatever they say. There is no higher authority to appeal to.

Mom's final word on the subject was: "Tough taffy. You're a Claus and you have certain responsibilities."

I told her I hated having certain responsibilities and climbed the stairs to my bedroom wishing I'd been born to polar bears.

Want to know what turned me around? A dress. A beautiful new dress my mother had surprised me with just for the occasion. Hanging from the pole of my canopy bed frame, a big pink bow tied to the hanger. The dress I had wanted for my sweet sixteen. What wouldn't I tolerate for a new outfit like that.

I breathlessly tried on the floor-length, strapless gown. Thin lines of glittery crimson guarded a thick ribbon of glistening, beaded peppermint that swirled around my body diagonally, right shoulder to left hip and around the back to my right ankle, cutting into the frame-hugging, sugary white silk like a dream.

Despite all the craziness he had going on in the kitchen, Chefy found time to come up and braid my white-streaked, cherry-red hair into an elegant, twisty updo. I could marry a penguin like that.

To top it all off, or bottom it off I should say, I stepped into my favorite candy-cane heels and looked over the results in the mirror. I had to blush. From head to toe, I practically *was* a 5′ 9″ candy cane. With boobs.

The guests showered me with sweet-tasting compliments, like honey dipped in sunshine, as they filtered into the party. *Said Sugar Plum to Santa's little girl, "Do you see what I see?"* The town's terminally giddy dental hygienist plucked my cheek so hard I wanted to run back to my room to reapply my makeup. "I don't believe my eyes! You were littler than the littlest elf around. And now, look at you. You're all grown up!"

"You're rockin' it, Candycane," said Rupert the Squirrel, president of the North Pole Savings and Loan.

"My stars, you look scrumptious," Silly the Elf said.

"Thank you." I smiled back at Tinsel's mom's child-sized boss.

Even you-know-who, the great, grand guest of honor, looked impressed for a second. Not that I cared.

Rudy and his bald-headed, stooped-over, bespectacled father still had that through-the-looking-glass confusion plastered on their faces a full ten minutes after Chefy had formally announced their arrival. Mom called it culture shock.

To be fair, lots of people tripped out the first time they came into our house. From the outside, it appeared no different than any other home on Gingerbread Lane—quaint and good enough to eat. Crossing the threshold gave off a disarming, Escheristic effect, as though you'd wandered into a giant's palace. The Tuttis seemed to dwell on this illusion a little longer than normal people.

They looked like two bugs that had crawled into a giant gumball machine—they in their colorless attire slogging through a rainbow of festive Poleans in our brightest formal wear. Their bronze, sun-soaked skin made them look sickly next to our pale, doughy flesh.

Chefy ushered Rudy and his father through the antechamber to our opulent drawing room, where the traditional Claus family lineup awaited. Mom always greeted the visitors first in the royal receiving line, followed by Wizard the Elf, Judge Dickens, and Officer Brownbear, then me and Frostbite, and finally His Majesty.

Daddy had on his everyday suit. Major diss. The truly important dignitaries got the royal blue version. If he donned his gold-colored outfit, well... Suffice it to say, he saved that one for only the rarest of occasions—like the time I was eight and this nanny came to NoPo to sub for a vacationing Chefy. She'd floated in on an umbrella all the way from Great Britain. She and Chefy had mutual penguin friends. Frostbite and I had a blast with her, but that's another story. For the Tuttis, it was ho-hum traditional red-and-white all the way.

"Welcome to our home," my mother said. She handed Rudy's father the first gift, officially commencing the Welcoming ceremony. "It's so nice to finally meet you."

Dr. Anthony Tutti, D.D.S., who looked more like an accountant than the new North Pole dentist, blanched as he peered down the line. "Oh, I didn't..." he mumbled. "I beg your pardon, but I didn't bring anything for you."

Chefy cleared his throat and whispered, "That's not how it works."

The Welcoming ritual called for each VIP to present each guest of honor with a wonderful present in lieu of the common and downright mundane clasping of hands. Daddy took care of the gifts, bringing them home from the Workshop, of course. None of us ever knew what was in them because, as a rule, the recipients had to wait until the next morning to open them. Again, it was all about Daddy showing off his most fantastic skill. I never had to do anything more than hand out a few pretty boxes.

Dr. Tutti thanked my mother and moved on, squatting to

help Wizard the Elf place another gift on top of the first. And so on. As the bear and the judge plunked two more colorful packages onto the doctor's haul, Rudy accepted his first gift with a disinterested grunt. His father's dark, beady eyes turned into narrow slits as he shot Rudy a dirty look with the trademarked Tutti family scowl.

Rudy continued down the line, refusing to scrunch even a smidgen for Wizard, forcing the exalted elf to stretch onto his tippy toes and shoot the next present into Rudy's arms like a basketball free throw. I wondered what Rudy's dad had to say to get *him* to come, considering I needed to be bribed with, like, the most amazing dress ever.

When my turn came, I politely gifted Dr. Tutti, then chewed on my tongue while I waited for Rudy to navigate around the big brown bear blocking me from his view.

"Candycane?" he squeaked when he finally reached me. His brow arched and his almond-shaped eyes widened into coconuts that took a round trip up and down my body.

I thought he might actually crack a smile, but he quickly erased any trace of it. Thank goodness. I gathered from the weird, fleeting, near-human emotion he emitted that Silentnight hadn't told him who I was. "Duh, that's my name," I shot back at him.

"So, the jolly red chimney sweep here is your father? That explains a lot."

I giggled and stuffed my present onto the top of his stack. "Welcome to the North Pole, Rudy," I said as cheerfully as I'd been taught, complete with the obligatory rosy-cheeked smile.

"Oh, that's right," my mother said, clasping her delicate hands beneath her pointed chin. "I forgot you two are already friends."

"Lords a-leaping! That's a laugh!"

"Keep them, princess," Rudy said as he shoved his presents back at me, then let go of them before I could get a grip.

They crashed to the floor and I stood over them with my arms folded. I probably harrumphed—loudly. Maybe I even stamped a foot.

"Rudy!" His father glared at him.

"What?"

A mean staring contest erupted between the two Tuttis until my overlooked brother broke the uncomfortable silence.

"Hey, you'll like my presents. I kinda broke the rules this time and made them myself. I'm Frostbite. I'm Candy's little brother. You can open my presents right now. Right here. Go head, open them." At ten years old, Frostbite still hadn't grown out of his I-want-to-be-an-elf-when-I-grow-up phase.

Dr. Tutti knelt to scoop Rudy's discarded treasure off the blue-gray marble floor. While down there, he tousled my brother's light-brown faux elf-lick and accepted the package the annoying runt had thrust at him. "Thank you, Frostbite."

"Open it! It's a gumball!"

Dr. Tutti peeked inside at the brightly colored jawbreaker the size of a volleyball. His teeth clenched into an uneasy grimace.

"I hope you don't already have one," Frostbite said.

"It's very kind of you," he replied. Then he made the queerest request of my brother. "Open your mouth and say, 'Ahh.'"

"Ho-ho-ho," Daddy interjected, reaching into his pocket for a handful of jelly beans. Nervous habit of his. So when something upset him, he could chew it over, so to speak. "Chefy, why don't you take our guests' coats?"

"Where shall I take them," Chefy asked, "the furnace?"

"Ho-ho-ho!" Beads of sweat started to form on Daddy's brow.

If his discomfort this early in the affair wasn't amusing enough, you should have seen Dr. Tutti struggle to balance the twin mountains of presents he was holding—his and his son's—while Chefy worked to extract his drab overcoat—tugging, nipping, untucking—until finally he yanked it off cleanly, like the old tablecloth trick.

Underneath his coat, the doctor had on a dreary brown argyle sweater, a dreary brownish necktie, and dreary brown dress slacks. The sad thing was, he'd probably actually made an effort to dress nice. He looked like he was going to the bank to ask for a loan. And would probably get turned down. Was brown the brightest color he could find in his closet? I didn't really want to know the answer to that.

Rudy tossed his trench coat at Chefy. "Be careful with it, penguin." He hadn't bothered to change out of the fatigues he'd worn to school that day.

"I assure you, young man, I shan't allow a drop of golden sun to be wasted on letting this garment be seen more than it has to. By anyone."

"Ho-ho-ho," Daddy said as Chefy waddled away.

Dr. Tutti leaned close to my dad. "Good help is so hard to find, huh?" Then he chuckled as if he'd just told some kind of joke.

Honestly, I didn't get it.

Sugar Plum, along with several of Daddy's favorite little helpers, overheard the remark and burst into tears.

"Why would you say that?" my father asked him.

"You know, 'cause Chefy, he's... you know, the way he... it's just an expression."

"I don't understand this... *expression*. Chefy's the best there is."

"Well, I'm sure he is. I only meant..."

"You meant me," Sugar Plum said, her eyes all pink and puffy. "Didn't you, Dr. Tutti?"

"Oh, dear," my mom said. "Are you not satisfied with your new assistant, Dr. Tutti?"

"For crying out loud, that's not what I…" Dr. Tutti loosened his tie. "Is it getting hot in here?"

"Oh, sure, change the subject." Sugar Plum jabbed her chunky fingers into her boss's chest, upsetting the stacks of presents in his arms. "You don't like the way I take X-rays in 3-D to make them more exciting, or the way I sing to the patients to take their minds off your awful drill, or the way I make the molds for the crowns out of whipped cream, so you talk about the weather. 'It's too hot.' 'It's too cold.' Anything so you don't have to face me and tell me I'm the worst hygienist you've ever had, and you think you're the only one who has to make adjustments because you're new in town, but I got news for you, buster, I've had to make plenty of adjustments too, having *you* as a new boss. And I'm a darn good hygienist. You can just ask around about that, Doctor. You won't find a better dental hygienist anywhere around these parts!"

"I swear I wasn't talking about you!"

"There, there, Sugar Plum," Daddy said. "I'm sure Dr. Tutti didn't mean it. He just has… different ways of expressing himself." He let the frazzled fairy cry on his shoulder, then sneered at her employer. "Are you happy now?"

"Yeah, good going, Dad," Rudy said.

The nerve of him to call out his father like that in public!

Rudy pushed past all of us and said, "I thought this was supposed to be some sort of feast. Where's the grub?"

"Yeah, let's eat," Frostbite echoed.

"Moved and seconded," said Flip, our pet puffin, skidding his webbed, yellow feet across the smooth surface of the floor.

19

"Ooh, I'll take seconds!" said his counterpart, Flop.

The drooling duo hopped up and down at Frostbite's side, their black-and-white-feathered wings all aflutter.

"All in favor," Flip continued, "say, 'Feed me.'"

"All opposed," Flop added, "we'll take yours."

"Great pumpkin pie," my mother said. "Who let you boys in?" She lowered her blue eyes at Frostbite, who shrugged and grabbed Flip by his bright orange beak. Then Mom pointed at the door and said, "Out."

"C'mon, guys," Frostbite said as he led the pair of auks out into the cold.

"Can't we get some to go?" said Flip.

"Leftovers would be sweet too," Flop chirped hopelessly.

The birds had a point. Tummies started to rumble. Mom called for Chefy to start the first course, and the guests, many still stung by Dr. Tutti's "joke," followed her to the banquet hall.

"Is *he* staying?" Sugar Plum blubbered into the furry white trim of Daddy's coat.

"I assume so."

Dr. Tutti's hangdog expression peeked over the top of his presents. "I really am sorry."

Sugar Plum spun around and pushed her copper-tinged hair out of her face. "A Welcoming Feast is no place to be sorry. Let's go have the greatest time ever, okay, Dr. Tutti?"

Just like that, all was forgotten. She jammed her elbow into her boss's side and it took him a moment to understand she was waiting for him to escort her to the table.

Keeping his gifts balanced, he leaned forward so she could hook her arm through his. "Shall we, Miss Plum?"

"Ooh, call me Sugar Plum. 'Miss Plum' is great too. But Sugar Plum is greater. Or Sugar. Sugar would be super."

His thin lips formed a small smile. "I'm starving, Sugar… Plum."

My father's wary gaze followed them as they joined the other guests still draining out of the greeting area. When Daddy and I were the last two left, he gave me a weary smile. "Did I mention how absolutely stunning you look tonight?"

My apple cheeks swelled. I curtsied like a princess for her king. "Thank you, Daddy."

He coiled his arm around me warmly as we adjourned to the dining room, where my anticipation of tasty delights quickly gave way to the dread I'd hoped to avoid all along. I mean, really. How was I expected to enjoy even one morsel of Chefy's incredible specials with Rudy's atrocious scowl fixed directly opposite me? Ugh.

four

Boughs of holly decked the hall, while beautiful neon poinsettias glowed and flickered at each place setting along the formal dining table.

Most kids on the planet would have given their two front teeth for this kind of meet-and-greet with my dad. But grumpy old Rudy would have been happier at a dinner with the Abominable Snowman—even if he were the main course!

I was still rejoicing in the grisly image of Yeti sticking a fork into Rudy's brain when my mother daintily adjusted her tiara of red and yellow roses and said, "I understand you and Rudy are in some of the same classes. Isn't that nice?" Her subtle way of reminding me of my duty as a Claus to spread good cheer.

"Perhaps," I answered coyly. "Was that you brooding in the back row in Ornaments class today, Rudy?"

"I didn't think you could hear my brooding over all that merriment."

"You say that like it's a bad thing. What's wrong with being merry?"

"Nothing, if you have a reason to be merry. But to be merry just because the calendar says so is nothing but a big fat lie."

I couldn't help laughing at him.

"What's so funny?" His widened eyes shifted uncomfortably.

"You're not so different from us as you thought, Rudy Tutti. We don't believe in waiting for Christmastime to be merry, either. We practice merriment every day here at the N.P."

"That is not what I said, Candycane Claus." He curled a furious lip, baring his teeth.

I made sure my mother wasn't looking, then stuck out my tongue at him.

Frostbite licked a stray drop of toffee-caramel salad dressing off his sticky index finger and said, "She's telling the truth, Rudy. I got a hundred on my merriment quiz in school today."

"Goody for you, Frost-butt. Go be the merriest kid in the world for all I care."

"Thank you!" Frostbite sat up straight and beamed as though he'd been granted permission to be awesome. "I certainly will try."

Rudy shook his head in disgust and gave up on talking altogether, until he took his first taste of the soup. His lips pursed as if he'd just eaten a yellow Sno-Cone. "What is this?"

"It's called gazpacho," I told him. "It's *supposed* to be cold."

"Believe it or not, your highness, I know what gazpacho is."

"Then maybe you've never had it with real marshmallow seeds before."

He pushed his bowl away and Chefy came to collect it.

Sugar Plum took a break from her ear-splitting slurping to fawn over the proprietary penguin. "Mmm, so yummy. Do you think I could get the recipe? Please? Pretty please? Pretty, pretty please with lots and lots of sugar and cinnamon on top?"

Rudy smirked. "I think that *was* the recipe."

She ignored Rudy and winked at Chefy. "I've been a good girl this year."

"That only works with me, Sugar Plum. Ho-ho-ho!"

Cue the sycophantile laughter from the high-ranking elves and their spouses that followed whenever Daddy would say anything remotely witty. *Yawn.*

And so it went, course after heavenly course, while Rudy grinched about them all. What did he expect, curds and whey? This was a Welcoming Feast, after all.

Meanwhile, I had to suffer through Daddy's tiresome anecdotes that I'd heard so many times I could tell them in my sleep.

"…and she said, 'Of course I lied, Blimpy. I'm the Tooth Fairy, not the Truth Fairy!' Ho-ho-ho!"

"You really know the Tooth Fairy?" Dr. Tutti shifted closer, a devoted puppy ready to lick Daddy's face.

"We go way back," my father said, laying it on thicker than his waist. "Why, I had lunch with her not two weeks ago. I'll introduce you some time. Only, don't tell her what you do for a living."

"But, I'm a dentist."

"Exactly. You have any idea how much your cleaning and drilling devalues those teeth she spends her whole life collecting? How happy would your little boy have been if you'd wiped all the pictures from those baseball cards you gave him when he was six?"

"Rudy had chicken pox." Dr. Tutti leaned back and blinked, a faint memory landing softly on him like a fly. "Playing with those cards kept him from picking at them. The pockmarks, that is. How did you know I…?"

"I may be hundreds of years old, but I've still got a few things running around up here," Daddy said, sliding his cap off long enough to scratch the shock of white curls underneath.

For dessert, Chefy brought out a flaming baked Alaska so humongous it could have set off the fire alarm. Instead of simply loosening his belt like everybody else, Dr. Tutti opened his mouth only to say, "I don't know where I'd find the room."

A hushed silence fell over the table. The clinking of

silverware stopped. The *oohs* and *yums* and *bring-it-ons* and other verbal anticipation of Chefy's *pièce de résistance* were transformed into gasps of horror at the guest of honor's slight.

"I'll take his!" my brother shouted.

"Ho-ho-ho, Frostbite. What our esteemed visitor doesn't realize yet is that he needs to put on an extra layer of fat to survive our cold temperatures."

"Be that as it may," Dr. Tutti said, "all this sugar is not really good for the tee-heeheeheehee..."

Dr. Tutti exploded in laughter, unable to finish his thought. He turned to his hygienist, seated to his immediate left, and asked with a puzzled expression, "What was that for?"

"What was what for, funny bunny?" Sugar Plum stared at him, innocent and wide-eyed, betraying no sign of having done what we all very well knew she had done. "You must have thought of a joke, Doc."

"I don't know any jokes. I'm not that funny." He eyed her suspiciously, then turned back to my father. "Anyway, as I was saying, you really shouldn't eat-tee-hee-heeeeee."

It happened again.

"Will you *please* stop that!"

"Sure thing, Doc," Sugar Plum said.

The hapless dentist tried to continue. "Listen, Santa—"

"Mr. Claus," Daddy corrected him.

"I hope you'll come in soon and let me look at your teeth because—"

Sugar Plum lunged at Dr. Tutti, tickling him with both hands this time. And not under the table anymore, either.

Dr. Tutti couldn't help but collapse in a fit of laughter. Sugar Plum quickly caught his contagious giggles. Some of the elves laughed too, while the rest of us watched in bemused silence. Dr. Tutti soon gained his composure, but Sugar Plum continued her hysterical howling.

"What is *wrong* with you?" the doctor demanded.

"L.O.L., Dr. Tutti. That was a good one!" Then Sugar Plum picked up her napkin and flung it to the floor. "Whoops! I think I dropped something." She vanished somewhere beneath the sea of dirty dishes.

Left up top next to an empty seat, Rudy's bewildered father shook his head, his mouth hung open. He glanced over at my dad.

"Why don't you help her, Doctor," my father coolly advised. Daddy punctuated his instruction with a nod.

Dr. Tutti caught on fast that it was no idle suggestion. The dentist joined his flighty assistant under the table, but we could plainly hear their conversation.

"Don't you know why you're here, Dr. Tutti?"

"Under the table?"

"In the North Pole."

"Sure I do. I was hired to come here and fix teeth."

"You didn't think you were our first dentist, did you?"

"What are you talking about?"

"Don't you know what happened to the last dentist?"

"How would I know that?"

"He was *banished*."

"Banished?"

"Do you know why?"

"I don't even know *what!*"

"He was banished for telling the big guy to lay off the cookies."

"And?"

"What do you mean, 'And?' Cookies are his bread and butter. Think about it. Would you deliver toys to a billion houses in a single night if you didn't get to eat all the superly delicious cookies they leave out for you at every one of them?"

"Well, I don't—"

"Found it!"

Sugar Plum's cherubic head popped up above the tabletop. She took her seat as though nothing strange had happened at all.

"Ouch!" The plates jumped. Rudy's father rejoined us topside, massaging a bump on his bald head as he took in the grave expressions around him.

Daddy gave him another nod to confirm what he'd heard down there was true. "You were saying?"

The doctor cleared his throat and straightened his dessert fork. "Um, thank you for your gracious hospitality, Mr. Claus, sir. You've made me and my son feel most welcome."

The flames burned themselves out as Chefy began to swap each dinner plate for a generous helping of the delicious baked Alaska.

He came to Rudy, who had barely touched his main course. Technically, he did touch it. He played with it. For the last twenty minutes he had toyed with the pink wad of stuffing on his plate. Now he stretched it out between his fingers and said, "Is this bubblegum?"

"Yep," I said. "And it was super yummy, Chefy."

"Well, it must have been, like, a *million* calories."

Had he learned nothing from the interaction that had just transpired with his father?

"I beg your pardon, young man," Chefy said. "Tonight's meal was no less than the boss's minimum requirement of fourteen million calories per person."

While Chefy replaced Rudy's uneaten dinner with his soon-to-remain-uneaten dessert, I blew an enormous pink bubble with my stuffing. That last dish was one of Chefy's most famous specialties and I desperately wanted to rub it in Rudy's face how he didn't know what he was missing. I might have taken it too far, though. My sugary balloon stretched more than halfway across the table before it burst wide open, sending globules of gravy-soaked, marzipan-coated bubblegum all over Rudy.

Frostbite wiggled and snorted so much it made him let loose a loud belch. I laughed along with him, expecting Rudy to blow up any second.

But strangely, he didn't.

That's when it happened. I can't explain it. The way he looked at me. With a trace of a smile. Like we had just shared a secret or something. One that I didn't fully understand. His blueberry eyes peered out at me past the gunk I had childishly sprayed on him, and for just a flash of a moment, I saw Rudy as a different boy from the greasy outsider who had strutted into class demanding to be left alone. A boy who somehow belonged here even if he didn't know it. A boy who was— OMG!—he was *cute*! Rudy Tutti was actually, kind of, sort of not so bad looking.

What had come o'er me?

What would my friends think?

I mean, it's not like I fell in love with him or anything. Please!

He wiped my sticky mess from his face and those weird feelings were washed away with it. Or at least I thought they were. I couldn't be certain because I'd kept my eyes on my baked Alaska for the rest of the Feast. As I devoured the meringue and pistachio-flavored delicacy without daring to look back up at him, all I could think was, *I hope nobody noticed.*

five

"Now class, watch what Tinsel does with the bows," Mr. Polar Bear said.

I flushed watching Tinsel's nimble elf fingers twirl in a brilliant blur. We had moved on from Ornaments to Presents. Somehow I'd managed not to think about Rudy Tutti in all that time. 'Twas Tinsel made me happy, and all could see why. He out-gift-wrapped anyone at North Pole High. He demonstrated on twelve presents at once, creating sensational, confettied ribbons, sprinkling each gift with magnificent snowflaked patterns of multicolored glitter. With breathtaking dexterity like that, imagine how many different places those fingers could tickle a girlfriend at one time. And that lucky girlfriend would be me!

Tinsel was a diamond in the Arctic, while Rudy could bring a girl nothing but coal. Rudy Tutti only cared about himself. Rudy Tutti had a chocolate chip on his shoulder the size of a white whale. Rudy Tutti was the kind of boy who... Well, maybe I wasn't doing such a hot job of not thinking about him after all.

"You get an A-super-duper-plus, Tinsel," Mr. Polar Bear said.

Tinsel bounced and jingled as everyone in class applauded his finished handiwork. Everyone, that is, except you-know-who.

I watched Rudy not give a carol about the amazing display of gift-wrapping genius he'd just witnessed.

No, I *stared* at him—and he caught me.

I froze.

And I smiled.

An awkward, goofy smile.

At him.

Tinsel noticed too. His jingly bells fell silent as his shiny green eyes traced a path between me and Rudy, his cheeks drooping halfway down his face like a sad, old puffin. I'm sure to him it looked like I was somehow flirting with Rudy from way across the room.

The last thing I needed was a jealous elf boyfriend.

Tinsel and I had been dating since the ninth grade. He'd been the star of all the sports teams since middle school— boy, was he fast!—but for some reason, I had played hard-to-get with him like, forever. Right up until we had to spend all that time together writing a paper on *Snow White and the Seven Dwarfs* for Miss Pandabaker's freshman English lit class. Strange how you can hang out with someone practically every day after school, playing sledball on Butterscotch Hills or whatever, and never really get to know them. Then you find yourself, you know, *collaborating* on something more serious and you see a whole different person.

Tinsel had been my Prince Charming ever since.

So now I went out of my way to make sure Rudy saw us together as much as possible. To send him a message: *Hey, loser. I'm not available. That look at the Welcoming Feast meant nothing. Go away. Forget all about me.*

Or was I secretly trying to make him jealous?

In any event, all it seemed to do was annoy my boyfriend while having no noticeable effect on the new boy at all.

I'd hold Tinsel's hand in the hallway between third and fourth periods and he'd make believe he had an itch to scratch so he could let go. Then I'd tell him *I* had an itch. Instead of scratching it for me like he used to, he'd look around first to make sure nobody was watching. Nobody ever was. Particularly not Rudy. Because Rudy couldn't care less. Which bothered me more than anything!

I started inexplicably breaking dates with Tinsel. I told myself it was only until I could figure this whole mess out. But it was more like, why do anything with Tinsel if Rudy wasn't there to see it? And was that fair to Tinsel? Was I even thinking about *his* feelings? No siree, Bobby Brady.

After Tinsel's awesome gift-wrapping display in Presents class, Snowflake and I hiked to the school cafeteria for lunch. We sat at our usual table with Delicious and Sugarcookie.

"There's the new guy," Delicious said with a giggle, pointing discreetly with her long, thick eyelashes.

The rest of us turned to see Rudy, all by himself, at the table by the trash can where nobody ever sat.

"Jiminy Christmas!" Snowflake said. "Look at him. He's all icky-picky." Her slender fingers mimed the way Rudy picked the lollipops out of his salad.

"What a loser," Sugarcookie said, brushing a cookie crumb off her snow-white Property of North Pole High hoodie. "You were so right about him, Candycane."

"He just likes to march to his own little drummer boy," I said.

Snowflake slapped the table. "Woo! Good one, Candy. I gotta remember that. Marches to his own little drummer boy. I like that."

"No, Snowflake. That's not what I meant."

"Hey, let's take him to the Fortress of Solitude," Sugarcookie tittered, her rainbow-colored freckles twinkling on her cheeks like candy sprinkles, "so he can jingle his bells in private, if you know what I mean."

Poor Rudy. All of the other children laughed at him and

called him names, and it was partly my fault.

Tinsel jingled up behind me. "Hey, babe. Ready to stand me up again?" He brushed his ticklers across my neck.

Not in a mood to be tickled, I pushed them away and said—as innocently as possible—"Did we have plans?"

"Oh, do we need to make plans first before you can cancel them? I wasn't sure how that worked. Heh-heh-heh."

Funny how Tinsel's habit of laughing after almost everything he said never used to bother me. "I'm not canceling anything with you, silly. Aren't you coming with us to Butterscotch Hills?"

Tinsel grabbed a handful of my mashed-Toll-House-cookie-dough-with-Skittles then spoke with his mouth full. "You don't have homework or something?"

"All caught up." I had been using homework as a catch-all excuse for some time.

"It'll be fun," Snowflake said, offering Tinsel her French-fried Nilla Wafers. "We're all going. Delicious and Sugarcookie and me."

"And Johnny Toboggan is coming," Delicious added. "And Cookiejar and Silentnight." Delicious never went anywhere with us if boys weren't involved.

"Yeah. Sure. Whatever," Tinsel said, his gaze falling on Rudy five tables away.

Did I cause that? Did I look over there and not know it?

Tinsel helped himself to a bite of my licorice dog. "Why don't we invite the new guy?"

He was testing me, waiting to see how I'd react. The other girls giggled. Delicious almost choked on a Skittle. But I kept my cool. Why should I act all guilty about someone I'd barely said ten words to other than in my head?

"Sure. If you want." I tried not to let on how much I was

burning inside or that I was starting to develop a headache.

Snowflake's eyes widened. "You're joking, Candy. You said he was nothing but a Danny Downer at the Welcoming Feast."

Did I say that? "Hey, it wasn't my idea. If Tinsel wants to invite Rudy Tutti to play with us, why should I care?"

"Yeah," Tinsel said. "It's about time we showed him what we're made of up here."

"And what would that be?" I asked.

"You know. Hospitality. Good will toward men." He tapped on the table, emulating a drum roll. "Extreme snow sports, hehehe."

"Oh, I get it," Snowflake said with a devious hoot.

So did I. They wanted to get Rudy up on the slopes to humiliate him. I couldn't have stopped them if I'd wanted to. And I can't say that I wanted to. Maybe seeing Rudy humiliated would finally push him out of my mind.

Delicious chortled, enrolling herself in the developing conspiracy. "This is gonna be tasty!"

"Then it's settled," Tinsel said, hopping over to Rudy like a mischievous polar bunny.

I couldn't hear what they were saying, but Tinsel gestured toward our table a lot. I waved at them once, when Rudy's gaze landed on me. He nodded to Tinsel, who grinned and slapped Rudy's shoulder.

Then Tinsel sprinted back to our table and stuffed another handful of my lunch in his face. "Gotta run, babe. See you after school. Heh-hehehe."

six

We loaded our gear into my red-and-white-striped Range Rover and piled in. Tinsel squeezed next to me, the girls in back. Rudy drove up with the boys—Silentnight, Cookiejar, and Johnny Toboggan. It took about fifteen minutes to get to Butterscotch Hills and another fifteen to unload all our stuff and start up to the top.

My brother's snow scooter, tricked out with flashing superglowstrips and a turbo booster, was way more power than Rudy would need. The first time he punched GO, he lurched forward a mere two feet before hitting a rock that sent him somersaulting over the handlebars into a neat faceplant in the snow.

Silentnight ran over to him. "Swans a-swimming! Are you all right, buddy?"

"I got it. I got it." Rudy picked himself up, refusing Silent's help, and shook the wet snowpellets from his jet-black hair.

Silentnight laughed. "You'll get the hang of it. The important thing is to get right back on."

"Whatever." Rudy righted the machine and gave it a gruff kick. "It's just a glorified Segway that runs on snow. Looks like it was designed by Dr. Seuss."

Silent's hazel eyes widened. "You have a doctor who builds snow scooters? Cool!"

"What is *wrong* with you?" Rudy climbed on and punched GO again. The scooter flew out from under his feet, dragging him a little ways before he thought to let go.

"No Rudy," Silent called out, "you need to lean forward

before it starts moving."

"Look, the day I need advice from a nutcracker like you, I'll sing you a Christmas carol."

"Sweet! Which one?"

"We're wasting time," Tinsel said, even though he must have secretly loved watching Rudy make a clown of himself. "Grab this. I'll tow you up." He tossed him one end of a bright green bungee cord and wrapped the other around his chiseled waist.

Rudy flung the line right back at him. "What do I look like, a broken sled?"

He started the snow scooter for a third time. To his credit, he picked it up pretty fast. By the time we reached the summit, he could weave expertly through the patches of Douglas firs and artfully dodge the wild candy canes that sprouted from the ground, some up to twenty feet tall. He almost looked like he was having fun.

The view from the snow-capped peaks was more beautiful than ever. Stars that hadn't been seen in months were just beginning to poke holes in the sky. The cold, distant sun would soon spoon with the horizon for the first time of the season as the Pole inched toward its month of constant twilight in anticipation of the persistent Dark that would ultimately take over for the long winter ahead.

"So what happens next?" Rudy said, slowing to a stop. "Snowball fights?"

"Hahaha," Tinsel cackled. "Tough guy, aren't you? From the land of summers and swimming pools. Let's see if you got the snowballs for a good old-fashioned race."

"Ready when you are, Tonsil." Rudy accelerated and leaned to one side, putting his scooter into a spin that I had to admit was impressive for a first-timer.

"Eh-eh," Tinsel snickered. "That ain't how we do it at the N.P."

By that time, Johnny and Cookiejar had reached us with two Snow Pods in tow.

"You want me to get in one of *those*?" Rudy asked.

An invention of Tinsel's uncle's on his mother's side from only two seasons ago, Daddy hadn't approved the Snow Pods for official Christmas distribution yet. They were far too dangerous.

The toboggan-shaped cage of roll bars held one rider in a claustrophobic embrace. Runners attached to all sides meant the Pod would keep moving, even in the event of a rollover. Steering was a challenge, more so when upside down, but stopping? Forget it. No brakes. You either made it to the bottom of the hill—or the bullseye of a tree.

The Pods came in two colors: glimmering red and shimmering green—primary colors around these parts—with a glow that left the most beautiful Christmassy streaks behind as they plummeted down the mountainside. Hence the glowstrips Frostbite had added to his snow scooter—the closest he could ever come to the thrill of a Pod, for Daddy would never let him anywhere near one.

He wouldn't exactly let *me* ride one, either—if he knew. He needn't worry, though. I'd only tried it one time. Those things are *insane*.

"Come on, Tutti," Tinsel prodded, "it's only scary if you hit something." He knew Rudy wouldn't back down in front of me.

Rudy paused, then said in a voice filled with unsure bravado, "Strap me in and let's do this."

Snowflake and the other girls jumped and cheered, while Silentnight helped Rudy stuff his broad shoulders into Red-11.

36

Tinsel squiggled into Green-13 with his pit crew, Johnny and Cookiejar, close at hand.

Rudy's cobalt-blue eyes narrowed and turned toward me while Silent hastily plied him with tips and instructions. "Pay attention, Rudy. You steer with your whole body. Like this." The mentor pushed his lanky frame forward to demonstrate. "Same when you're upside down, but you shift the opposite way."

"Piece of cake."

"Ooh, I like cake."

Sugarcookie approached the red Pod and whispered, "Cheer up, Rudy. Even if you lose, we can't possibly think less of you than we already do. Tee-hee-hee." She placed a kiss on her wool-mittened fingertips and touched them to Rudy's cheek through the bars.

Rudy surveyed the treacherous downhill path that lay ahead, his face turning white as snow. For the first time in the short time I'd known him, Rudy Tutti looked vulnerable.

I approached the big "13" emblazoned on the side of Tinsel's Pod. He pushed his apple cheek through the illuminated green bars, expecting the same fingertip kiss for luck that Sugarcookie had given Rudy. Instead, I told him, "Rudy's never done this before. Don't you think it would be fair to give him a practice run?"

Johnny Toboggan nodded. "She's got a point."

Tinsel searched for a third opinion. Cookiejar just shrugged and scratched his goatee.

After a pause, my magnanimous boyfriend sighed and called out, "Hey, kid. There's a bunny slope we can take you to, let you get in a couple practice runs till you get the feel for it—you know, in a safe place—if you want."

Rudy smirked, the color returning to his face. "It's just

down. How hard could it be if a half-breed can do it?"

Tinsel arched his golden eyebrows at me. I pressed my lips together, returning a look that told him to try again.

"There's more to Snow Podding than just plain gravity," he said.

"Scared I'll beat you, Pencil-head?"

No wonder I had so disliked Rudy Tutti from the start. I backed away from Tinsel, surrendering the new boy's fate to the gods of Butterscotch Hills, confident I could sleep at night knowing his maimed body would not be on my head.

"We gave you fair warning, Tutti!" Tinsel shouted. "Remember that first cane we passed coming up here? About five feet tall? Yellow stripes?"

"Didn't know I was supposed to be taking botany notes."

"It's the one closest to the cars. You can't miss it."

"What about it?"

"It's the finish line. First one to the candy cane. You have to pull it out of the ground to win." Tinsel howled his increasingly annoying laugh and winked at me.

"Piece of cake," Rudy said with a cocky grin.

Silentnight shook Delicious by her shoulders. "Where the devil is this cake he keeps talking about? Ooh, is it devil's food cake?"

"Okay, boys. Let's get the snow on the road!" I shouted as I stepped in front of the vessels, removing my candy-cane scarf.

Johnny and Cookiejar took their positions behind Green-13, all set to shove Tinsel over the start line on my say-so, while Silent and Snowflake readied themselves likewise at Rudy's Pod.

I raised the scarf high over my head and held it there for a long moment, gazing at the mask of intense concentration that hid the fear on Rudy's oval face—a strong contrast to Tinsel's

38

assured self-confidence as if he had already won.

Why wasn't I more proud of my handsome, virile boyfriend, poised for certain championship?

Oh. The candy cane.

So *I* was to be the prize?

I tightened a fist around my scarf, still in the air. If that was how Tinsel wanted it, then so be it. The turmoil that had clouded my brain for weeks on end would finally be settled in a matter of minutes. This race would determine, once and for all, which boy I liked.

I dropped my scarf and my suitors were off!

seven

"Woo! Look at them go!" Snowflake screeched, circling her arm in the air as if trying to stir the clouds.

Everyone cheered for Tinsel as he quickly took the lead.

The open space at the top of the course gave Rudy a chance to test Red-11's reactions to his movements before he'd have to worry about obstructions. He was doing all right. And by that I mean, he probably wouldn't die.

But Tinsel rode his machine like it was part of him. He knew the track intimately and could effortlessly take advantage of a small dip or minor jut to increase his momentum.

It was no contest.

Rudy careened down the steep mountain, through the fresh powder, as the first patch of trees started to rush past him.

Tinsel zigzagged, just to buy time, giving his opponent a fighting chance to catch up, out of good, honest, North Pole fairness.

But then he cut sharp in front of Rudy, forcing a swerve. Rudy's Snow Pod bobbed onto its side. He continued down the hill that way, an unstoppable bullet.

From our faraway perch, we could just make out a blurry red streak headed straight for a great big tree. Six snow scooter engines roared to life as we descended the hill for an up-close look at the impending carnage.

Red-11 wobbled from Rudy's desperate fight to upright her, as the immovable object before him rushed closer and closer.

Silentnight whooshed down the hillside on his snow

scooter beside me, his sleek butt involuntarily contorting itself in the direction Rudy's would need to move to survive. "Steer, Rudy! Twist your butt! Up, like this!"

At the very last second, Red-11 curved around the staunch, immobile fir—close enough for a shave.

I exhaled.

Another tree sprang up in his path. He had even less time to think about this one. He swooshed around it. A candy cane threatened him next. By sheer luck, he curled through a snowbank, coming down right-side up, and eluded the wrath of the thick, deadly cane.

Tinsel sailed over a snowy knoll, his loud cackle streaming past our ears over the whistling wind.

The two Pods raced side by side. Tinsel inched Green-13 closer to Rudy. He bumped the red Pod, but Rudy surprised us all as he maintained control and even took a slight lead.

Delicious and Johnny and the others shouted for Tinsel to go faster, faster, *don't let that freak beat you!*

I tried to stay neutral, keeping my cheers to myself. Frankly, I didn't know who I wanted to win. As they continued down the mountain, neck and neck, trading off the lead position like an evenly matched unicorn race, I would silently switch my allegiance to whomever was the underdog of the moment.

That may sound like a fierce lack of loyalty on my part, but I kind of wished they *both* could win. And no, not because I was spoiled and wanted two boyfriends. Lords a-leaping! One boy was almost more than any teenage girl could handle. It was more like the way my father wanted every child to have a new toy on Christmas. About not wanting to see either of them lose. Or get himself splattered onto a tree. Not over me, for goodness sake!

But both of them were playing for keeps. Mere seconds

ahead of another tree, neither would back off. In their high-speed game of chicken, one was about to get plucked.

Yet my friends kept whooping and hooting like they were in the Running of the Elves.

Tinsel veered closer to Rudy. Their runners touched.

Rudy almost lost control. Tinsel stayed on him.

Right at the tree's roots, Rudy peeled away.

I imagined a snort of self-satisfied laughter coming from Tinsel in the half-second before he banked around the trunk of that ominous fir. He'd waited so long, the back of his Pod took off a huge chunk of bark, shaking loose a clump of needles and flipping Tinsel's ride upside down.

"Did you see that?" Johnny Toboggan shouted.

Tinsel hot-dogged through a cluster of candy canes, still turned on his head, just to show off his tremendous skill.

Rudy adjusted course and gained a lead, heading for the finish line.

Tinsel casually flipped himself back over, then took aim at Red-11, destined to T-bone his nemesis.

Snowflake let out a loud whoop. If I hadn't known Tinsel better, I would have turned away. The terror Rudy must have felt. The bright green lights of Tinsel's bars coming at him like an arrow from a bow. Faster and faster.

Within an elf's foot of Rudy's Pod, Tinsel jerked his body back, sending Green-13 up into the sky, high over Rudy's head, spraying Rudy with a face full of icy snow.

Magnificent! No wonder the girls at school envied me.

Rudy's Pod tumbled out of control, arcing away from the finish line.

Tinsel stretched a spindly arm through his cage as he neared the baby yellow candy cane. He yanked the sapling out of the ground, roots and all, then slowed to a triumphant stop.

And just like that, my dilemma was over. Tinsel had won. Rudy Tutti was officially, decidedly, categorically a big dopey loser. I breathed deeply for the first time since the race had begun. And beamed. Tinsel was my hero.

Then dumb old Rudy managed to pilot Red-11 back on course—hanging upside down and traveling backward. He couldn't see where he was going. Or that he had just lost the race. Or that Tinsel's now-stationary Snow Pod was directly in his path.

A loud crunch shot across the mountain.

The impact sent Green-13 ricocheting down another embankment, while Rudy spun around like a top in the same direction. Both Snow Pods dropped onto Butterscotch Hills Road, the main road back into town. They sped right past a sign that read: "ABSOLUTELY NO SNOW PODDING BEYOND THIS POINT! By order of the N.P.P.D."

The band of snow scooters carrying me and my friends followed in their wake as Rudy flipped his Snow Pod back the right way over and caught up to Tinsel, who shouted something at him that we couldn't hear.

But Rudy wouldn't let up. He'd learned Tinsel's game too well. Every time Tinsel tried to slue away, Rudy jumped right back on his tail.

A slick film of ice glazed the curvy, hilly highway. The Pods reached crazy speeds. And now they were headed into the heart of downtown.

We zipped past the "Welcome to the North Pole" sign where Hills Road becomes Main Street. Dozens of Poleans glided down the festive esplanade on their ice skates, going about their daily business without a care in the world, until the scrape of runners against the ice made them look up at the two Snow Pods barreling down on them. They must have suddenly known what it felt like to be bowling pins.

They scattered in every direction, into the Sno-Mart, into the Igloo Depot, into the sled-repair shop, dropping their purses and packages and leaving them in the street.

Mayhem! Pandemonium! And my father, in the middle of the road, chatting with Billy Winterland's mom, oblivious, his back to the imminent doom. Mrs. Winterland screamed in terror. The Pods whooshed by them so fast they created a breeze that blew Daddy's cap clear off his head.

We were past the point of no return, our snow scooters moving much too fast to stop on that ice. Cookiejar's scooter grazed the plush red target bending over to pick up his hat.

Daddy toppled like a defective Weeble.

I shut my eyes and kept scootering, too afraid to think what he would do if he noticed me in the pack. And how could he not? I had the only candy-cane-striped snow scooter in town.

Cookiejar kept going too. We all did. The N-List had just grown a little bigger this year, but there was nothing we could do about it now.

The Snow Pod racers zoomed further down the boulevard. Red-11 forced my boyfriend through a dense patch of tinselbushes. He plowed out the other end, covered in the same silvery strands he was named after. The stuff draped his face, blinding him. He flew like a rocket down the slippery street as he pulled the sticky tinsel out of his mouth and away from his eyes. He regained his vision just in time to discover his chariot had diverted itself onto Hop Scotch Road.

A dead end.

With no time to react, he threw his hands in front of his face and crashed Green-13 through the fence at the end of the road. He skidded all the way across Yuletide Park, soaring through the air over the whipped-creamed shoreline of Hot

44

Fudge Pond.

"Oh, *fudge!*" he screamed, as his long journey at last reached its end with a big splosh in the bubbling, syrupy sludge. As his ship slowly sank, he kicked open the hatch and emerged unharmed, but unamused, and covered in gooey, fudgey tinsel.

"Are you okay?" I shouted as soon as I reached the edge of the pond.

"Get me out of here!" he screamed back.

I looked around for help because I didn't want to get fudge on my snowshoes. They were new. They had pretty little candy canes on them.

But Tinsel was my guy now, so I was obligated to help. "Use the candy cane," I suggested.

Tinsel sloshed his way through the viscous confection and held out the marker that had made me his prize. I reached for the hook and pulled with all my might.

All our friends pointed and laughed at my messy, grumpy elfman while Rudy leaned against his Pod with that sly smile of his. The smile that sent shivers coursing through me. I blushed and lost my grip on the candy cane. A loud splash erupted behind me, accompanied by Tinsel's angry, high-pitched obscenities.

Oops.

DUSK

"Hang a shining star upon the highest bough."

\- Hugh Martin

eight

What was the deal with Rudy and food anyway? Who doesn't love *fruitcake*, for goodness sake?

"Just because you put it on a pizza doesn't make it any more edible," Rudy said. He flicked the nuts off his slice then plopped it back into the serving pan.

Pizza at T.G.I. Fruitcake was one of our usual post-snowgames rituals. The girls had begun to swoon over Rudy thanks to his daredevil stunts in the Pod. Snowflake campaigned to invite him. We took a quick vote and he was in. The miracle-on-thirty-fourth-street was that he had deigned to accept.

Tinsel, on the other hand, had already gone home to clean himself off just prior to Rudy's promotion from Quasimodo to James Dean of the North. I offered to go with—you know, the supportive girlfriend and all—but he snapped at me as if the whole fiasco had somehow been *my* fault!

"Let's hear it for the Snow Pod champion of the Pole!" Johnny Toboggan shouted to boisterous cheers.

"But I didn't win," Rudy said with a twisted grin.

Leave it to Rudy Tutti to snow on his own parade.

Snowflake reached for a second slice. "Technicality, Rudy. Look around. Tinsel's the one at home licking his Fudgesicle."

Silentnight nearly choked on a raisin. "Ha! That's a good one, Snowflake!"

"Thank you, Sy." Snowflake's eyelashes fluttered, making Silentnight blush and quickly look away.

I could so picture the two of them making snow angels together. How cute!

I washed down an enormous bite of my fruitcake pizza with a delicious peppermint milkshake and said, "You could at least try some, Rudy." I waved the rest of my slice under his crooked nose to no avail.

"I got a better idea," he said. "I heard about this place called Rocks that sounds pretty cool."

"Oh, it's *cool* all right," Sugarcookie said, sprinkling extra sugar over her piece.

The rest of us tittered knowingly.

I broke off a small piece of crust and played with it in my fingers. "How'd you happen to hear about that place, Rudy?"

"Let's just say a little bird told me."

"That's silly. Birds don't talk."

"What about your butler? I heard him talk."

"Chefy? He's a penguin."

"Yeah. And penguins are birds."

"Yes. But they don't fly."

Rudy paused, then shook his head. "Whatever. Is anyone else for gettin' out of this dump?"

Yay! I'd won *that* argument. I lodged the pizza-crust crouton between my teeth and chewed.

A crease formed between Silentnight's dark bushy eyebrows. "Are you sure you want to go *there*?"

"What's wrong with *therrre*?" Rudy stretched out the last word with uncalled-for sarcasm. "Do they only serve reindeer or something?"

"We don't go *there*, Rudy." Silentnight lowered his voice to a whisper. "That's in Eggnog Alley."

"So?"

Everybody knew about Eggnog Alley, though none of us had ever been. It's like, a place for grownups and stuff. Then again, *we were sixteen*. We weren't kids anymore. We were juniors in high school. And someday soon, we'd be old enough to go wherever we wanted. Wouldn't it make sense to find out now if Eggnog Alley might be one of those places?

Besides, we were probably already in deep polar bear poo with Daddy for all the chaos we'd caused on Main Street. And I didn't exactly care for Rudy barging into our little world treating us like a bunch of big babies—like he was better than us or something.

"Rudy's right," I announced. "This place is for the puffins. Who else feels like a little adventure?"

A round of blank stares met my unexpected enthusiasm. The seediest part of town was the last place my friends expected their sweet little Candycane Claus to lead them. But darn it, it was high time for this princess to grow a pear tree.

I waited for someone to break the silence. When that didn't happen, I polled them. Johnny had homework. Delicious was tired. Silent, too chicken. The two Cookies gave no excuse at all. Each "no" vote made the idea seem more and more foolish, while at the same time stoking some burning desire to prove something to someone.

I couldn't very well go to Eggnog Alley alone. Not with just Rudy. So I sucked down some more of my peppermint milkshake and tried not to think about how boring a night at T.G.I. Fruitcake had suddenly become.

Boring because *he* saw it that way.

He leaned back and balanced his chair on its hind legs, bored out of his mind. Bored as Thanksgiving. *Bored with me.*

Swans a-swimming! Who was I kidding? *He* was the one I was trying to prove something to!

The conversation journeyed to other topics and by the time the food was gone, everyone had forgotten all about my silly suggestion. Rudy stuffed his wavy, dark-chocolate hair into his black knit cap and stood as he thanked us for the treats he didn't even eat. He planned on going to Rocks with or without us. I made him promise to wait for me and Snowflake to get back from the bathroom before he said goodbye.

Yes, we have bathrooms up here. Someone actually asked me about that once when I was traveling with Daddy. We're regular people, you know. We're not cartoons!

Anyway, I asked Snowflake about her plans for the rest of the night as she rinsed the sticky fruitcake residue from her hands with the powdery cinnamon-scented soap in the ladies room.

"What do you mean?" She peered oddly at my reflection in the mirror before breezing over to the electric hand dryer. "This was it."

"I meant after. What do you want to do next?" I had to raise my voice and repeat myself to be heard over the loud whirring noise, which made me self-conscious.

Snowflake furrowed her brow at me as if I had just refused a Christmas present. "Candy, what's with you tonight? This is what we always do."

"Tell me about it." I folded my arms across my chest and pouted. "We hang out here all the time. Then we go home and study. Rudy's right. It's boring."

Snowflake blinked twice and shook her head, hopelessly lost. "*Rudy's* right? Rudy's *trouble*, is what Rudy is."

"No. I think you had it right the first time, Snowflake."

"What are you caroling about, Candy?"

"His first day here, when you said you thought he was hot chocolate. You were right…" The warm pocket of air shooting out of the wall fell into echoey silence just as I blurted, "Rudy *is* hot chocolate!"

Snowflake giggled at how loudly that had come out.

I watched my cheeks go bright cherry-red in the mirror and covered my face to hide them, peeking through my fingers as if watching a horror movie. I half-expected Rudy to appear in front of the bathroom door holding his belly from laughing so hard, though he couldn't possibly have heard my embarrassing admission over the noisy restaurant clatter and the PA system blaring a version of "Let It Snow! Let It Snow! Let It Snow!" by Kenny G. (Egad, no wonder he wanted to leave this place!)

When Rudy didn't materialize, I turned back to Snowflake and waited.

"You really think so?" she finally said, twirling the notion through her brain the same way she twirled her long strands of honey-blonde hair through her fingers. "He is, isn't he?"

I closed my eyes, relieved to have finally unburdened myself, to have shared my weird secret crush with my best friend. I knew she'd understand. "I think we should go with him to Rocks," I told her. "Tonight."

"We should!" She turned to her giddy reflection and began to apply some blush to her beautiful porcelain skin. "Do you really think he likes me?"

Huh? I swallowed hard and blanched. "Um, I don't know. I kind of meant *I* think he's hot chocolate." My voice dropped to such a mumbly whisper, I wasn't certain she'd heard me.

"You?" She frowned and froze, a dab of sparkly pink-lemonade lip gloss on her fingertip, ready to dance across her full lips. "But you're the one who said he was bah-humbug."

"He is."

"And you said he was rude and that's why he was called Rude-y."

Haha. I barely remembered telling her that one, but I did say it. Or rather, I'd repeated it after hearing my father say it at breakfast following the Welcoming Feast.

"I know. He's all those things," I said.

"And now you *like* him?" She stared, her cat's eyes now as wide as saucers.

I made a pathetic grin, laced with insecurity, and felt the fruitcake pizza bounce around inside my stomach like a pinball.

Snowflake went back to her lip gloss. She puckered in the mirror when she finished, then said, "That's too bad, Candy. I liked him first. And I think you turned me off of him on purpose so you could have him for yourself!"

"It wasn't like that, Snowflake. I would never do that to you."

"And you already *have* a boyfriend!" She was starting to screech.

I sneaked another peek at the door, waiting for all my friends to plow through and yell at me and pelt me with used marshmallows. I didn't have a good case for them not to.

"And now you want me to go to Eggnog Alley and be a third wheel to you and *him*? Next you'll be wanting me to lie to Tinsel for you too!" She banged her fist on the hand dryer and clomped around me to one of the stalls.

I stared after her, stunned, my emotions swirling like the noisy fan in that dryer bolted to the fluorescent fuchsia wall. I shouldn't have needed someone to remind me I had a boyfriend who didn't deserve to be lied to. But Snowflake was right. Rudy would have to explore Eggnog Alley on his own. All I wanted was to go and hug my best friend and apologize and thank her for finally snapping me out of whatever stupid spell I'd been under.

I strode across the pink-tiled floor as Snowflake yanked on the toilet paper roll and began to stuff wadded-up squares of tissue into her bra. I held onto her wrists and almost laughed in her face. "You don't need to do that, Snowflake. Trust me."

She let the paper snowballs drift to the floor. "So now you won't even let me go with you at all, huh?"

"First of all, no, I meant you're beautiful the way you are. Boys have always been attracted to you."

She crossed her arms and rolled her emerald eyes.

I put my lips by her ear, pushing her hair out of the way, so I wouldn't have to shout—that dryer was bound to shut off again at the next inopportune moment. "And second of all, no boy is hot chocolate enough to come between us. Especially not Rudy Tutti."

Her chin wobbled the way it did that time we were nine and she'd heard that awful rumor about my family and I had to convince her that her best friend wasn't imaginary. Finally, she dropped her arms back down to her sides, allowing me to stretch mine around her and hold her tight like a lifelong friend should.

"You know what? I think I'd better go see how Tinsel's doing getting all that fudge out of his hair."

Snowflake smiled and began to laugh. "He was pretty gooey, wasn't he?" We left the bathroom giggling like sorority sisters and headed back to our table, the weight of a Christmas goose lifted off my shoulders. "I really appreciate what you're doing," she whispered. "It'll be so much easier to get Rudy to notice me if you're not there."

She zipped through the restaurant so fast, I didn't have time to say, *wait, that wasn't what we decided, was it?* I never expected her to still want to go without me. I practically had to jog to keep up with her.

Rudy had one foot aimed at the door. Impatient from having waited exactly as long as I'd made him promise, he gave us a weak half-wave goodbye.

Snowflake pinched his elbow. "Hold on a sec. So who's all

going to Rocks?"

Silentnight examined a spot of dirt on his leather snow boots. "We could get in trouble."

"What's a little trouble?" she taunted.

Silent hemmed and hawed and searched for a safe way to wimp out while the others re-voiced their earlier reasons for wanting to head home.

Rudy's face lit up with that night-before-Christmas twinkle in his baby-blues. "Looks like it's just me and the girls then."

Snowflake inched closer to Rudy, her eyes minty pools of puppy love pleading with me to beg out, to let her have this adventure with the new bad boy in town.

I have a boyfriend, I reminded myself. *And Snowflake doesn't. And I don't really like Rudy anyway, do I?* "I just remembered, I have to do something for my father tonight."

Rudy smirked in a way that signaled either disappointment or relief—I couldn't decide which—and said, "Wouldn't want to get Santa's little princess into hot water. Let's go, Snowbird."

My whole body stiffened, enraged, as my bestie blithely bumped past me, pulling Rudy away as if they were in the path of a looming avalanche. Before they were halfway to the door, I cleared my throat and shouted, "*Excuse me?* This little princess does whatever the heck she wants!"

nine

Snowflake glared at me as I stabbed my arms into the sleeves of my red-and-white-striped parka. But whether she wanted it or not, she deserved my protection from this boy who literally didn't know her name. My fleeting, teeter-tottering infatuation had nothing to do with it. I swear.

Delicious and the others filed out behind us and splintered off in their own directions, calling out their have-funs and see-ya-laters until only four of us remained. Silentnight had decided at the last minute to come with, our quartet trudging through the slush as lavender wisps of twilight began to paint the sky.

The short walk took us two blocks down Kringle Avenue, then left onto Pipers Lane, and right onto Coal Street. Midway down that block, on the right-hand side, just past the North Star Bucks, lay the small, dead-end row of clubs and establishments tucked neatly out of view from the kind of Poleans who might be content with a fruitcake pizza and a movie rental for their nightly entertainment. We had officially retired from that category with our first hesitant steps into the alley.

Snowflake shouted and whooped and acted super excited, trying to mask her fear—or perhaps her lingering resentment toward my presence—until a filthy mound of snow startled her. The city's enormous snow-whitening machines unable to squeeze through the narrow alleyway, the ground in this tiny passage remained the only part of town blanketed in dirt-flecked snow. The large gray lump that had stopped Snow in her tracks, and dimmed her woo-hoos and we're-heres, however, was *alive*.

The sad little polar bear, asleep in the gutter, looked as if he hadn't bathed in a week. His grimy, matted fur blended in with the muck-colored mush that surrounded him. His chest rose and fell rhythmically, his lungs filling with air then releasing it in a groan-filled sigh. As we tiptoed around the slumbering ursine mass, his paws began to twitch as though he might have been hunting in his dream.

A line of unfamiliar storefronts dotted the left-hand side of the alley, anchored by The Naughty List. A sign over its door claimed they sold books and toys. But rather than display their bestsellers in the front window to entice shoppers to come in, the glass was painted over in pitch black. Right next to that stood the Maids A-Milking Massage Parlor. We couldn't see inside there either, but I started to get a sense of why the boys in choir would sometimes giggle whenever we got to the eighth day of Christmas in my all-time favorite carol.

Opposite those two businesses, some older boys crouched in a dark, recessed doorway doing foots. I half-expected Rudy to change his mind and try to detour us all into the massage parlor or join the 'toeheads, but to my surprise, none of that seemed to interest him.

"That must be it," he said, pointing to the crystalline palace perched at the far end of Eggnog Alley.

Rocks. Staring brightly and invitingly at any passers-by who might choose to venture down the squalid aisle.

"Duh," I said, like I'd been there a hundred times. In truth I must have gone by this alley a million times with nary a second glance. Never in my life had it occurred to me I might be missing something here until Rudy first brought it up an hour ago. The long and lively queue waiting to get inside surprised as much as enticed me, like the call of a brand new roller coaster at Candyland.

A large, imposing Inuit gentleman guarded the door, controlling who could enter and who had to wait outside. Everyone there appeared older than us, but we were among the tallest. We sheepishly took our places at the end of the line and whispered amongst ourselves, "How are we going to get in?"

"Relax," Rudy said with a cool confidence that made Snowflake swoon. "I've gotten into tougher places than this."

"We really shouldn't be here," Silentnight groaned.

"Miss Claus," a husky voice barked from the front of the line. I shuddered and looked away from its source. "Candy Claus. Get over here!"

I felt dozens of beady eyes fall on me. I turned to Snowflake for help, expecting her to be super angry: *How could you be so stupid? Everyone in town knows who you are. Now you've ruined it for all of us!* But instead, her jaw dropped just like mine and her only instinct was to tell me to run, to save myself.

I didn't have time. Grubby, tiny hands reached up and passed me forward to the next in line like a block of ice in an igloo-building brigade. They threw me at the feet of the brawny Eskimo bouncer who tore my cap off my head and mussed my gingery tresses. "Child, you don't remember me?"

I searched his wide face, his oval cheeks, his neatly trimmed eyebrows, until his two different-colored eyes—brown on the left, hazel on the right, hidden behind their narrow slits—finally jogged my memory. "Nagloolik!" I cried. Of course I knew him. He had wandered from his tribe about three years ago, lost in a blizzard. Blitzen and Donner had come upon him while they were out exercising. They brought him back to our house and Mom fixed him up with Chefy's famous chocolate noodle soup. Nagloolik decided to stay in our village and we held a splendid Welcoming Feast for him where he told stories about all the sled races he'd won as a boy.

"Santa's little girl don't have to wait in no line," he said as he launched the door open for me.

I looked for my friends. Silent cowered in a ball, his eyes hidden in his sleeve. Snowflake tugged on his earmuffs to clue him in on our reversal of fortune—from underage trespassers to VIPs.

Already pushing his way past everyone else, Rudy was all too eager to indulge in my cutsies without so much as the courtesy to wait for my say-so. Not that I would have left him out in the cold, but still.

I waved Silent and Snow over and fished a cookie out of my purse for Nagloolik. The four of us then crossed the chilly threshold together.

I'd heard Rocks was made entirely of ice—that was the inside joke we had giggled about when Rudy referred to the place as "cool"—but if I'd known how beautiful it was inside, how stunning, beyond anything I'd ever dreamed, I would have insisted we check it out years ago.

Chiseled blocks of ice formed frozen tables and seats. Smoothly powdered ice columns rose from the floor. Curtains of glistening icicles dangled across space in intricate, criss-cross patterns. Drinks were served at a long, translucent bar. Every piece of ice glowed in an ever-changing array of swirling hues that flashed and pulsated with the driving beat of the music being spun by Kanye North, the DJ seal. On the slippery stage next to him, three dancing-girl seals performed all manner of flips and loop-the-loops over vertical ice rings, like floppy, breathing, bendable Hot Wheels cars. What a sight!

The clientele included polar bears, walruses, and several other humans besides us, but mostly the place was crawling with elves. Elves everywhere. Climbing the barstools, sliding across the floor, hanging from ice sculptures.

Only a few steps inside the door, a large, feathery flipper landed on my shoulder. My heart leaped out of my parka. I spun around, relieved to find a stern but familiar penguin face bearing down on me. "Chefy!"

"Does your father know where you are, Candycane?"

My nerves frayed again. I pressed my lips together and stared up his beak with hopeful, pleading eyes. "He won't find out from you, will he?"

"Now let me think," the penguin pontificated. "He never did find out about the time you filled his cap with molasses, did he?"

"I never did anything like that!"

"Oh, that's right. *I* did it. Your father is so much fun to prank. But it seems I've let the cat out of the bag, and now *you* have a secret on *me*. Quid pro quo."

"Quid pro quo, Chefy."

He held out his flipper and I tapped my fist against it.

"It's Silly Hour. Come, I'll buy you a candy-cane eggnog."

"Super!"

We followed him to an ice cold table. A bearded seal in a striped tuxedo waddled over with a fresh bowl of gingerbread cookie pieces. I nibbled on a foot while Chefy ordered us eggnogs all around. Rudy tilted his head back and tossed himself a gingerbread head, prompting the waiter to clap his flippers at his seal-like behavior before leaving to fetch our refreshments.

Rudy pointed to a giant ice sculpture at one end of the bar, shaped in the form of a larger-than-life-sized elf-god. An ice cube container rested atop its pointy head, holding a hundred pounds of a glowing orange substance. "Looks like someone dropped Garfield in a blender," he said.

A burly panda bartender dispensed the smelly concoction from a nozzle on the side of the cube. He slid small bowls of the stuff, one after the other, down the bar's slippery surface. Speedy elf fingers darted at the passing snacks, cleaning the bowls dry before they reached the far end without ever slowing them down.

"*Elf*nip," Chefy said with a hint of indignation.

"You wouldn't like it, Rudy," Snowflake added. "Trust me."

"The lady is correct. Although, I am told it is the best in town. Hence the swarming popularity of this establishment with those miniature toymakers."

Rudy took in the vast number of wee folk bouncing off the frozen walls like a thousand dwarfs in a Busby Berkeley musical in super-fast-forward mode. "I get it. Heroin for Munchkins."

"Not exactly. You've come on a very special night. Or had you not previously noticed the tenor of the sky?"

"*Twilight Eve!*" Snowflake, Silent, and I blurted in unison. Then we squealed in embarrassed laughter.

I tried to bring Rudy up to speed as delicately as I knew how. "You know how it's been daylight all the time since you moved here?" He nodded. "And did you notice the sky turning purple while we were walking here?" Another nod. "This is the first night of twilight. It'll be like that all day and all night. It lasts about a month. Then it stays dark for the next five months."

"I took astronomy at my old school. I know how it works. I didn't come here thinking the earth was flat."

Snowflake decided I wasn't getting to the point fast enough, so she leaned in, touching his forearm, and squawked loud enough to be heard over the music: "Twilight is the mating season for elves."

I blushed at the sight of an elf I thought I recognized

turning a quadruple somersault on the dance floor just as our seal returned with our drinks. Chefy raised his glass and we toasted the ribald elfin holiday.

Right from the first sip, the eggnog tasted funny. Funny in the sense that it made me want to laugh more than usual. It smelled like regular eggnog, but with the volume turned way up on the candy-cane flavoring. My mother's 'nog never tasted like this.

I laughed at Silent's and Rudy's milk mustaches and licked mine away before they could see it. Then I cracked open one end of the paper wrapper on my straw and blew the other end into Rudy's face. I laughed again as it bounced off his square chin and landed in his drink. He looked at me stone-faced as he plucked it out.

I stabbed the straw into my frosty glass and drew up a longer sample of that unusual taste when a spherical elf rolled into my legs like a bowling ball, mid-sip, making me jump. He unfurled himself, blanching when he realized he'd torpedoed his boss's daughter. I assured him Daddy would never hear about our collision from me. The little guy seemed not to grasp how I would be in way more trouble than he if my father knew where I was. Especially on Twilight Eve.

He apologized profusely until Chefy shoved him back across the ice like a shuffleboard weight. A young elfette then whirled him in a circle. As the music got faster, they danced like they were on fire.

"I think he liked you," Snowflake teased.

"Shut *up!*" I hid my beet-red face behind my hands and rocked with laughter.

Then she added, "It's too bad Tinsel isn't here, this being Twilight Eve and all."

My mouth flew open and I flung a gingerbread torso at

Snowflake's head, which rolled down the front of her shirt.

Although we'd been dating for two years, Tinsel had never even talked about doing *that* with me. He knew how to suppress his elf urges. In fact, he used to strive so hard to be more human that in sixth grade we started calling him Spock behind his back.

Snowflake had made her crude insinuation purely for the sake of bringing up my half-elf boyfriend's name in front of Rudy. She still thought I was trying to steal the boy she'd called dibs on. And I swear, I wasn't. I was so over him by then, I seriously considered calling Tinsel and demanding he get his bells over there to share in all the fun and excitement.

So I don't know what made me take another swallow of my delicious drink and say, "Um, Sy, why don't you ask Snowflake to dance?"

Snowflake ignored me and dug the cookie piece out of her bra. She looked at it and said, "I can't believe you threw a gingerbread boy's you-know-what at me!" Then she put it in her mouth and bit down hard on it.

"Ew! I can't believe you just *ate* a gingerbread boy's you-know-what!" The unusual-tasting eggnog was making me act more juvenile than usual.

And maybe it was the eggnog, too, that made Silentnight decide to take my advice. He finished his beverage and boldly faced Snowflake. "Let's dance."

"Do I look like an elf?" she snapped.

Silent shrank onto his block of ice. "Sorry. It sounded like such a good idea when Candy said it."

"Then go dance with Candy."

"But she has a boyfriend."

Snowflake chirped and stuck out her tongue as if she'd scored some huge victory—having gotten it out there, the

B-word, in front of Rudy and everything. "That's right. She does." She slammed her hands on the wet table to push herself up. "Okay, let's dance. And you'd better be good."

Silentnight shot up from his seat like a jack-in-the-box and sprang to the dance floor so fast he nearly forgot to take Snowflake with him. Chefy and I cracked up at the ridiculous sight of two full-grown teenagers dancing in a sea of manic elves. But to Snowflake's astonishment, Silent really had the moves. He twirled on his head, kicking out his wiry legs, then popped up and whipped Snowflake high over his head like a windmill.

I poked Rudy. "Don't they look adorable?"

"That's not the word I was thinking of."

"Don't worry, Rudy. I wasn't going to make you dance with me."

"Of course not. We wouldn't want your pointy-eared *boyfriend* to get his tights all in a twist, now would we?"

I cast an angry glance back at Snowflake, then against my better judgment, prodded Rudy further on the subject. "Are you peanut butter and jelly?"

"What?"

"You know. Jealous."

"Of Tonsil?"

"Tinsel."

"Why should I be?"

"You shouldn't."

"Then I'm not."

"Good."

Did that count as flirting? I wished I could take it all back. I allowed another long draw of the strange liquid to run down my throat and felt a buzz in my head that was part brain freeze and part something else.

"Besides, Tinsel doesn't own me," I heard myself saying over the throbbing beats that came from either the DJ or my racing heart. "…If you wanted to dance with me, I mean."

"In a room full of elves in heat on some kind of Keebler Viagra? I'll pass."

Chefy howled at that. He must have misread my squirming as a sign that I wanted to be alone with Rudy, because he picked that moment to excuse himself to use the restroom.

"Rudy, the elfnip doesn't make them, you know…" I paused. His marble-blue eyes pierced into me so sharply I had to look away. "It makes them want to dance. Word on the playground is, the dancing takes their minds off of… *that*. Like it speeds up their metabolism or something. And somehow, this whole suppression of… you know… and all that dancing gives them the energy to make all the toys they need to make between Twilight Eve and Christmas Eve. The busy season."

I sipped some more eggnog before continuing, "They say Daddy never could have gotten his workshop business started without the elfnip."

Rudy shook his head. "I've heard a lot of stupid stuff since I moved here, but that is definitely the stupidest."

A pang of nausea hit me. Whether caused by whatever mysterious ingredient was in that drink, or the exhilarating discomfort of being laughed at in the face by this strangely captivating outsider, my head began to throb louder than the pounding music. Why had I wasted so much energy thinking about him in the first place?

I rummaged around the gingerbread-parts bowl. Nothing left but discarded gingerbread bones. Yuk. "Why *did* you move up here, Rudy?"

"Believe me, it wasn't my choice." He took a giant gulp of his eggnog, then added, "It's a little too 'Ho-ho-ho' for me, you know?"

"What's that supposed to mean?" I scowled and shifted slightly on my ice block, wondering how much longer I'd have to endure his Rude-y-ness, then glanced at the dance floor. Silent and Snowflake were still kicking it up. I was stuck with Rudy the way my pants were beginning to stick to the ice, and for a second I regretted not having let Snowflake go have her own miserable time with Ebenezer Tutti.

He stirred his eggnog with his straw. "You're the smartest one in class. I don't think I need to spell things out for you."

I grunted loudly at him, certain I would never figure him out. Why would he call me smart a minute after insulting me? I pressed my fist into my hip. "You're impossible, Rudy Tutti."

"Impossible for what?"

"To have a simple conversation with!"

"Oh? What do you talk about with Tonsil?"

"Could you please stop talking about him, *please*?"

"Whatever."

An awkward minute passed without any more painful words.

When, oh when, would my Chefy come rescue me? I panned to the bathroom, catching sight of him at the bar engaged in some hilarious anecdote with a small group of captivated puffins. I'd been abandoned. My tall feathery friend just might end up with a lump of coal from me this year.

Silent and Snowflake showed no signs of slowing. I'd made my igloo, now I had to sit in it—with *him*—until the ride came to a complete stop.

"So what do you want to talk about?" he asked.

And my ironic answer only served to confuse him as I turned back to look at him and instead found the very half-person I'd just insisted I didn't want to discuss—stalking behind him, glaring at the two of us, waggling his long, elfish fingers in a way that made them look creepy.

"Tinsel," I said.

ten

"I thought you said you didn't want to talk about—" Rudy fell silent once he caught my gaze bouncing past him. He turned slowly to face his adversary, all cleaned up now and mad as heck. "Well, speak of the glandular leprechaun. If it isn't Fondue Man himself."

I tried to hide all emotion. "When did you get here?"

Tinsel's nostrils flared, ready for trouble. "Time to teach you a lesson, Tutti." His anger brought his voice to a loud, high-pitched fury.

Kanye North stopped spinning records. Lights stopped flashing. A thousand pairs of elfin eyes trained on the two boys who were about to go at each other big time—over me. I should have been flattered. Instead I had a sickening feeling in the pit of my stomach and decided I was not yet grown up enough to handle this kind of excitement. I badly wanted to go home.

"I don't need to learn how to wrap Christmas presents, Tinhead," Rudy answered back.

A few elves gasped. A few others tittered.

Tinsel guffawed with faux cackles at Rudy's bravado.

"What's so funny, elf-man?"

"You're about to find out." Tinsel stuffed his ticklers into his mouth and made a shrill, cartoonish whistling sound that summoned six abnormally strong elves to sneak up out of nowhere and grab hold of Rudy.

They had him pinned to the tabletop like a damsel on a railroad track before he had time to flinch. His struggles were of no use—these guys were enormous for elves.

"Don't do it, Tinsel!" I cried.

"Stay out of this, Candy. It's got nothing to do with you." Tinsel advanced toward his supine victim.

"You're being foolish. You have no idea." I didn't like this new side of Tinsel at all. My knees were shaking but I had to say something. "Rudy and I can barely stand each other."

"Gee thanks, Candy," Rudy muttered.

"Seriously, Tinsel. You've got it all wrong. It's not like this is a date or anything. We were just waiting for Snowflake and Silentnight."

"She's telling the truth." Snowflake had somehow materialized at my side without my noticing. Silentnight and Chefy had returned as well and I felt a little stronger.

My boyfriend waved his snake-like fingers in Rudy's face.

I grabbed him by the waist and tried with all my might to pull him away but his bells made nary a jingle for my effort. "Tinsel, stop! You can't do this!"

"Watch me!" he screamed.

Then he did something I never would have expected of him in a million years. He pushed me off of him. Hard. So hard my feet flew out from under me and my bottom made an audible thud on the icy floor. The pain and humiliation of a bruised and banged up buttock was nothing compared to the hurt of a swift, careless shove coming from someone who supposedly...

I thought he loved me? I thought he loved me?

The thought kept running through my head, unable to reconcile itself with his brutish act. I imagined everyone laughing at me. If I hadn't been on such a stupid quest to be more grown up, I would have cried.

"How *dare* you!" Chefy bellowed at my attacker as he

70

gingerly placed me back on my feet.

"Take her home, Chefy. This is between me and Tutti."

Two of Tinsel's thuggish elves released their hold on Rudy and thrust their claws menacingly at Chefy. The remaining four tightened their grip.

Tinsel encroached further on his prisoner. "You're not getting out of this," he hissed.

"That ain't fair," Silentnight protested, worried beads of sweat forming across his wide forehead and trembling upper lip.

"I can't watch." Snowflake turned away. So did Silent.

Rudy grimaced, bracing for Tinsel's wrath, helpless, so undeserving of his predicament.

I had to look away too. I shut my eyes tight when I heard the screaming start. Those horrible screams. He sounded like a little girl.

You know how out-of-control it feels when you don't want to laugh but you can't help it? When you're trying to stop but your opponent won't let up?

Tickle fights are just about the worst thing that can happen to anyone at the N.P.

Poor Rudy. "Ahahahahaha! Stop it! Stop it! Teeheeeheehahahaha-heeheehe-hehe!" he squeaked impotently.

I pried my eyelids open into a squint. I couldn't stand not knowing what was happening. Tinsel was ruthless, his merciless ticklers wiggling vigorously under Rudy's square chin, in the pits of his strong but immobilized arms, across the soles of his feet, in itty-bitty curlicues over his tight muscular belly. Those incredible fingers that could reach every tickle spot at once. Rudy didn't stand a chance.

A wave of contagious laughter emanated outward from the tickle torture's epicenter as Rudy's limbs spasmed wildly. One of the thugs lost hold of a kicking leg. He called for the two who were holding Chefy back. They rushed over to help keep their captive anchored to the ice slab.

On Chefy's command, Snowflake, Silent, and I rushed in with him to tickle the six super-elves. Within seconds, three of them had let go to tickle us back. We were all laughing insufferably, but Rudy was almost free.

The tickle fight quickly escalated to a Tickle War. Elves tickled walruses, who tickled polar bears, who tickled puffins, who tickled elves. The deafening laughter drowned out the silly symphony record Kanye North had found to accompany the mayhem.

Cackling elves slid everywhere. Across every frosty surface. They knocked into each other like hockey pucks, setting off chain reactions. Chefy ricocheted into Tinsel, and the two of them went at it—Chefy taking full advantage of his tickly feathers against the maniacal elfman—giving Rudy the opening he'd been waiting for to finally break free.

Rudy lunged at his rival, but revenge eluded him—well, sort of. He slipped on the ice and knocked a laughing seal across the floor and up an ice buttress, nearly to the ceiling. The jovial gray mammal floundered through the air, gravity hurling her full weight down to smash Tinsel with enough force to propel him clear across the dance floor.

Like an elfin cannonball, Tinsel shot onto the stage where he zoomed through a loop-the-loop, the momentum sending him high over the heads of the hysterical crowd.

Amidst my tickle-induced shrieks, I shook off all my torturers in time to see Tinsel land on the ice bar, speeding down its surface like a human luge, picking up speed, his arms and legs flailing, until at last he slammed smack-dab into the elfnip dispenser, crotch-first.

Right in the bells!

eleven

"I bet that didn't tickle," Chefy quipped.

I fought to see if Tinsel was alive, but couldn't get close. Doused in elfnip, a swarm of his elfin half-brethren had promptly pounced on his bruised and aching body.

No one was ever supposed to get *hurt* in a tickle fight. Poor Tinsel ended up with a couple bruised ribs, a big lump on his forehead, and worst of all, a broken funny bone. It would be some time before he'd be able to jingle again.

He had no one to blame but himself, really. And the way he had treated me was inexcusable. Still, I couldn't help but wonder—maybe it had something to do with Twilight Eve. Maybe his elf hormones and human hormones had gotten all mixed up, turning him into a were-elf or something. Like some force he couldn't control that might go away in a day or two, and he would turn back into the perfect boyfriend he'd always been.

But honestly, the change had been building since before Twilight Eve. Going back to when I'd first started acting all nutcracker over Rudy. So I supposed it was partly my fault too. And let's face it, Rudy wasn't so blameless either. He could make anybody nutcracker with his bah-humbuggery. Daddy always says it only takes one bad partridge to spoil the whole pear tree.

Or was I just making excuses for Tinsel? Conflicting emotions jumbled my brain. I needed to see him face to face to clear it all up, but it was late by the time the ambulance took him away.

Chefy brought me home, where I feared much worse than a tickling awaited me. Luckily my father had gone to bed early with a toothache. My mother made no mention of the incident on Main Street. Either Daddy hadn't said anything, or she'd agreed to let him spring it on me himself in the morning with the full-on lecture-and-punishment combo.

I tossed and turned all night as visions of tickle fights danced in my head—only *I* was the one being tickled against my will, while Rudy sat under a gumdrop tree reading a book.

As it turned out, Daddy hadn't slept well that night either. When I came down for breakfast the next morning, he was grumpier than I'd ever seen him. Mom demanded he let Chefy make him an appointment with Dr. Tutti right away.

"It's no emergency," my father grumbled, holding one side of his face. "In fact, I don't need a doctor at all. Chefy, bring me my jelly beans."

"Right away, boss."

Chefy and I exchanged the slightest of nods as he set Daddy's favorite comfort food on the table.

"Good morning, princess," Daddy said when he saw me in the doorway.

I quietly sat and grinned, afraid to say anything that might upset him. He threw a fistful of bright red jelly beans into his mouth, then yowled in pain the moment he started chewing.

My mother put her foot down. "You are *going* to the dentist, dear, and that is all there is to it."

"Look outside, for Christmas sake!" He gestured out the window at the orangey pinkish purple horizon. "It's already Dusk! Don't you realize how much work I have to do?"

"The whole world knows how much work you have to do. And you certainly won't be able to do any of it with that toothache."

"My teeth can wait until after Christmas."

"Oh, poo," she said, pursing her ruby-red lips. "You're afraid to go to the dentist and you're going to make Christmas suffer because of it, you stubborn old fool." She pulled the lightly chilled dish of sweets out of his reach, leaving him with just the few beans that had gathered on his spoon.

"I am not being stubborn. I don't trust that Tutti fellow. I can chew on the other side of my mouth until Christmas." He emptied the spoon into his wide-open maw to demonstrate. After a tense minute of extremely careful chewing, he swallowed. "You see? I'm fine. Ho-ho-ho."

Chefy served us breakfast—poached caramel apples wrapped in bacon and sprinkled with nuts and Milk Duds. Daddy frowned at the goodies and rose from his chair. "You know what? I have so much to do, I'm going to skip breakfast today. I'll grab something at the Workshop."

He bent over to kiss me, his prickly white whiskers softly brushing my cheek. It was all I could do to keep from leaping up and down like a child who'd gotten exactly what she'd wished for for Christmas. That wonderful, blessed toothache must have given him amnesia! Or maybe he hadn't noticed me on Main Street after all. Either way, I wasn't about to bring it up. Ever.

"I'm glad you're feeling better, Daddy. And for what it's worth, I don't trust those Tuttis either."

He turned to my mother and held out his hands with another I-told-you-so look. "I'm telling you, there's something the matter with those people. Who's a better judge of character than our own beautiful daughter?"

"Thank you, Daddy." I blushed and beamed.

"Fiddlesticks," my mother countered. "You're looking for an excuse to get rid of them so you won't have to get that toothache looked at." She smoothed a crease on her white chiffon blouse, then passed me the peppermint jam to spread on my apple. "And you, young lady, have a responsibility as a Claus to help that nice boy fit in."

Ugh. The responsibility speech again.

The door flew open and Frostbite breezed in, with Flip and Flop in tow. "Guess what! Guess what! Tommy Toboggan just texted me. There was a huge tickle fight last night at Rocks and—"

"Tickle fights are boring," I said before he could spill any incriminating details. I faked a yawn to illustrate my point, then added a bribe: "Want a ride to school today?"

"Nah, I'll take my snow scooter."

I bristled at the mere mention of snow scooters, but that didn't seem to jog Daddy's memory. He crouched down to pet Flop and tickle Flip's belly, still trying to mask the pain in his tooth with his forced gaiety.

"Ooh-hoo-hoo!" Flip giggled. "I beg to differ, Miss Candycane, but how can anyone find tickle fights boring?"

"Flip's right," added Flop. "They're hilarious. They make *everyone* laugh."

"And chuckle."

"And chortle."

"And snortle."

"And wheedle."

"And guffaw."

"Oh, that's a good one, Flip. Guffaw!" Flop then proceeded to guffaw as loudly as he could.

"And that's not all." Frostbite hadn't finished the breaking news he'd heard from Johnny Toboggan's brother. "Tommy said that someone got—"

He was about to blab about Tinsel being sent to the hospital when Chefy roadblocked his words with a poached caramel apple, twice as big as my brother's mouth—if that's possible.

"Your father didn't want his breakfast today," Chefy explained. He winked at me when no one else was looking.

Frostbite munched on a mouthful while making some exclamatory response I couldn't decipher. He'd literally bitten off more than he could chew. Loose nuts and Milk Duds rained at his feet. The puffins vacuumed up the scraps, then flipped and flopped, begging for more.

With the three of them occupied, Daddy announced he was running late for work and took off. I was safe.

At school, everyone kept asking me about Tinsel. All day long, I repeated the same answers: Yes, he was hurt pretty bad. Not yet, but I'm planning to go see him after school. No, Rudy did not pull a knife on him!

Walter the Asthmatic Walrus made him a get-well card that looked like an arts-and-crafts project constructed by a second-grader. Mr. Polar Bear passed it around for the rest of the class to sign, then instructed us to pair up and start working on our tree assignment.

The Christmas tree pageant at the annual Snow Ball was a big deal at North Pole High. Tinsel and I had designed the winning trees in both our freshman and sophomore years. I had a new design I couldn't wait to implement, and the thought of working on it with Tinsel excited me for the first time in forever.

Mr. Polar Bear, however, had other plans. "Candycane, since Tinsel will be absent for the better part of the term, I would like you to work with Mr. Tutti."

No!

"Mr. Polar Bear? I'm sure I can work on it at the hospital. With Tinsel, I mean."

The bear scratched at the fur behind his small, coin-shaped ear. "Mmm, you could. But Rudy needs a partner and everyone else is already paired up. That won't be a problem, will it, Miss Claus?"

"No, sir."

"Will that be satisfactory with you, Mr. Tutti?"

"Super," Rudy said with that awful whiff of sarcasm he always had.

Neither of us wanted to make the first move. Rudy stared at the clock as Mr. Polar Bear padded away to collect Tinsel's card. I considered doing the project solo—a solution I was sure would have appealed to Rudy as well—but eventually sucked it up and waved him over. I waited while he dragged his desk across the linoleum. The horrible scraping sound signaled the start of what I fully expected to be a miserable collaboration. But I knew I'd better not pout.

I pulled out some sketches I'd made ahead of time. Rudy had never built a tree like the ones we cook up at N.P.H., so I would have to start him off with the basics—standard skeletal structure and stuff like that—before overwhelming him with my advanced design techniques. Regardless of who my partner was, I still intended to win.

"I didn't start that fight," he said.

"I know," I said, trying not to snap at him, trying not to look at him—trying to put the whole humiliating fracas out of my mind and focus on the task at hand.

He slouched. "Why are you mad at me?"

"I'm not."

"You haven't said one thing to me all day."

He had a point. We hadn't spoken since last night. I never even saw him leave Rocks. And our last conversation—before "the incident"—hadn't been going too peachy. So, okay, I *could*

78

have shown him some sympathy. After all, it was *my* insanely jealous boyfriend who had attacked him.

"Are you okay?" I said.

"Oh, you mean from Twinklebell?" He wiggled his fingers in the air, mimicking Tonsil. I mean Tinsel. "Not a scratch. You guys have a strange way of fighting here."

"I'm really sorry about that, Rudy. It was all my fault."

"No it wasn't. It was Tinkle's. What do you see in that guy anyway?"

"Rudy, focus." I felt my skull tightening. A numbness shot through my arms, starting at my shoulder blades and running all the way down to my candy-cane striped fingernails. "This tree is fifty percent of our grade."

"So? Why does every subject in this place have to be Christmas?" He flipped his pencil in the air, over and over.

"What's more important than Christmas?" I asked.

"I don't know. Math. History. Normal stuff."

Would Rudy ever see the Christmas lights? I sighed. I'd have to make that my goal for extra credit. What kind of Claus would I be if I couldn't get one pathetic, lonely boy to discover the joy of Christmas *in the middle of the freezing North Pole?*

"You want math?" I snatched his spinning pencil out of the air and used it to point to my diagrams. "I used the Pythagorean theorem to get the height of the tree. Are you looking?" I poked his hard bicep with the eraser end of his pencil. "Pay attention, Rudy! You want history?"

His piercing gaze penetrated my soul. I almost forgot to breathe for a second. My voice softened as I went on with my lesson.

"In the eighth century, Saint Boniface came upon a pagan ritual. An oak tree was about to be cut down and made into stakes to sacrifice children to the Norse god Thor. In protest,

Saint Boniface felled the oak tree with one blow of his ax. It split apart and a Christmas tree sprang up in its place. That's its history."

Rudy plucked his pencil from my fingertips.

"What are you doing?"

"I'm writing this down. It's an incredible story. Is there gonna be a quiz?"

"It *is* incredible," I said, ignoring his sarcasm, "but you can learn all that from Wikipedia. This assignment isn't about that. It's about each of us personifying our trees with our own Christmas Spirit."

"Sounds real... spiritual." He went back to playing with his lead-based toy.

"Do you want me to do this project by myself?"

He weighed the pencil in his hand for an eternity before he let out a deep sigh. "I didn't ask the teacher to pair me with you."

"I know that."

I wished I could read his mind. A strange chill traveled through me as I waited for an answer. It reminded me of the very first time I'd worked on a homework assignment with Tinsel.

Rudy scooted closer to get a better look at my diagrams. "Let's focus," he said.

For the rest of the period, I couldn't think straight. I vaguely recall babbling *ad nauseam* about the four main theories of tree trimming until the bell rang. I don't think he was listening anyway.

twelve

Bells chimed out the "March" from *The Nutcracker Suite* to signal the end of the school day, their dinging and donging still lingering in my ears when Snowflake swooped in on me, demanding to hear every last detail of whatever Rudy and I had been talking about.

Strictly schoolwork, I assured her. I had neither the time nor desire to relive that awkward hour. I was eager to get to the hospital to visit Tinsel. Snowflake tagged along to pump me for gossip anyway.

"There's nothing to tell," I insisted as we marched down Holiday Hill. "We're just tree partners."

"So you're gonna tell Tinsel, right?"

"Yeah, *that* would be smart." I bit my tongue, horrified I'd been infected with Rudy's sarcasm. "Seriously, don't tell him, all right?"

"Wanna switch?" She colored a light bounce into her step. "I'll take Rudy!"

"You know Mr. Polar Bear won't let us. Besides, you'll get a much better grade with Delicious."

"Oh, I get it." She hugged her schoolbooks and kept walking.

Cranberry sauce! I'd forgotten all about her dibs on Mr. Hot Chocolate. "Snowflaaake!" I rolled my eyes, quickening my pace until I caught up to her, then tugged on her elbow and turned her to face me. "You're my best friend. If you want to chase after Rudy Tutti, be my guest. I swear I don't like him."

She pulled away from me.

"Wait. I'll help you. Okay?" That made her stop. "I'm gonna have to spend like a bajillion hours with the loser on this assignment. I'm sure I can get him to ask you out. Trust me."

Her face got all goofy like it couldn't decide which of twelve emotions to express first. She lunged forward into a great big hug and squealed in my ear. "Oh, Candy! You would really do that for me?" She let go and gazed dreamily through the stars in her eyes. "Do you think you can get him to ask me to the Snow Ball?"

"You never know." I resumed our trek, anxious to get away from my lie. I honestly couldn't picture Rudy going anywhere near the Snow Ball—with anyone.

In a way, taking on the Snowflake Challenge solved one of my problems. As long as I concentrated on hooking them up, maybe I'd stop having my own weird thoughts about him— and keep him from getting any about me.

Plus, it couldn't hurt the Tinsel situation either. As we approached Yuletide General, I realized how much I'd been dreading this visit. I hadn't yet figured out what I wanted to do about the way he had acted at Rocks. Snowflake called his behavior "typical territorial boy stuff," as if she found his thuggishness romantic—even chivalrous. "And besides," she added, "he'll get over it once me and Rudy become an item."

His cramped hospital room overflowed with a forest of balloons sent by his relatives to cheer him up. A grotesque, vice-like contraption pinned his swollen head back against a stiff pillow. Tightly wound bandages encased his entire midsection and purplish bruises stained the rest of his body. At first, I didn't know if he could even talk.

We found him fighting a losing battle with a crazy straw and a peanut butter smoothie. I helped him set the difficult protein drink on the tray next to his bed as I told him how concerned all the kids at school were. I had to hold the get-well card in front of his face because he couldn't turn his head.

He scanned the signatures and all the cute comments his friends had written. He stopped at one. His lips formed as much of a frown as they were able. With great difficulty, he managed to lift his once-beautiful fingers—now withered and curled into ugly knots—and flick the card out of my hand.

Snowflake picked it up and looked over the personalized greetings. "Aww, isn't that sweet. Rudy signed it." She showed me where.

In the middle, plain as day, he had scrawled: I'M RUBBER, YOU'RE GLUE. LOL. BEST WISHES, RUDY.

"Mr. Polar Bear did say everyone had to write something," I offered. Tough crowd. I'd forgotten Tinsel had a broken funny bone, which would greatly affect his ability to appreciate irony.

"You think you can make a fool of me?" he mumbled. "Why did you come here, Candy?"

"I came because you're my friend, and you're hurt."

"Your friend. Not your boyfriend?" His expression went from pitiable to daggered eyes in the twinkling of a star. "You're seeing him."

"Do you really want to talk about this now?"

"I want you to leave."

My eyes began to mist.

"It's probably the drugs," Snowflake whispered to me, then shouted to him, as if he were deaf, "Did they dope you up? Put you on painkillers? Tell me if this hurts." She raised her Advanced Caroling textbook to the ceiling, ready to drop it on him like an atomic bomb.

"Snowflake! No!" I caught the book as soon as it left her fingertips and clutched it safely to my chest. "If anyone should hurt him it should be me."

"You already have," he said.

Incredible. We'd been there less than five minutes, and twice he'd tried to make *me* the villain. I made up my mind to quit thinking and just let words pour out of my mouth. "You know what, Tinsel? I came here to give you a second chance. But I want to go on record that what I'm about to do has nothing to do with anyone but you and me."

I leaned over him so he couldn't look away as I tore his classmates' handmade, heartfelt well-wishes into shreds. He didn't deserve them. Snowflake's jaw dropped.

"Rudy and I are just friends," I continued, "so don't think this has anything to do with him. It's hard for me to say this, Tinsel, but from what you've shown me, there is no chance of having a normal relationship between the two of us." I swallowed hard and shut my eyes before delivering the final blow. "I don't want to talk to you anymore. That's the reality of the situation. That's the way it has to be."

Then I ran. I didn't want to give him the chance to apologize. I didn't even look back when I heard the snap of balloons popping from all the anger I'd left hanging in the air.

I cried all the way home. Snowflake tried to tell me that Tinsel would come around in a few days, that we'd both calm down and talk it out and things would go back to normal. It's just a fight, she said. Every couple has to have a fight once in a while. And if we didn't make up, then we weren't meant to be.

Where the heck had Snowflake gleaned all this relationship knowledge? She'd never even been on a *date* before! I chose not to question her. I just held her hand, grateful to have her friendship.

I hardly said a word during dinner that night. Daddy mentioned how his workers were all abuzz about the melee at Rocks and I got even quieter.

"Those elves," he grumbled. "I'm lucky I can get them to do any work at all."

My mother frowned as I twirled my fork absently. "Is something the matter, dear?" She eyed my untouched mesquite-grilled ice cream kabobs.

"I'm not hungry," I said.

"Are you feeling all right?" Her gentle voice warmed me a little.

"I just want to lie down and then maybe do some homework."

She promised to look in on me later and reminded me to let Chefy know if I got my appetite back. I went up to my room and closed the door. As soon as I lay on my bed, comfortably surrounded by all my favorite stuffed animals, my phone rang.

"Are we still on for tonight? No skin off my back if we're not. We have a lot of groundwork to cover, according to you."

Jingle bells! I'd forgotten I had told Rudy I'd get together with him tonight to show him the rest of my designs for our tree.

thirteen

Dr. Tutti greeted me warmly when I arrived at their Noël Valley condo. He ushered me through the living room, dimly lit and cluttered with piles and piles of books, past the messy kitchen filled with the watery aroma of flavorless, sugarless vegetables, down a beige-carpeted, barren-walled hallway that led, finally, to Rudy's bedroom.

I thanked him for the tour, trying to hide my shock at being left alone in a bedroom with a boy, but relieved when he made a show of arcing the door all the way open before disappearing back to somewhere within earshot (I hoped).

Rudy's room lacked all the hallmarks of a typical teenager's room. No clothes crumpled on the floor, no toys or games or collectible lunchboxes or action figures, no posters on the walls. A simple desk, a nightstand. The bed neatly made. Unopened moving boxes stacked unobtrusively in a corner. The soulless interior giving away none of its owner's interests, his life, his personality—save for a shelf stuffed with novels by J.D. Salinger, S.E. Hinton, Ernest Hemingway, and Kurt Vonnegut, and a single framed photograph atop a dresser showing a beautiful woman with auburn hair and high cheekbones who could have been a movie star.

We got right to work. I started by showing him some photos of the trees I'd made with Tinsel the last two years, to give him an idea of what we were shooting for. Then I presented him with the early design ideas I'd already sketched in my spare time for the new one. The root theme would be candy canes, of course. I had envisioned a tree as tall and as thick as Paul

Bunyan's blue ox, blanketed in red and white flowers arranged in brilliant candy-cane patterns. I'd dreamed of that tree since I was three, but had not been allowed to bring it to fruition in my freshman or sophomore years because, as underclassmen, we were assigned themes by our teachers while we mastered the more fundamental mechanics of Christmas tree engineering.

Rudy called my candy-cane-flowers tree "pretty." My face flushed with warmth. I'm pretty sure he only meant the drawing, because then he came up with an idea that made it much better. He suggested curving the top like a candy cane instead of having it point straight up like most Christmas trees. I *loved* that idea.

We'd been discussing the tree for almost an hour when Rudy's father poked his head in to check up on us. "How's the project coming?"

Rudy rolled his eyes and leaned back in his chair. "We just started."

"I'm just asking. Don't bite my head off or I won't be able to—"

"—to clean you out of my teeth," Rudy said, finishing his father's dental joke. "I know that one."

I smiled politely and said, "Rudy already came up with some excellent suggestions, Dr. Tutti. But this is a long-term project. It'll take us the rest of the semester."

"You see, Dad? We're just getting started."

"I'm really glad my son has someone like you to work with," his father said, addressing me as if Rudy weren't in the room. "He's a good kid. He really is. It's been a little rough on him being in such a different... a new environment, I should say."

"Dad! I'll call you when we're ready for milk and cookies."

Dr. Tutti gritted his teeth and backed toward the door.

"Sorry. I'll leave you two kids alone."

Rudy held his breath, eyes aimed at the ceiling, and mentally counted the footsteps till his father had traveled a sufficient distance from the cave. *Eight... Nine... Ten!* He hunched back over my drawings. "So where were we?"

"Your father's sweet."

"Do we start building this floral leviathan, or do we just sit around and keep talking about it?"

I blasted him with a loud laugh. He gawked at me, not getting the joke.

"All we have so far is a premise," I said. "I love the improvements you're coming up with, but there's more to a collaboration than that. We haven't designed any of *you* into it."

"Why ruin a good thing?"

"Rudy, a Christmas tree by itself is just a tree." I set down my colored pencils and imagined the biggest, brightest tree imaginable as I explained to him how it worked. "Each soul who hangs a bauble from its bough, or threads a string of lights through its needles, or tops it with a shining star, is teaching it to sing its own unique song of joy. A Christmas tree, when it's finished and all lit up, with lots of presents cuddled underneath it, reflects the magic inside each person who trimmed it."

I waited for a scoff while his unblinking gaze confronted me, urging me to go on, to enlighten him.

"The tree that you and I create together will expose our very hearts to the world. No one else will ever be able to duplicate that." I leaned forward, tempted to reach for his hand. "Close your eyes, Rudy. Picture it."

He folded his arms and did as I said.

"You have to really think. See it in your mind's eye." I waited again, giving him space for his tree to flourish. "Now tell me, what's in your heart. What does Christmas mean to you?"

He was quiet. I held my breath, ready for something special, something magical, to bubble out of him. Goosebumps sprouted up and down my arms.

Then he spoke. "I see our grades. They're threatening to jump off a tall building if they depend on me buying into all this 'Tis-the-season jazz." He opened his eyes and grinned.

I knew he'd never take this seriously.

"You're a poo-head! I'm not talking to you anymore." I swiveled my chair, only pretending to be angry, when my eyes landed on the picture on his dresser. I went over and picked it up for a closer look. I half-waited for him to stop me, but he didn't. The woman's eyes were so much like Rudy's, I had to ask, "Is this your mother?"

"Uh huh," he answered quietly.

"She's very pretty."

"She was."

"I'm sorry."

"Cancer. When I was ten."

Hearing that Rudy's mother was in heaven made me appreciate never having to worry about that, since my parents would live forever. But the sadness overwhelmed me. "What kind of Christmas tree would she want to see?"

"She's in the ground." His words took on a terseness that made me shudder. "She's not watching us from anywhere and there are no such things as Christmas miracles."

So, his dark side was no act. I'd obviously opened a door I shouldn't have. Not knowing how to go back and close it, I quietly stood his mother's picture back up on his dresser. "Maybe we should take that milk-and-cookies break now," I said.

"I was kidding about the milk and cookies." He got up and tucked his mother's picture into a drawer. "Maybe we should call it a night."

"If you say so." I went back to the desk and carefully slipped my drawings into their portfolio. "Rudy?"

"What?"

"I don't care what you think of me, or my friends, or my family, or my town. But what exactly do you have against Christmas?"

"It's getting late. Why don't we save this for later."

My heart beat faster. I should have gotten out of there. I should have run. But I couldn't let it go. "I think you're here—you and your father—for a reason. One that you're not even aware of."

"Go home, Candy."

I almost melted when I heard him say my name, so softly, so at odds with the way he said almost everything else. "At least tell me you're not one of those people who doesn't believe in Santa Claus."

"I had dinner with him. Remember?"

We both smiled. He wasn't a heretic.

Relieved, I started packing the rest of my stuff into my backpack.

"I just happen to think your father's ideas are ridiculous," he added.

Our game went into pause mode.

"What ideas? Spreading joy to the world?"

"What do you know about the world?" he snapped. "You live up here in a fantasy land, and once a year, your old man flies around the globe handing out toys—'One for you, and one for you, and one for you.'—as if an electric train set could make up for all the wars and death and misery people suffer in the real world." He hovered over me, his words so forceful. His hot breath hit me like a right hook with every disgruntled thought he threw at me. "I have news for you, princess. The world doesn't work that way."

He made me scared and confused and curious all at once. "What do electric trains have to do with suffering and death?"

He didn't answer. Whatever he'd been ranting about, he clearly hadn't meant to direct his anger at me. For in another five seconds, he was almost certain to make a pass. And in each of the first four of those long seconds, I glimpsed an entire future dashing through my mind. We'd kiss, get married, have kids. Or we'd kiss, get married, and he'd leave me. Or we'd kiss, get married, and he'd cheat on me. Or we'd kiss, my dad would find out, and run him over with the sleigh. Three of the four imaginary scenarios ended badly, but all four had started with a kiss. I was still frozen in that fifth second, our lips inches apart, ready to let his mouth collide with mine, when my phone buzzed. I came out of my stupor just enough to fish the intrusive device out of my backpack. Still flustered, I looked at the display.

A text message. From Tinsel. An apology. It was the best of timing, it was the worst of timing. "Um, it's from Snowflake," I lied.

Snowflake! I was supposed to be getting Rudy interested in her!

"You gonna answer it?"

"Um, no. I forgot, I'm supposed to meet up with her." I shoved the phone back in my backpack.

"Good thing we stopped then."

"Yeah. Good thing."

"Can I come with?"

That was the last thing I expected him to ask. "Uh, no, we're just gonna hang out at her place. Girl stuff. Nails. Hair.

You know."

"Right. Girl stuff. Sounds boring. Have fun."

We stood there for an awkward few seconds more, as if we both thought a hug—or maybe just a polite handshake, or possibly that missed-out-on kiss—might be forthcoming, but neither of us made a move. In the end, we both came up with a lame wave goodbye and I turned toward the door.

"Hey," he stopped me. "Does Tinsel know you're here?"

"It's Tonsil. No, you're right. It's Tinsel. And what do you care anyway?"

"I don't, really." He smirked.

"Good. I'll see you tomorrow." Disoriented, I stumbled into the door jamb like the biggest klutz in the world. It was all I could do to force myself not to look back, knowing he'd be snickering at me. I kept moving, facing forward, barely managing to utter a goodnight to Dr. Tutti as I passed him on the sofa. I didn't breathe again until I was back outside in the crisp dusk air. Not even the ethereal greenish glow of the sky could tame the butterflies in my stomach.

I raced into a hot shower the minute I got home. As the water fell on me, I tried to sort out what was happening. I had broken up with my boyfriend for getting all peanut-butter-and-jelly over a boy I didn't even want to like, but with whom I was virtually cheating when I was supposed to be getting him to fall for my best friend.

This wasn't me. I'd never played the drama queen before. I needed advice. When I was little and had problems, I could always go to my parents. But my father's solution to boy trouble would probably be to lock me up in my room till I was a hundred. And I couldn't take a chance going to my mother, because she might tell Daddy. Besides, she wouldn't understand anything about boys.

I slid into my warm, flannel footsie pajamas and crept downstairs to the kitchen to try my luck with Chefy. "If I've always loved vanilla ice cream, and you suddenly brought home chocolate, and I didn't think I'd like it but I kind of wanted to try it because maybe I'm a little tired of vanilla, or vanilla made me sick once but other than that it's always been good to me, and chocolate so far hasn't—should I give vanilla another chance or should I make the switch to chocolate and hope for the best?"

Okay, now, in my own defense, Chefy had always been a very astute penguin. And after what he'd witnessed at Rocks, I assumed he'd get what I was babbling about, that I was talking in code in case my parents overheard. But by the time I finished posing my lengthy hypothetical, he had already placed in front of me a large dish with one humongous scoop of vanilla ice cream and one ginormous scoop of chocolate. While the hot fudge and caramel and whipped cream and Oreo cookies and M&M's and bananas and Pop Rocks and Twinkling Sprinkles he topped it with were not the answer I was looking for, it was all very yummy and helped me get right to sleep that night.

fourteen

"Just like that?" Snowflake shrieked when I recounted how Rudy had tried to invite himself to our fictitious girls' night. Two freshman girls mistook her squeal for the tardy bell and scurried to their classes. "You didn't even have to drop a hint or anything?"

I hadn't volunteered the misinformation right away. Not until she started pummeling me with questions about our study session. *Did you get a lot of work done? What kind of tree is he? How was he dressed? Did he ask about me? Did he mention a girlfriend back wherever he came from? Where did he come from?*

If you think that's bad, you should have heard her go off *after* I'd given her that pearl of false hope. *How did he say it? What were his exact words? Did he actually say my name? Do you think we'll go on a double date when you and Tinsel make up?*

The more she went on about it as if they were already hanging their stockings by the same chimney, the more my head filled with my own litany of questions. *Why would he ridicule my most cherished ideals and then try to kiss me? Did he really try to kiss me, or did I imagine it? If I imagined it, was it because I wanted him to? Why did I want him to! And what if he really did ask to go with just to see her?*

Snowflake slammed her locker shut. "Candy, why didn't you say yes?"

"Because I wasn't really going to your house. Remember?"

"So? I wasn't doing anything. We could've all watched a movie or something."

"You don't want to appear too eager, Snow."

"Right. Gotcha. I'm playing hard to get. Good thinking." She squealed and jumped up and down, her porcelain face glimmering brighter than the Northern Lights.

We hit up the supply shack before Mr. Polar Bear's class to sign out the raw materials we would need for building our trees. I had already begun shaping the wire frame around the zealous sapling I'd been given when Rudy trailed in and, without a word, slapped a black Moleskine notebook onto the lab station's lacquered countertop.

I creaked open the cover. There on the first page was a drawing of the most messed-up Christmas tree ever. Pine needles as black as a magician's top hat dripped dark, inky blood like a wounded squid. Skulls hung as ornaments, red blood oozing from their eye sockets, which meant only that the blackness of the rest of the tree was not some accident precipitated by a lack of colored drawing utensils. The trunk had a section missing, like someone had tried to chop it down but gave up, leaving the crippled tree to fend for itself against its own weight. A cluster of fiery trees surrounded the protagonist, their bright orange flames threatening to whip it into submission. Instead of a star, Rudy had topped his tree with a finger of white-hot lightning that stretched to the dark, billowy clouds above.

It made no difference how bleak his interpretation of the most wonderful time of the year looked on paper. That could be fixed.

Showing me his artwork was his way of saying he was *all in*. He'd decided to give himself to the project with his whole heart, no matter how gunky that organ might be on the inside. Melding our opposing imagery into one cohesive theme might present a challenge, but at least we had something to work with.

I looked over at Snowflake and Delicious crafting their tree, Snow still beaming as if she'd found a million cookies, then gazed back at Rudy waiting patiently for my reaction. "It's definitely you," I said.

He hopped onto the stool beside me and rocked back on two legs. "I knew you wouldn't like it."

"I told you, Christmas trees aren't about liking or not liking. As long as the feelings are real—"

"Who cares?" he said. "It's not like I'm expecting the polar bear to do any handstands over this."

"Goodness, no. Not the way it is now. But when your ideas come together with mine, they'll each elevate the other to a whole new level and something magical will transpire." I studied his drawing for a few seconds longer, struggling to suppress my own doubts. "It's bound to. You'll see. Trust me."

I went to see Tinsel again after school because I'd made up my mind—it was time to go on a diet. I didn't want chocolate *or* vanilla ice cream anymore. I accepted his apology and said I hoped we could still be friends. Unfortunately, somebody from school—I never found out who—had blabbed about me and Rudy being paired up for the tree assignment and Tinsel got all peanut-butter-and-jelly all over again. He called me such horrible names that when I got home I took all the vanilla ice cream from the freezer and jammed it down the garbage disposal.

Chefy stopped me from doing the same with the chocolate but I made him promise not to serve it to me anymore. He put his flipper around my shoulder and told me that one day I'd find another flavor I liked even better. So he *had* been paying attention to me the other night. Or he could have still been talking about the ice cream. Who could tell?

Now all I had to do was (1) focus on my schoolwork, (2)

get Rudy and Snowflake together somehow, and (3) get used to being lonely until boys stopped being so complicated.

Rudy committed to working with me every night. Any time I thought he was being flirtatious with me, or any time I caught myself being attracted to him, I'd launch into some funny but endearing anecdote about Snowflake. I got the feeling he put up with those stories only because he liked the way I told them. That flattered me endlessly, a detail I conveniently left out of my daily reports to her.

I waited to tell my parents about being paired with "that awful Tutti boy" until the day before Parents' Night, when they would have found out anyway.

My mother couldn't have been more delighted. How fortunate for him, she said, getting the most talented girl in the Pole as his personal guide through the rigors of tree design. Mom only sees the bulbs that are working in a string of Christmas lights, not the ones that are burned out.

Daddy, on the other hand, worried about my grades getting dragged down to the equator by this outsider. He found the timing of my revelation quite convenient, however, as he could now easily have a word with Mr. Polar Bear and get me reassigned to someone normal. I assured him that wouldn't be necessary as we were already making good progress—which was true—and it would be a lot harder to catch up if I had to start over with someone new.

As the dusk skies darkened, Rudy and I settled into a comfortable groove. I began our thematic merge by changing my cheerful red flowers into licorice-black ones, but kept the colors striped in my original pattern. The result was an elegant, tree-shaped, black-and-white candy cane.

"See? We put a little bit of you into it, all dark and dreary, and we've made it much classier. Like a black-tie tree."

From there, creative decorating ideas blossomed practically by themselves. We rested a top hat upon the curve that Rudy had come up with earlier. With the new color scheme, the curved top became crucial to maintaining the recognizability of the candy cane motif. Then we added shimmering crystal teardrops and baby candy canes with much deeper reds than the ones Chefy grows: crimson, burgundy, maroon, ruby, carmine. My mouth watered as I looked forward to inventing these exotic new flavors.

This was all still on paper, mind you. Next we went down to the Igloo Depot to stock up on extra jars of daylight, which we'd need in order to grow our flowers and tree during the all-day nights of winter fast approaching. While our official tree was still forming, we continued to experiment with new design ideas on a clay maquette.

Things were going rather peachy. Rudy was keeping up with me and contributing to the cause. The weirdness between us had lessened, though I did sometimes tingle when he said my name, or catch myself wanting to run my fingers through his dark, wavy locks, or occasionally imagine he was thinking the same about *my* hair when he looked at me in a certain way. Then he'd go and say something Scroogey and those fleeting moments would evaporate like snow in a sauna.

I heard through the cupcakevine, because it's such a small town, that Tinsel had been released from the hospital. I hadn't gone public about our breakup, hoping to avoid the million-and-one painful questions everyone would ask. So now when friends wanted to know why Tinsel still hadn't returned to school, I'd have to make up an answer—he was staying at home to catch up on the schoolwork he'd missed, and besides, he didn't have a tree partner, and so on. Sometimes my friends would urge me to dump Rudy, which would freak me out for a second because I thought they could tell how badly I was crushing on him, which I didn't think I was, and then I'd get that they meant to dump him as a lab partner. I was careful to keep any follow-up responses vague.

Rumors about our breakup eventually surfaced. Sugarcookie said that Johnny Toboggan told her that Tinsel had vowed to win me back. I sometimes missed what we'd had so much that I almost wished for some quixotic gesture on his part that would convince me to give him another chance. Then I might actually be able to get somewhere with the Great Snowflake-and-Rudy-Matchmaking Experiment. But Tinsel never did show up outside my window holding a music box over his head like John Cusack. So my increasingly undeniable crush, or infatuation, or whatever-you-want-to-call-it with Rudy Tutti kept blossoming, like our tree.

And I liked it.

I just never imagined the whole thing snowballing out of control so fast.

fifteen

'Twas Mexican night at the Claus family dinner. I gobbled the last of my banana-cream burritos with refried grapes. Frostbite let out a loud, smelly belch that made the puffins roll on the floor and laugh their tail feathers off.

"Ew, gross. Can I be excused?" In a hurry to start my homework for the night, I sprang from my chair as if my question had been a rhetorical one.

"Off to Rudy's again?" my mother asked with a smile.

"Mm-hmm," I replied, perhaps a bit too cheerfully.

"Just a minute, young lady," Daddy said. Somehow I knew he wasn't trying to tempt me into staying for dessert. "I don't think I like you spending so much time with that boy."

Without missing a beat, I fell right into what had worked before. "Blech! I'm not crazy about it either, Daddy. Believe me. But I have to. It's for school." I giggled and poised myself for a quick exit, but paused to make sure I had won his blessing.

"Hmm." He combed his fingers through his bushy white beard. Flip sneezed. Flop flipped himself to his feet and shook himself off like a dog. Daddy spoke again, slowly, as if he were daring me. "Invite him here."

My eyes widened. "Here?"

"Sure. Why not? You can do your homework right here." He tapped the dining room table.

"But why?"

"It would make your mother more comfortable."

Mom's snow-white eyebrows rose toward her silver beehive. Her comfort obviously had little to do with Daddy's sudden disruption of the fragile melodrama that had become my social life. She shrugged at me, then brimmed with her usual bright, wide smile. "Why, that's a wonderful idea. I'll have Chefy make a snack for when you kids get hungry."

Daddy furrowed his brow. "Unless you have a problem with that, princess?"

Nothing came to me but a queasiness in my throat from having been put on the spot. "I guess it doesn't matter where we do the work, as long as we get it done." I strained not to appear as frazzled as I felt inside.

"Then it's settled." Daddy grinned and leaned back in his throne. "You'd better go call him."

"Oh, did you mean tonight?"

"Sure. Why not?"

"It's just that…" Somehow I thought he'd meant it in a more general sense, like sometime in the future, after he'd had time to forget he ever brought it up. He didn't. I was back to not having a single decent argument. "No reason."

Chefy came in to clear the table and Mom placed her order for a fresh batch of cookies. He grumbled about it, even though we all knew how much he loved to show off, whipping up mouthwatering cookies and scrumptious cakes and splendiferous pumpkin pies at a moment's notice.

Frostbite only cared about one thing. "All right! We get cookies!"

The puffins hopped onto his knees to join in his victory.

"Yippee!" said Flip.

"But they're for Candy and her friend," Flop reminded him.

"But we're Candy's friends."

"That's right. I forgot. Yippee!"

Frostbite jumped up, the puffins tumbling down his legs.

"I wanna help!"

"I want to lick the bowl," said Flip.

"I want to lick the spoon," said Flop.

"Tut tut," Chefy said. "I do not require assistance. The last time I let you three help me we ended up with puffin-poop soup. No thank you and stay out of my kitchen!"

The boys fell in behind the waddling chef anyway, begging him to reconsider, while Daddy had my mom fetch him his after-dinner jellybeantini.

I went to my room to tidy it up, even though Daddy had clearly designated the dining room as the sole Santa-approved study area. Not that I would ever dream of bringing a boy up to my bedroom. Frankly, I still felt a little funny studying in Rudy's room. Sometimes I'd make him bring our work outside so we could take in the refreshing, frosty air. He hated that because he still wasn't used to the cold. Then we'd usually end up having a snowball fight. And let's face it, I had tons more experience at snowball fighting than he did.

I called Rudy to let him know about the change in venue. He was cool about it and said he'd be over soon. I slipped into my comfiest watermelon Juicy Couture sweatpants and matching hoodie to make it look like I didn't care about my appearance, then tied my hair into a cute, messy bun, leaving two curly tendrils loose in front to frame my cheekbones. I was touching up my makeup when Daddy knocked on the door.

"Ho-ho-ho. Who has a minute for her proud old man?" His heavy boots sank into my thick, candy-cane-striped carpet as he trod across it and settled on top of my fluffy pink comforter.

"Um, his beautiful little princess?"

"That's my girl." He sat there and looked down at his twirling thumbs.

"What's on your mind, Daddy?"

He patted the space next to him. I hopped onto his knee instead, like a kid in a department store, and tugged at his whiskers. You know, to see if they were real. Our little joke.

He winced from my weight, dreading the avalanche of chubby kids he would soon have to contend with in the malls. Then he took a deep breath. "Candycane, I know you're a good girl."

"I know you do." I snuggled my head against his pillowy chest and serenaded him: "You see me when I'm sleeping. You know when I'm awake. You know if I've been bad or good—"

"Candy, sweetheart, I'm trying to be serious. It's this Tutti fellow. I'm really sorry you got stuck with such a loser for this homework assignment."

"But it's not your fault Rudy's such a loser." I looked my dad in the eye. Mom always said I had his eyes. But no, there they were, still in his head. LOL!

"What I mean is, I know how much the tree pageant means to you. I should have stepped in and made your teacher reassign you to that half-elf kid, the one you tree'd up with last year. You guys did pretty well, didn't you?"

"You mean Tinsel?" I regretted bringing up his name the second it escaped my lips.

"Yes. He wasn't so bad. His people are no slouches when it comes to Christmas-tree trimming."

I frowned. "You don't think I might have had something to do with those ribbons we won? I probably do have one or two of the family's special gifts to work with, you know."

"Of course you do, sweet pea." He stroked the side of my face with his warm, thick fingers. "I didn't mean anything by that. Why, I'm sure you'd win the pageant even if you were paired with a dumb old turtle dove. I suppose Mr. Polar Bear, in all his wisdom, figured it would be more fair to split you two up."

"Oh, he didn't split us up. Tinsel's been out of school since his injury—" Word vomit! The elves knew how to keep a secret. Why couldn't I have shut my stupid mouth when I had the chance? I crawled off Daddy's lap and toyed with one of my ten thousand Barbies.

"Oh, that's too bad. How'd he get hurt?"

I shifted my weight back and forth on each leg like I had to pee. "Remember that silly little scuffle at that bar last Twilight Eve?"

"That was your friend?"

Was he toying with me? I watched Daddy in my makeup mirror as he reached into his pocket and popped a few beans. "I think so. I don't know too much about it." Now I really did have to pee. I needed this conversation to end.

Thank goodness the doorbell rang. "That must be Rudy!" I lunged for the hallway.

"Just a minute." Daddy's eyes shifted. "I need to ask you something. Father to daughter." I nodded for him to go ahead. "Has this boy ever tried anything—" he winced again as he bit down on a jelly bean, "—*funny* with you?"

Lords a-leaping! Daddy finally noticed I was grown up enough for him to think he had to start worrying about stuff like that. Things were going to get a lot stickier for me in boyland from now on.

I thought fast. "No, Daddy. I don't think Rudy's ever told a joke in his whole life!" I left a quick peck on his forehead, then bounced down the stairs, nervous but giddy to start our first study session with a home-court advantage.

sixteen

We worked in near total silence for the first forty or so minutes. Rudy had never been one to start a conversation, and I felt kind of funny knowing Daddy was lurking nearby.

Perched between us on a corner of the dining room table, our two-foot-tall prototype shaded our view of each other. I worked on my half, he worked on his. Not very conducive to true teamwork. In other words, I couldn't easily check his work and fix his mistakes. I much preferred sitting side-by-side, like at his place, but it would have been awkward to get up and move closer once we'd started.

Frostbite came in to bother us a couple of times, whining that he wanted to help. I reminded him this was for a grade, but he didn't care. I didn't get super-duper annoyed until I noticed Flop slobbering all over Rudy's boots. I hauled my brother into the kitchen and asked him straight out what it would take to get him to go play with his friend Tommy Toboggan and take the puffins with him. We struck a deal. I had take the brat to the movies on Saturday. My treat, to boot.

I went back to the dining room to declare our victory. The three little pests would no longer be bothering us. Rudy just shrugged and said, "They weren't really bothering me that much."

"That's because you weren't really *working* that much," I snapped, having expected a thank you for my sacrifice. I abruptly apologized, then got mad at myself for apologizing. Why did my thoughts always turn upside down whenever I was around him?

We went back to painting our model. We had discovered a few days earlier that bringing in one ultra-fine ribbon of raspberry-red flowers, nestled up the center of the thickest twirly lane of black roses, would heighten the sense of dressed-up stylishness we were going for.

Rudy and I dabbed our brushes painstakingly across the appropriate black flower tips to effect the change. With my side done, I set down my brush and took a moment to admire the overall flow. The colored line bent gracefully up the gentle slope of the feathery triangle. She was a beauty all right, but it felt like something was missing. I paged through our sketchbook for clues. The answer stared me in the face, right there in Rudy's first drawing.

"You know what we forgot? Your skulls."

Rudy knocked on his head. "Nope. Still there." He went back to painting.

"Not the one in your head, you dope." I showed him his drawing. "We were supposed to incorporate these skulls into our theme. Remember?"

"I was never married to the idea." He stayed glued to his reddening flowers, his brush never missing a stroke. "It's not like I'm some emo goth freak."

I didn't want to give up. I'd be letting him down if we dropped the skulls entirely. A tiny piece of Christmas lived, buried alive, somewhere deep inside his heart. It had to. How else would I have been able to tolerate him as much as I had so far? I knew the key to a truly enchanted tree design lay in drawing that out of him.

Those skulls. He drew them. That meant they were inside of him, just like the real one he'd rapped his knuckles against. If only I could find a way to Christmasize that thick skull of his. To make it a symbolic representation of that thing that, if it existed in him, exists in everyone. If our tree could say all that, then surely we would get an A-super-duper-plus.

"What if we made them shiny!" I yelped. "In gold and silver and red and green. Like traditional glass-ball ornaments. And transparent ones too!" I sputtered out crazy, disconnected ideas. Tiny, shiny skulls would dot our tree, sparingly, endowing it with a subtle message of inner tranquility as the pathway to global harmony or something precious like that.

Rudy dug into his pocket and produced two peppermint balls wrapped in cellophane—the kind you take from the little dish by the cash register when you're leaving a restaurant—and plopped them onto the table in front of me.

"Are you trying to tell me I have bad breath?" I asked.

"Eyeballs," he said.

"I have bad eyeballs?"

Rudy laughed. It was rare that I could make him laugh. Laughing looked nice on him. "No, we can use these as eyeballs for the skulls." He grabbed his notebook and started sketching furiously.

"You poo-face."

He kept scribbling without looking up. "What did you call me?"

"You're making fun of me."

"No I'm not." He turned the sketchpad around to show me.

I felt prickly all over. He had engraved an adorable little pair of candy-cane-striped eyeballs onto one of the skulls. He'd never responded so enthusiastically to any of my ideas before.

"I figured if we're gonna put a face on this thing, we gotta keep the candy-cane theme going. So it looks like you're the poo-face now."

My cheeks burned. I must have gone twelve-and-a-half shades of red. "Shut up. You're not supposed to be funny. My dad said so."

"Oh, yeah?" The corners of his mouth turned slightly upward.

"Yeah. He came into my room and asked me if you ever tried any 'funny business.'"

Rudy leaned forward, holding back a chuckle. "What did you tell him?"

"That you're a poo-head and I hate you and I'm never talking to you again." I stuck out my tongue.

He curve-balled one of the after-dinner mints around the tree at me. "Have an eyeball. You need it. You have poo breath."

"No I don't. You're nothing *but* poo!" I flung the hard candy back at him with rotten aim. He tracked it as it whizzed past his head. I took advantage of the distraction and tickled him below the ribs, just as I might have if I'd been hanging out with Tinsel.

Rudy flinched. He whipped around and got me right back. With both hands. I squeaked. I gave him another prickle on his knee, which flew up and banged against the bottom of the glass dining table, making our tree hiccup. He returned fire on my thigh. I squeaked again and cracked up. Rudy was finally having fun, like a normal Polean.

My father appeared just as I was calculating my next counter-attack. "Ho-ho-ho. Hello, children."

We choked back our giggles and cease-fired our merriment. Rudy bolted up, straight as a board, and donned his usual blank, leaden face.

"Hi, Daddy. What's up?"

Daddy's gaze darted back and forth between us, scrutinizing, reminding us wordlessly that he was always on watch. Satisfied he had accomplished his objective—to slaughter the innocent amusement he'd overheard—he inspected our prototype. "That's some tree you got there," he finally said, examining it up and down. "Elegant."

I beamed. "That's exactly what we were going for!"

Daddy nodded. His lips formed a tight smile of approval. "Don't mind me," he said. "I was just looking for my jelly beans." He found them, a glass bowl filled with his favorites resting on top of the sidebar. He tossed a couple in his mouth before he noticed the stray peppermint ball at his feet. He knelt down to pick it up.

"Oh, that's where that went," I said, feigning ignorance of how ever that important piece of art might have ended up there. "We need that. It's for the tree. See?" I showed him Rudy's newly enhanced skull sketch.

Daddy took a cursory glance at it, then back at the maquette. He shook his head, frowning, but abstained from further comment. He simply placed the wrapped candy at the base of the tree and said, "I'll let you kids get back to work."

"See you later, alligator!" I answered like a dork. I watched him stroll down the long hallway to his den, jelly beans in hand. As soon as the door closed, I felt Rudy's sneaky fingertips dance over my belly. I let out a shriek of laughter but tried to keep it as quiet as possible. "No funny business!" I curtly reminded him with a pleased grin.

"You know he planted those jelly beans here on purpose, don't you?"

"Duh." I tickled him back, which made *me* laugh more than it did him.

The kitchen door swung open. I leaped about a foot in the air. Daddy couldn't have gotten from his den to the kitchen without reappearing in the hallway. Then again, if he could get into houses with no chimneys, he could do anything. But Daddy never used his Christmas Eve tricks at home.

It turned out this latest interruption had come from Chefy, who cleared his throat loudly as he waddled in with a plate of warm gingerbread cookies and a pitcher of cold milk. "Your mother thought you might need a break from all your, ahem, hard work."

"Yummy!"

He'd brought us a whole gingerbread family, with a mommy and a daddy and a boy and a girl and a dog and a cat and aunts and uncles and grandpas and grandmas and cousins and nieces and nephews. With just one bite you could taste the rich backstory Chefy had baked into each one of them. I chewed on the mommy—she had a Ph.D. in fruitcakes, liked to sing in the shower, and loved all of her family and friends dearly. She was delicious.

I pushed the plate to Rudy and said, "Go on. Take one. While they're still warm."

He chose the daddy and obligingly chomped its head off.

I hopped out of my seat and grabbed Rudy's arm. "Come with me. As long as we're on a break, I want to show you something."

I pulled him through the sliding glass door and into our backyard. A chilly breeze nipped at our noses. I tugged at my bun and let my silky waves cascade around my shoulders to keep my neck warm. The way Rudy studied the gentle sway of my hair warmed me even more, but that wasn't what I wanted to show him. I pointed at the byzantium sky. Traces of muted cerise and dulling mustard blended together, fading fast into a quickening chocolate darkness beyond a sugary shower of millions of brilliant stars.

"It's the last night of dusk. By the time we wake up tomorrow morning, it'll be night." I laughed at myself. "That sounded strange, didn't it?"

"That's hardly the strangest thing about this place." He was being flip, but he stared for a good minute at the vibrant expanse in what could only be described as appropriately awed wonder.

"In about a week, the moon will come out and stay for two

weeks straight. C'mere." I gently took his hand in mine.

He stiffened, like maybe he thought I was going for a cheap tickle shot, but then relaxed when he realized it was safe and let me lead him to the stable.

The girls all perked up at the sound of our footsteps. Except for Cupid. She was the youngest and still always very active during the day, so she was already curled up, snoring away like a big bear. Comet tapped her hoof repeatedly to let me know she was hungry. I rushed over and petted the bridge of her nose to calm her.

Rudy stayed rooted by the door as if his feet were held in place by a giant magnet. A dim light bounced in from the starlit snow outside. I could just make out the hint of a faint, happy boyhood memory pouring back into him, lifting his spirits, ever so briefly, despite his efforts to fight it. He silently counted out all eight of the doe. Dasher and Dancer, Prancer and Vixen. I could tell he knew them all. "But where's...?" He pointed to his nose.

"Oh, come on. Don't tell me you..." I couldn't believe what he was asking. "Hello? This is reality. Think about it, Rudy. A deer with a glowing red nose? That was so obviously made up by a guy in a department store." I belly-laughed loudly. Rudy still hadn't moved from his post. "You're allowed to come in, you know. Come say hello to Comet."

He took a cautious pace forward. Blitzen wheezed at him, and he two-stepped away from her.

"Don't be a baby." I waved him in further.

"Hi, Comet." He resumed his approach, gingerly stretching his arm past my chest to scratch her behind the ear with a silly grin as if he were about to go *gootchy-gootchy-goo*. Comet snorted. Rudy yanked his hand away.

I chortled. "She's hungry, is all."

"I gathered. Hence my cowardly jerking motion away from her mouth."

I went over to the feed sack on the wall and brought him a cocoa bean the size of a kiwifruit. "Go on. Feed her."

"Am I gonna get in trouble for this?"

"Watch me." I held the cocoa bean in my flat palm and shoved it under Comet's nose. She slurped it up like a vacuum cleaner, then licked the remaining residue off my hand. "Gee, whiz, Comet. Did Frostbite skip you at lunch today or something? Try chewing next time, why don't you?"

I fetched another and gave it to Rudy.

"I can't believe I'm doing this," he said. He repeated exactly what he'd seen me do, only slower. This time Comet picked up the cocoa bean in her teeth and chomped away. Rudy wrenched his hand back while he still could and wiped the reindeer slobber off on his jeans.

"See? You do have Christmas Spirit after all, Rudy Tutti."

"I wouldn't go that far."

"Like it or not, mister, you just contributed to Christmas this year."

"That's a stretch."

"Admit it. I'm finally rubbing off on you."

"Not even. I could feed a hundred reindeer and build a thousand Christmas trees and it wouldn't change a thing."

He could pretend to hate Christmas all he wanted. I'd seen through the cracks now. If only I could poke at those holes and command him to tear down that wall like that old, important guy said in that video we saw in our world peace history class. But Comet came up with a far better retort when she blasted a loud fart out of her butt.

"Ha! That's what Comet thinks of you!" I literally fell down laughing as her perfectly timed gas leak was followed by a plop, plop, plop sound on the floor beneath her.

"Eww!" Rudy made a face like he'd swallowed a bug. He

pinched his nose and said, "I'm going back inside."

"You silly dodo. Open your nostrils." I breathed in the heavenly aroma then vaulted into Comet's stall to scoop up her special present.

"Whoa, what do you think you're you doing?" Rudy backed away from me, ashen-faced, as I tried to bestow the precious droppings on him. "Okay, game over. You win. I'll wear jingle bells to school. I'll eat fruitcake pizza. I'll do anything you want. Just don't start throwing that at me."

"Rudy, what's wrong with you?"

"I'm warning you, Candy! This isn't funny anymore!" He found a snow shovel leaning against the wall and brandished it like a weapon.

"Would you calm down? It's *chocolate*!" I squeezed off a nugget of Comet's leavings and dropped it on my tongue.

Rudy turned a million shades of green. He retched and fell on the floor in convulsions while the stuff melted sublimely in my mouth. I tore off another piece and offered it to him.

"No, really. I'm full from the gingerbread man." He held his fingers in the shape of a cross as I advanced on him. "Back off, Claus!"

"Don't they teach you anything where you come from? The magic cocoa beans are all they eat. The magic makes them fly. The rest they process—*into chocolate*." I swallowed his portion, then closed my eyes and rubbed my belly. "You don't know what you're missing. It's wonderful!"

I inched nearer to him, but he kept his defenses up. "Honestly, Rudy, do you think I would eat actual reindeer poop? Just open up." Getting him to taste the indescribable purity of this delicacy became my new mission—so that, at the very least, he wouldn't think I was some backwoods loon.

I drove another sample toward his tightly closed mouth.

113

He didn't push me away so much anymore, but it was still a struggle to shove that piece of fudge through his clenched teeth. Half of it got all over his face before I finally managed to get some in there.

As soon as he felt it touch his tongue he swung his head the other way, prepared to spit it out, but the magic hit him super fast. He stopped squirming and let the unique confection glide down his throat. "Hey! That's one damn good piece of chocolate," he declared.

"I told you. There's no other chocolate like it in the whole wide world." I opened my hand to let him enjoy another chunk. I was feeling really good about myself, like I'd broken a wild unicorn.

When he finished chewing, he dipped his finger into what was left of the mound I had scooped up. "You know something, Candy? I've always wanted to say this to you..." He shoved his sweet dollop in my face. "Eat poop!"

He got some of it on my nose because I wasn't expecting it, but I didn't mind. I savored the taste of what had made it into my mouth as I smushed the rest of the creamy pile in his face. I got it all over him. "Now you really are a poo-face," I said. We were laughing so hard I thought I might pee.

"And you really do have poo breath," he said.

I thrust my tongue at him like a child, then bent the wet, pink tip toward the chocolaty smudge he'd left on my nose. I might have been able to reach it if I hadn't been jiggling so much with laughter.

I crawled into Prancer's stall and returned with a fresh load. We took messy turns feeding each other until our faces were painted with the most prized melted chocolate in all the world. When our main supply was exhausted, Rudy picked some off my chin and held it out for me.

I let my lips linger across his extended fingertip. I could barely think about the chocolate anymore. He took his finger away after what seemed like a hundred years. He spotted a bit of uneaten chocolate left on it, covered in my unexpected kiss, then rubbed it deliberately across his lips before licking it clean.

"Amazing," he whispered. "You make even the best chocolate in the world taste sweeter."

The wind blew a tree branch against the outside of the stable and eight tiny reindeer breathed in and out all at once, but all I could hear was my own heart thumping against every nerve in my body. Rudy gazed into my eyes, in a trance. Every possible thought I could have had about Tinsel or Snowflake or homework or Daddy made way for the most important question of all: Was he going to kiss me now?

I honestly believed I might become paralyzed if he didn't. I stopped breathing. I wished I had some secret, as-yet-undiscovered Claus power to push my desires into his brain and make him make that slightest move toward me that I so frenziedly awaited. *Count to three*, I told myself. *No, five—no, ten.* If he didn't make his move by the time I reached ten, and if I were too chicken to do it for him, then the moment would pass and it wasn't meant to be.

One... Two...

Too fast. *Two and a half,* I decided, even though I still had eight more counts to go.

Three... Four...

That was it. That was all it took. Four. I saw it. I swear I did. Time slowed to an impossible standstill. I became more aware of every tick in the sequence of events that followed than anything in my life. That minutest twitch of him coming closer to me, sending me forward to meet him halfway. We were almost there. My lips parted. His head tilted. Goosebumps blossomed. A flash of lightning. My body involuntarily pulling away. My awareness that the lightning was actually the stable lights flickering on and that we were no longer alone. Rudy reeling away from me at the same instant. The deep, jolly voice of my father wafting through the musty air, forever spoiling the most perfect moment.

Santa Claus interruptus.

seventeen

His ho-ho-ho sounded more like a fee-fi-fo-fum.

I never should have let Daddy trick me into bringing a boy home. My head throbbed. My body went numb. The walls of the stable closed in on me.

For two years I'd been able to hide countless of Tinsel's tickle-hickeys from Daddy. I get within an elf's breath of Rudy's lips and—*BLAM!*—he barges in out of nowhere. Bad enough he'd finally caught on that boys might be noticing me. If he knew I liked them back, you know, like a normal teenage girl—

Look, I know I promised not to spill any secrets *about* my old man. Well, here's one *for* him—and all the other dads reading this: *Kids don't date.* We hang out. With our friends. Sometimes that means we're hanging out with our friends. Sometimes it doesn't. Fathers can never know which. Especially fathers of daughters. Can you imagine if they did? Every father of every teenage girl would band together to segregate the whole world by the sexes. Not one of my friends has ever told her parents when she was dating a boy. But we do date. We date a lot.

So I'd never told my father about me and Tinsel. I played Daddy like a xylophone. *I'm going to the library with Snowflake. I'm going to the mall with Delicious. I'm going to a sleepover at Sugarcookie's and we're gonna build a girls-only igloo clubhouse.* As far as he knew, I still thought boys had cooties.

If he'd have walked in a second later, it would have been all over for me forever. I'd be forced into eternal spinsterhood and Snowflake would get all the boys. And technically, I wasn't even dating anyone. I mean, Tinsel and I were way over by then, and I didn't know what to call what Rudy and I were doing.

Fortunately, Daddy hadn't actually seen anything. I slapped on a candy-coated happy face to cover the minor stroke I was having. Our fudge-smeared mouths made it easy for him to swallow my story that I'd only brought Rudy out there to show him where chocolate came from while the paint on our model dried.

"I think I'm gonna take off," Rudy said, shifting nervously from one foot to the other. I pictured him running to tell all the boys at school not to bother ever trying to hook up with Candycane Claus; she's more trouble than she's worth.

Daddy paced down the length of the stable, checking to make sure the girls all had enough water. "Just a moment, son." His voice crackled like the cocking of a gun. "I was thinking, maybe I could help you kids. Not to brag, but I do know a thing or two about Christmas trees."

Great. Now he wanted to watch us do our homework. With a slight twitch, Rudy wisely or cowardly yielded to me.

"Thanks, Dad. But that wouldn't be fair to the rest of the class, now would it?"

He patted Donner's neck. "No, you're probably right, princess."

I breathed. Rudy thanked me for the chocolate again and turned to head for the hills.

"Oh, before you go..." My father stopped him for a second time. "A little word with you, if I may?"

Rudy folded his arms and pretended to shiver. "Sure thing, but can you make it quick? I'm freezing my—" my father's hard glare made him edit himself, "—nutcrackers off here."

"I'll make it brief then," my dad said. "Things are a lot different here in the N.P. than what you're used to."

"No kidding."

"I know what happened to you at your last school. You'll find we're just as strict about that sort of thing up here. Maybe even more so."

"I'll keep it in mind, *Mr. Claus.*"

I didn't like the sound of that. "Do you want some chocolate, Daddy?" I said.

"Don't mind if I do."

I brought him a fresh treat from Dancer's stall. He dipped a jelly bean and chewed. Within seconds, the sensational taste sent him off to some faraway dreamland where someone had given him the most incredible Christmas present he could ever hope for.

"Can I go now?" Rudy asked.

Daddy held up a do-not-disturb hand while he enjoyed the full richness of the morsel. I turned to Rudy and angrily put a shut-the-heck-up finger to my lips.

When Daddy came out of his chocophoric reverie, he fixed his gaze back on Rudy and resumed his lecture. "Now where was I? Oh, yes. You're on real thin ice here, son. That stunt you pulled with the Snow Pods, for instance..."

I shrank into a shadow. Daddy had known all along. *He sees me when I'm lying. He hears me when I flirt...*

"That won't fly here," Daddy continued. "Taking my sixteen-year-old daughter to Eggnog Alley wasn't such a good idea either."

My heart wanted so badly to shout out that that was my idea, but my brain wouldn't let my voice make a peep.

"Now this class you're in... you're learning something useful. I can see that. But it's my understanding they give you more than enough lab time to get your work done at school. Outside of that, it might be best for everyone—including your father—if you didn't spend so much time with Candy."

See? He said it. Like he was Wyatt Earp or something. No Candy for the boys' team. I can't even describe how much I wanted to die.

To his foolish credit, Rudy didn't even blink. "With all due respect, sir, I haven't sat on your lap to ask you for anything in a long, long time. You're just an old man to me." He kept his voice cool and steady. "And maybe you can get me kicked out of school. And maybe you can get my dad fired. And maybe you can run us out of town. But there's one thing you'll never be able to do, Obi-Wan. No matter how many toys you deliver in a lifetime of Christmases, you'll never stop your daughter from growing up."

My father replied, just as evenly, "Is that so?"

"Yes," came a voice I didn't recognize at first, until I realized it had risen from my own tight throat—a newfound courage, inspired by my lab partner's fearless defiance of my father, buoyed by his sudden defense of my maturity. "That's so, Daddy! Just because you and Mom stopped aging doesn't mean I'll stay a little girl forever."

My outburst startled a few of the reindeer. Dancer lifted off the ground and kicked her hooves against the rail.

Rudy ducked.

Daddy ho-ho-ho'd him. "Scared of a little doe, are we?"

Rudy puffed out his chest and said, "I'm out of here."

"Wait!" I started after him when a big strong limb coiled around my waist and lifted me into the air.

"Let him go," my father warned, clutching me against his spare tire with his thick paw as Rudy disappeared through our yard.

I fought against Daddy's stomach-crunching grip. No use. He held me there till I ran out of breath from kicking and screaming at him about how he was ruining my life.

"Nothing was going on," I swore as the blood rushed to my head. "If you must know, Snowflake asked me to find out if he was interested in *her*." (Not that I was following through on *that* plan.) "Now will you please let me down? You're hurting me!"

By then, Rudy must have already grabbed his things and let himself out the front door. I had to promise not to run after him before I could finally convince Daddy to release me. Of course I took off the second my feet touched the ground. I didn't even stop to catch my breath, not until I was back inside staring at our beautiful maquette. The empty space on the table where his books had sat a short time ago punched me square in the chest, and I knew then what it must feel like to wake up Christmas morning to an empty stocking and no presents under the tree.

Daddy caught up with me, all out of breath, his face blue from the icy cold. He peeled off his cap and glared at me, shiny beads of perspiration rolling down his forehead. One side of his mouth was swollen, inflamed from crunching his jelly beans with his bad tooth. He ignored the pain. "You and I have a lot to talk about," he said.

All I wanted was to gather my papers, have a hot bath, and go to bed. I stood there for a good minute trying to formulate an exit strategy. "When did you find out about Eggnog Alley?"

"Give me some credit. I'm Santa Claus, for rice cake."

"Then you saw me on Main Street on my snow scooter that day too, didn't you?" He pressed his lips together and nodded. "I'm sorry, Daddy. I know it was wrong. I should have said something sooner."

"Sit."

I slumped into my chair with a defeated sigh. It took Daddy

a little longer. He gripped the ledge of the table and carefully lowered himself into the seat next to me, his eyes shut tight, with a frightful grimace and a deep arthritic growl.

Mom came in, letting out a tiny gasp at how terrible he looked. "Is it your tooth? I'll call Dr. Tutti. I'm sure he'll make a house call. Why, he has to swing by anyway to pick up—" She did a quick head count. "What happened to your friend?"

"Daddy made him go home." I folded my arms and sulked.

"That's silly. Why would he do something like that?"

"We went to Eggnog Alley," I confessed.

"Oh." She shook her head, confused. "I thought you two were just out back."

Daddy pounded his fist on the table top. "Not tonight! A month ago. On Twilight Eve. And she kept it from us all this time!"

Mom relaxed and rubbed Daddy's neck. "How nice. Did you kids have a good time?"

"Did you hear what I said? She lied to us. How can you say, 'That's nice'? Our daughter, exposed to all kinds of mayhem. She's only sixteen years old!"

"Don't forget, dear, you and I were sixteen once upon a time." She smiled knowingly at him.

"That is precisely my point. Now, please. I'm the father. I shall handle this."

"Oh, okay. This ought to be good." Mom sat herself opposite my dad, her tiny lips pressed together, her soft hands folded neatly in her lap. "Don't mind me. I'll be right here, should you happen to need a mother's perspective." She winked at me.

Not helping, I thought.

Daddy took out a handkerchief and wiped the sweat off his brow. He smoothed his beard with his fingers, as if trying to buy time to figure out where to start. "Candycane, you're a very beautiful young girl."

"Thank you, Daddy." I smiled politely.

"You're welcome, honey. But… the point is… there is much you don't understand about life yet. To you, this is all just a fun school exercise." He tapped our fashionable tree mock-up. "But believe me, that boy is not the type to put in all this work for a grade. Do you understand what I'm saying?"

I rolled my eyes, then faked a look of confusion. "You think he wants something else?"

Daddy plucked the gingerbread boy and girl off the plate of cookies that was still sitting where we had left it. "Take this gingerbread girl, for example. See how she's fresh and soft and perfectly happy staying a pretty little gingerbread girl her whole life? And see how this gingerbread boy that's been sitting here just as long has already hardened? That's because gingerbread boys aren't like gingerbread girls."

"Duh! Chefy makes the girl cookies with sugar and spice and everything nice."

"Okay. Good. But pay attention now. See how crumby the boy cookie is?" He snapped off the gingerbread boy's right leg, then pointed with his eyes at the crumbs that fell like gingery snowflakes from his broken kneecap. "Gingerbread boys want different things than gingerbread girls, and they don't care if they hurt gingerbread girls to get it. Watch."

Daddy smashed the gingerbread boy into the gingerbread girl, tearing her into two pieces like a magician's assistant being sawed in half. Then he weeped in a falsetto imitation of a little girl screaming for Superman to save her.

Tears leaked out the corners of my eyes. My whole body throbbed trying to hold back the ripples of laughter. I finally lost it and fell backward in my chair. My head could have split wide open, my brain wobbling out like a glob of apricot Jell-O, and it still would not have diminished the hilarity of it all.

Mom doubled over with the snorty-sillies as well. She tried to help me up, nearly collapsing on top of me.

"This is not a joke. This is serious." Daddy folded his arms and scowled at our howling laugh-fest. "I demand you both stop laughing this instant and tell me what is so freezing funny?"

I lifted my head, which must have turned purple by then, and imagined what I would have made of his gingerbread-birds and gingerbread-bees talk if he had given it when I really didn't know anything—*like when I was six*. I might have grown up terrified of cookies. And then where would I be?

"Swans a-swimming, Daddy! I'm sixteen! I've been dating for, like, two years!"

And that, boys and girls, was how my long-held secret spilled out of me like so much apricot Jell-O. Weakened by prolonged, uncontrollable titters. Would Daddy have preferred to first find out I had boyfriends when he got my wedding invitation in, like, fifty years?

"Boys?!" he bellowed as he shot to his feet, pumping jelly beans down his throat at an alarming rate.

"I hope so!" I said, still unable to contain my fits-of-funny.

His insanity stoked by the pain of his decaying tooth, Daddy ranted incessantly about banishing Rudy and his toothmonger father and all his fancy drills and spit sinks. I swore to him for the jillionth time, on all twelve days of Christmas, that Rudy and I were not dating. My mother backed me up on that.

"Good heavens no," she said. "How could she be dating Rudy? What would Tinsel say?"

"*Tinsel?*" Daddy wobbled. I thought he might faint. "You're dating that *elfman?*"

"Not anymore."

"You two broke up?" my mother asked.

I really didn't want to get into that. I suspected she'd known about us all along, even though we'd never spoken about it. And for good reason. I could never chance Daddy finding out (as you can now see why). But Mom had always had a pretty good intuition. Uncanny, really. It had always been an inside joke in our family that Mom should have been the one deciding what all the boys and girls of the world wanted for Christmas.

Daddy wagged a finger at her. "You knew about this?"

"I thought it was fairly obvious," she said.

He went on for another ten minutes about all the terrible things he would do to Tinsel involving long, sharp icicles at the deep end of a glacier if he ever found out the rotten elf-boy had so much as touched my cookie. He wasn't making a whole lot of sense. Even to himself. It occurred to him that no matter what he did to Rudy or Tinsel, there'd eventually be other boys. "Lots of them. Nasty gingerbread boys. With nasty gingerbread boy parts. We'll ground her. I'll home-school her myself if I have to. She'll never have to leave her room for anything."

"We are not grounding our children for growing up," my mother insisted.

"Honey, trust me. Look at the suit." He tugged on his heavy red coat. "Kids are my specialty."

"Our daughter is not a tot waiting in awe for you to land on her rooftop with a stuffed giraffe. She's a woman."

"You deal with *elves*. This is entirely different." He was referring to my mother's employ as the Workshop's in-house social worker. For little people, elves have big problems.

"That's right. It *is* different. I'm her mother, that's how it's different."

I'd never seen my parents fight over me. I had no idea what the protocol was. I was too afraid to open my mouth again. I couldn't even tell how much trouble I was in anymore.

Mom kept him from grounding me outright but he did take away my keys to the Range Rover for the rest of the year; punishment for snow scootering through town with my hooligan friends, he said, which didn't make a whole lot of sense if you ask me. Because now I'd have to rely even more on the snow scooter for basic transportation. But his power-mad tizzy had left no room for logic.

As for the bigger kettle of popcorn, Daddy promised to draw up a set of very specific ground rules for dating. Not that it would matter for some time. After the way he scared off the boy who'd almost kissed me, I figured Rudy would sooner ask a strawberry moose to the Snow Ball than me.

My life sucked.

DARKNESS

"We've been good, but we can't last."
- Alvin, Simon, and Theodore

eighteen

Millions of multicolored lightbuds shone through the darkness of the permanent midnight skies as the fir trees that lined the streets all over town began to bud like they do every year on the first day of winter's night. Wondrous starfalls provided further illumination as Snowflake and I walked to school in the chilly arctic morning. I had on my warmest parka in our traditional family colors—bright red with furry white trim. Snowflake's parka was the happy powdered blue of a newborn baby boy's blanket, framed with pretty orange sunflower patterns that spun musically in the wind.

Amidst all that beauty, I was miserable.

I was dying to walk my best friend through all the painful events of the night before. Obviously, I couldn't tell her everything. I could safely recount how Daddy thought he'd caught me and Rudy making out in the barn, because I could also include the part about how I then had to explain to him that I was trying to fix Rudy up with her. She liked hearing that. I just had to leave out a lot of the littler details, like that we almost did kiss and that he made me feel warm inside whenever he touched me. Lying to my dad had always come naturally, but lying to my best friend left an icky taste in my mouth and I hated myself for it.

I told Snow how I had come to spill the beans about my relationship with Tinsel and how my dad had overreacted and how I'd tried to call Tinsel to warn him and how Tinsel had refused to take my call, which I just didn't get. I mean, I thought he'd be happy to hear from me about anything, after

I'd gone and shut him out of my life and he'd vowed to win me back and everything. But now he didn't want to hear my voice at all. I just couldn't deal with that any longer. I wouldn't have cared if Daddy *had* sent someone over to kick the tinsel out of him. In fact, I'd have gladly sent Frostbite to do it if Santa had thought to bring me an older brother for Christmas ten years ago instead of a younger one.

I became less chatty the closer we got to school, rehearsing in my head what I wanted to say to Rudy. I had no idea if he was mad at me, or if he couldn't wait to see me. Or if Daddy had sent the Tooth Fairy over to their condo to rip out their teeth while they slept. But getting him alone to discuss anything that mattered would be tricky. Snowflake had grown impatient with my toothless Cyrano performance, so she adopted a new plan—stalking him.

She spotted him under his favorite gumdrop tree, his nose in a book, from about a hundred ice blocks away. "Let's go talk to him," she said. "We can drop some hints about the Snow Ball and maybe he'll ask me."

I tried to think up a good excuse to prevent *that* awkward conversation from happening, but Snowflake sprinted ahead of me.

"Woo! Hey, Rudy! Whatcha reading?"

"A book," he grunted at her.

"L.O.L., Rudy. That's a good one." She punched the air, grinning like a Cheshire cat.

I considered burying myself in the snow. "Hi, Rudy," I said.

"Hey." He barely looked up from his book.

"Sorry my dad got all weird and stuff."

"No big deal." *What did he mean by that?* His breath steamed out of his nostrils into the frozen air.

"Snow Ball tickets go on sale today," Snowflake announced,

subtle as a kid reading Daddy a ten-page list of toy demands. "To the ball. Not to actual snowballs that you can pick up off the ground for free. Ha ha ha."

"Did somebody say 'snowballs'?" The voice came from up in the tree. Silentnight popped his fuzzy head through the branches. A gumdrop shook loose and dropped onto Rudy's head. Silent swung down, two big snowmounds in hand. "Everybody was snowball fight-*ting*. Huh! Hah!" He launched his missiles directly at Snowflake.

"Silentnight! What is *wrong* with you?" she screamed.

Rudy slapped his book shut and grumbled, "I've been asking that since day one."

Silent hovered over Snowflake. "Hey, did you guys study for the stocking-stuffer exam?"

"Of course," she answered, rolling her eyes.

"Ooh, good, we can quiz each other!"

Snow shook her head. "I don't think so, Sy."

He dug his hands in his pockets and kicked at the snow just as the bells chimed the "Dance of the Sugar Plum Fairy"—the school's way of telling us we had sixty seconds to fly like fairies to first period.

Halfway between the gumdrop tree and the schoolhouse, Rudy said, "So, we're not studying tonight, right?"

I so wanted to stop and interpret that, but Candycane Claus was not allowed to get tardies. If I were late, they'd have to stop all the clocks and that would screw up everyone's day. So I didn't have time to decipher whether Rudy was blowing me off or saying something completely different in some secret code he thought I understood. "It's for the best," I told him. "I mean, because, you know." *You know, because my father laid down the law and he meant it and I hate him for it and you look sooo freezing adorable today I can't stand it.* "Besides, most of the rest of our work has to be done in lab anyway."

"Good." He looked a little stung. I couldn't really tell.

I sat through my first two classes with the feeling of angry dragons in the pit of my stomach scratching to get out. Twelve hours ago, Rudy and I were diving headlong into first base. One bad call from a grumpy umpire and—poof! Game over.

I had to start acting more like a grown-up. I needed to march right up to him in third period Inuktitut Lit and tell him the truth: I liked feeding him chocolate and I wanted to do it again, and I wasn't afraid of my father and he shouldn't be either. And then he might say: *Don't you get it, Candy? I'm sick of all your silly drama.*

By the ninety-ninth time I'd asked myself how this one boy could be so much more confusing than anything else I'd ever encountered in my life, I found a new tragedy to consume me—a zit.

I hid in the bathroom between second and third periods dabbing concealer over the red, blotchy blemish threatening to erupt from the crevice beside my right nostril. The makeup would probably make it worse, but what else could I do? I had enough working against me already. I blended in some foundation and applied a little powder, then covered my lips in licorice lip gloss. I eyed the toilet paper and thought about stuffing my bra, but decided against it. I was fine in that department and Rudy, despite his many faults, had never come off that shallow.

I made it to Mr. Iceland's class about a minute before the school bells chimed the "Dance of the Reed-Flutes"—start of third period. The extra minute didn't buy me much. Rudy sat in his usual spot in the back row. Snowflake boldly occupied the seat next to him. She was letting him copy her homework. He may not have been shallow when it came to pimples or boobs, but I could totally see him picking a girl who gave him the answers over one who helped him learn them for himself. When did Snowflake get to be so crafty?

With no other empty seats near them, all I could do was wave at them like a seal as I shrank into a desk at the front of the class. I had to force myself to pay attention to Mr. Iceland as he diagrammed sentences from a translation of O. Henry's "The Gift of the Magi." Even in Inuktitut, Jim and Delia's quandary sounded immeasurably more solvable than mine.

At lunch, Snowflake was All. Over. Him. I made up a story about needing to go to my locker for something and asked Rudy to come with.

"What for?" he asked.

So I can talk to you alone, you idiot. "I have something for you."

"Oh, yeah? What?"

"You left something at my house." *My heart.*

"Woo, girl, just bring it to botany," this crafty, new Snowflake said.

"Good idea." I fake-smiled and skipped off to my locker all by myself. I screeched to a stop when I came to a poster for the Snow Ball. If I didn't have a date by the end of the week, I'd be the biggest loser at N.P.H. Cookiejar was taking Sugarcookie. Delicious was going with Johnny Toboggan. And it looked like my now-ex-bestie was halfway to happily-ever-after with my Prince Charming wrapped around her finger like a Christmas bow. To top off my patheticness, I probably couldn't get Tinsel to take me now even if I'd wanted him to, which I most certainly did not, thank you very much.

The way I saw it, I had one hope. He was snoozing in the Cotton Candy Lounge. I stormed into the quiet area set aside for students to relax in during free periods and drifted over to the fluffy blue cloud where Silentnight was lounging. I tapped my toe against the bottoms of his mandarin orange Skechers.

His tired, hazel eyes widened, his big teeth shining bright. "Hi Candycane," he whispered. "Pull up a cloud."

"Do you like Snow?" I demanded. Two baby shushbirds swooped down to remind me to keep it to a whisper.

"I like everything about the snow! I like making snowmen and snowwomen and snowchildren and snow angels. Once after a blizzard I had enough snow to make a snow hippopotamus."

"I'm talking about Snowflake. The girl you have a crush on. Don't deny it, Sy."

He quietly scanned the other cottony clouds for spies. "Does she know that?"

I bopped him lightly on the shoulder. "You have to tell her." The shushbirds buzzed by me again.

Silentnight curled up like a polar cub and shook his head. I thought he might start sucking his thumb.

I pulled up a soft pink cloud and lowered my whispers. "You two are so perfect for each other. But if you don't tell her, she'll never know it."

"I don't know."

"She thinks Rudy likes her."

Silent scrunched his face. "I don't think Rudy likes anybody."

"He doesn't. And when he doesn't ask Snowflake to the Snow Ball, her heart will be broken. Unless you ask her first."

"You mean, I should ask her before he doesn't? That gives me like forever."

I swallowed a small grunt. "No, Sy. You need to ask her as soon as possible. She'll be so thrilled, she'll never have time to build up her hopes about dumb old Rudy."

He fidgeted, tapping his toes like a wind-up toy. "But I'm

shy. I wouldn't know what to say."

My plan was beginning to look a lot less hopeful. "Well, why don't you practice on me? Pretend I'm Snowflake. Ask me out."

He considered me for a moment, then turned his head to hide a blush. "Ooh, that made me so nervous just now, thinking you were her."

"Come on, Silent." I tried to imitate Snowflake's voice. "Woo! Silentnight! How's it going?" One of the shushbirds torpedoed me in the head, beak-first. "Ow! Okay, I get the point!" I shouted.

Heads popped up from the other clouds, then went back to their books.

"Hey, you do a good Snowflake," Silent said. Then he made me high-five him like we were still in grade school.

I spoke in even more hushed tones. "You're not trying. Remind her about the time you two danced at Rocks."

"I really liked dancing with you at Rocks, Snowflake."

"Now you're getting it. Woo! Yeah, baby. I had fun that night too." It was harder to do Snowflake in a whisper. She's not much of a whisperer.

"We should do it again. Would you like to go to the Snow Ball with me?"

"Woo!" I threw my arms around him, still in my Snowflake. "I thought you'd never ask. I would be honored. I'm so happy. I always said you were the handsomest boy in school."

He let go of me and stared in terror. "Really? She *said* that?"

"Maybe," I said, my breath held tight. "See how easy that was?" I mussed his frizzy yellow hair. He mussed mine back. We smiled at each other. He laughed and rolled backward off the edge of his cloud, but caught hold of the vapors and quickly pulled himself back up.

Just then I noticed Snowflake in the corridor outside the lounge, her hands pressed up against the glass, looking in on us like we were wallabies in a zoo. "There she is now," I said. "Go ahead and ask her."

He froze when he saw her, then slithered with his bashfulness back into the middle of his dewy cumulus until only the heel of his sneaker broke the surface like a mouse-sized iceberg.

"I guess I'll have to bring her to you. Stay here." I floated toward the door, but Snowflake was gone. I went back to the chicken's shoe to whisper that it was safe to come out. I'd have to work on his fear problem later. I still had the awkwardness of tree class to look forward to.

Rudy gave only one-word answers to any questions regarding our artwork, and that was the safest topic. We hardly said anything as we molded a chintzy green bauble into a skull for a proof-of-concept ornament. We. Ha. I did most of it. He seemed to take pleasure in poking its eyes out. I snapped the peppermint balls into place and held it up for his approval. No reaction.

"Did I do something wrong, Rudy?"

"How could you do anything wrong?"

Mr. Polar Bear padded by to check on our progress. He emitted a low, rumbly growl and walked on to the next workstation.

"He's seeing it out of context," I assured my partner-in-crime. "Daddy couldn't see how it fit with our theme either."

"Hmm."

Yeah. I know. *Hmm.* That's what I had to put with the rest of the day. He spent half the period studying the clock. Thirty seconds before the bell, he gathered his stuff, ready to shoot out of the starting gate like Seabiscuit.

"Will you walk me home?" I asked.

"Got things to do."

And they're off! He crashed into Silentnight at the door. Taking a step back to let Sy go first, he looked back over his shoulder at me like I'd ripped all the stuffing out of his favorite teddy bear.

Was he peanut-butter-and-jelly of *Silentnight*?

Sugarcookie tapped me on the shoulder. "Hey, I heard Silentnight asked you to the Snow Ball."

"*What?*" It must have been all over school!

She gave me a little hug and a pat on the back. "I'm so happy for you, Candy. I never thought of you with anybody but Tinsel, but I guess I could see you with Silent."

I hung my new skull prototype on the black-and-white-and-raspberry maquette and suddenly it all looked kind of stupid and out of place. Me and Rudy. No wonder nobody could see the harmony in our tree.

But me and Silentnight?

nineteen

The suckiness of the day continued dragging me into a vortex of angst the likes of which were hitherto unknown in my world. I wanted to kick myself for having told Daddy how long I'd been dating. When it comes to fathers, what they don't know won't make them bananas.

In all his specialized wisdom about what makes children happy, my genius dad had decided to help me solve my "dating problem"—by which he meant *his* problem with *my* dating. So he took it upon himself to find "proper" boys for me to date. Wasting no time, he had Chefy set an extra place for dinner and brought Bachelor Number One home with him that very night. I wanted to rip my stomach out with a fork so I could skip family dinners for the rest of my life.

Smiley was the most polite snowboy I'd ever met. "Gee, thanks for having me over, Mr. and Mrs. Claus," he said, sounding not unlike Barney the Dinosaur after a lobotomy. He wore black-rimmed glasses and an N.P.H. Narwhals baseball cap. His lifeless eyes were black like a doll's, his carrot nose plump and juicy enough to be on the lookout for a bunny attack. His body was handsomely chiseled, yet something was oddly amiss with his eerily perpetual smile.

Midway through appetizers of coconut-frosted iced milk balls, Daddy leaned back in his chair with this brilliant conversation starter: "Say, Candy, didn't you used to collect snow?"

"When I was five," I said. And I want to go on record right now that I didn't actually collect the stuff. I went through a phase, like a lot of kids up here. I'd bring it up to my room by the bucketful—and I would eat it. Like I said, I was five. Now I ask you, was that an appropriate detail to share with someone like Smiley?

"Gee, that sounds like a nifty hobby, Candy. I love snow."

Daddy marveled at his insightful matchmaking skills. "You kids have something in common. Isn't that wild?"

"Do you still have any of your snow, Candy?" my date asked in earnest. "I'd love to see it."

Things snowballed from there. Chefy had been advised to keep the menu on the cold side to help with Smiley's digestion. But he'd gone and seasoned the chilled, strawberry-mousse-filled sushi rolls with a super hot wasabi. He didn't do it on purpose. He'd always made them that way. My brother and I used to pile on extra wasabi to see who could handle the most.

Frostbite noticed it first. He tugged on Mom's sleeve and asked, "Why is Smiley crying?"

"He's not, sweetie. Eat your supper." Mom kept chewing, trying to act like nothing was wrong.

"I'm all right," Smiley said. He used his napkin to sop up the sweat flowing off of him like a river. His voice became watery. "It's just that, gee, it is a little warm in here."

"Ugh! He's *melting*!" I couldn't hide my disgust any longer. Could this really be Daddy's first choice for a hot date for Candycane? Smiley the Melting Snowboy? I mean, he was a nice guy and all, but it would be like dating a Slip 'n Slide!

"No biggie," Daddy said. "After dinner, you two can run outside and play in the snow, like when you were little. Then Smiley here will be as good as new. Won't you, boy?"

Smiley didn't answer. His mouth was in his lap. He slid off the chair and drained himself out the front door. Luckily, Chefy was standing by with a mop to pick up the parts of our dinner guest that had been left behind.

The problem with Daddy having literally written the book on who's been naughty and who's been nice was that he'd gone all the way to the tippy-top of the Nice List without taking any other factors into consideration. Take Bachelor Number Two, for instance. Nice guy. No question about it. But let's face it— he cared even less about Christmas than Rudy. Honestly, who knew Hanukkah the Outcast Elf would even be on Daddy's radar at all?

Now I don't mean to sound picky, but I'll always love Christmas more than anything else in the world, no matter how mad I get at my dad. Considering all the heartache I'd suffered so far with the Ghost of Christmas-Can-Kiss-My-Butterball, I knew right away it would never work out with me and Hanukkah.

None of that fazed Daddy. He foraged through my precocious childhood memories to unearth more fodder for his supposedly pertinent anecdotes.

"So then my little Candycane said, 'Wouldn't it be neat to put candles in the Christmas tree?' Naturally I told her, 'No, princess, that would be dangerous.' So she sneaks down in the middle of the night, determined little rugrat that she is, and puts candles on every single branch—dozens of them, all shapes, sizes, and colors—and then she lights them. Phoom! We almost lost the whole house. Ho-ho-ho!"

In my defense, candles were used in Christmas trees long before electric lights were invented, and Daddy knew that better than anybody because he was around in those days. He made it sound like I wanted to turn our tree into a *menorah*!

Hanukkah's courtesy laugh shook the hundreds of tiny *dreidels* that dangled from every part of his body, making him rattle like a *gragger*.

"Say, Hanukkah, you're into candles, aren't you?" Smooth segue, Dad.

"*Oy*, you said it, Mr. Claus."

We all enjoyed the scrumptious potato *latkes* with mounds of cinnamony, chunky applesauce and nutmeg, but Frostbite made a sour face when Chefy dished out the main course. "What is this?"

"Now, Frostbite, behave," my mother scolded. "Hanukkah is our guest. This is what he likes to eat. It's like fish."

Flip and Flop perked up at the mere mention of F I S H. They bounced up and down on either side of my brother, first one, then the other, as if they were on an invisible, trampoline-powered teeter-totter.

"Let me see. Let me see," said Flip.

"Sounds fishy to me," said Flop.

"It looks different."

"Different is good."

"Unless it isn't."

Hanukkah scratched his head through his *yarmulke* when he saw what Chefy had plopped onto his plate. "Excuse me, ma'am," he said to my mother. "I don't mean to be rude, but this isn't what we normally eat."

"Why, don't be silly, Hanukkah. I called your mother special to ask her what to serve. She's such a lovely woman. So kind and helpful and friendly. She said this was your favorite."

"Begging your pardon, Mrs. Claus, but this doesn't look anything like lox."

We examined our plates. Each of us had been served a humongous bagel with a hot, steamed Christmas stocking spilling out the sides.

Chefy snickered. "Oops. My bad. I could find no recipe for this 'lox,' so I assumed you'd said *socks*."

To Chefy's credit, it was the yummiest Christmas stocking I'd ever eaten. Lots of fibers, and smeared with a generous amount of homemade mint-chocolate-chip ice cream cheese. Hanukkah didn't seem to mind the mix-up. Neither did Flip and Flop, but, well, truthfully, they'll eat anything.

Now, I totally got why nobody could picture me with Rudy. I wasn't born on an ice floe, you know. But seriously, how could anyone believe Smiley or Hanukkah were the answer? The more I was forced to look at what else was out there, the more I evaluated everyone in terms of: *What would Rudy do?* True, he never would have taken an interest in seeing my childhood snow collection. And no, he never would have enjoyed a tasty smoked Christmas stocking on a bagel that had been cooked up by mistake. But then, not one other person in the whole North Pole would have stood up to my father the way Rudy did that night in the stable. Except maybe my mom.

None of that mattered. Throughout the Dark Days of Daddy's Mortifying Setups, Rudy kept his distance from me at school. He even ditched lab, leaving me to mold and shape our sturdy young tree into the beautiful vision of our combined Christmas Spirits all by myself.

Snowflake started avoiding me too. She must have caught on that I hadn't tried all that hard to bring them together, and apparently she didn't need my help anymore. I saw them together in the lunch room. I saw them together in the Cotton Candy Lounge. I saw them together under the gumdrop tree. I didn't have the heart to get in the way of their blossoming whatever.

So when Snowflake came running up to me in the lunchroom, clutching my arm and shaking me like a bottle of cupcake juice, I was relieved to know she was talking to me again. But her news made my heart sink.

"Woo! He asked me! I said yes! To the Snow Ball! Woo! He asked me to the Snow Ball and I said yes!"

I forced a smile and told her how happy I was for her. Then I conjured up the heartbreaking image of her and Rudy waltzing elegantly at the most glamorous social function of the year, twirling and whirling right past me and my date—a puddle of melted snowboy mixed in with my tears—while Hanukkah boogied on the other side of town at the Matzo Ball. At least Snowflake still wanted to be friends with me, so that was something.

"Can you believe it? He's hot chocolate with whipped cream and a cherry on top. Eeee! I'm going to the Snow Ball with Silentnight!"

OMG. Silent-freezing-night! I could barely keep myself from slapping my forehead and going, "Duh!"

Out of nowhere, Silent zipped up behind us. He grabbed my shoulders and shook me even harder than Snowflake had. "I asked her! She said yes! Isn't that great? I'm taking Snowflake to the Snow Ball."

"Yay!" I cheered, with a real smile this time. "That is so hot chocolate."

"With marshmallows," he added.

"Uh huh." I nodded like a bobblehead from all the shaking. "Okay, Sy. I'm getting dizzy now."

He stopped. "I hafta go."

"You're not gonna sit with us?" Snowflake asked.

His shoulders scrunched up. He tightened his lips and looked away.

"What's the matter?" I asked.

He cupped a hand in front of his mouth and said into my ear, "What if I say something stupid? She might change her mind." He'd meant to whisper, but had to do it so loudly to be heard over all the cafeteria noise that Snowflake could easily hear him.

She stabbed her fists into her sides and stared him down. "So you're not going to talk to me until Christmas Eve?"

He shifted away from her, one eyebrow arched. "Maybe."

"That would be stupid," I told him.

He looked to Snowflake for a second opinion. She nodded. "Okay," he said. "Then let's have lunch."

Rudy's name didn't come up until much later in the day, when Snowflake and I were walking home. "All he ever talked about was how much he hated this place. How Mr. Polar Bear didn't know anything and Silentnight was a silly goose and blah, blah, blah."

"He said 'silly goose'?"

"Well, I don't remember his exact words, Candy. I'm not a tape recorder. But he sure hates your dad."

"What'd he say?"

"Just lots of stuff." She shrugged. "Mean stuff," she added, then squeezed my arm. "You were right from the start. I don't know how you put up with him for so long. You sure are lucky your dad made him stop bothering you. And I'll tell you, I'm lucky Silentnight asked me out. He's an incredible dancer. Woo! He's got real boyfriend potential."

Yeah, we were a couple of lucky schoolgirls all right. But our so-called luck wouldn't dissuade me. With Tinsel afraid to talk to me—the only good thing to come from Daddy's nuttiness—and Snowflake so happily disenchanted by Rudy's, uh, special charms, the only obstacle left between me and Rudy was Rudy. And my dad's nutty scheme to find me his version of the perfect boyfriend. Who would it be next? The Easter Bunny? No, even Daddy wouldn't go for that; we all know what bunnies want, and it's definitely more than cookies.

"Snowflake, will you ask your mom if I can come live with you? Pleeeeease?"

Unable to avoid the predictably unpredictable follow-up to the Great Hanukkah Debacle, I crept into my house ready to cringe and sneer at Bachelor Number Three. Daddy had failed to make a love connection two nights in a row. As Hanukkah himself might have asked, why should this night be any different?

True to form, Daddy outdid himself with his third consecutive choice of totally unsuitable, wholly incompatible gentleman callers. His ulterior motive could no longer pretend to be hiding in the shadows. If Daddy's precious little princess wanted to date, then by golly he would see to it that I only dated the kind of boys who would never dream of doing any of the things that, well, I or any teenage girl in the world would want to do with a boy on a date. In other words, someone safe.

Once again, Daddy presupposed victory from the start. "You know, forgive me, but I just have to say it. You two look so adorable together," he said as he steered me into the arms of Queero the Flamboyantly Gay Polar Bear.

Not that Queero wasn't the hottest polar bear in town. He wore a wicked pair of Ray Bans and a battery-operated ascot that lit up with little flashing pictograms of Daddy at work. The hair on top of his head stood up in spikes like fence posts, held in place with a thick gel and dyed hot pink. He had a rainbow-colored jingle bell pierced through his right ear. He told us that every time it rang, it meant a fairy had gotten lucky. That made my mother clap her hands and go *Aww*, just as in the dark about what kind of fairy he meant as Queero was about why he'd been invited to our odd little family show.

"You said it, Papa Claus." He had a lilting, breezy demeanor that made this third strike so much more bearable than the first two, no pun intended. He twirled my candy-cane earrings in his polished claws and said, "We got Candycane here, rockin' the candy-cane fashion, looking sweet as a peppermint latte. And I'm a pretty stylin' polar bear if I do say so myself. You know, we would look fabulous on a Christmas card, and we could send it to everyone in the North Pole."

Daddy fell in love with Queero's enthusiasm instantly. "Say, that is a good idea! Wait here. I'll go get the camera."

The house vibrated as he bounded down the hall to fetch an old Polaroid instant from his den. He hurried back and snapped a portrait, giddier than I'd seen him in a long time, as if he could already see the snapshot embossed on the cover of a photo album that would track the lifelong love affair of Candy and Queero.

"Daddy," I said as he fanned himself with the self-developing keepsake, "if it'll make you feel any better, I promise to bring Queero with me every week when I visit you in the *loony bin*."

"Sounds good," said the blithesome bear. "I'll pencil it in right after my facial."

Queero turned out to be a blast. I never would have gotten to know him if it hadn't been for Daddy's mental breakdown, because I didn't normally run with polar bears. He shared some recipe tips that impressed even our own Chefy, and we made plans to hit up the Borealis Spa together the following week. If only Rudy could have been more like Queero.

Daddy was pleased as pumpkin pie when I invited the hunky bear to stick around after dinner and watch *Glee* with me. Boy, my dad must have really thought he'd solved his problem. He practically carried us into the living room, then took Mom and Frostbite out for dessert so we could be alone. No worries about where this boyfriend might put his paws.

I confided in Queero about all my problems with Rudy. He was great about it. He suggested I bake Rudy a pie. Chefy helped us concoct an amazing dish out of Rice Krispies Treats with extra gooey marshmallows and lots of wiggly, squiggly gummy worms—because everyone knows the live ones taste the best.

The next day, I put on my most adorable cashmere sweater and tucked my best skinny jeans inside my thigh-high patent leather boots with custom-made, not-really-appropriate-for-school candy-cane-spike heels. I carried the pie with me in a pink bakery box. All morning long I worried the gummy worms might escape while it sat under my desk during class, but I had to keep it with me everywhere I went because I didn't know when I might run into Rudy. Just after fifth period, after I told Silentnight for the gazillionth time that he couldn't have any, I caught a glimpse of Rudy's leather jacket turning a corner.

I race-walked in that direction as fast as I could manage without falling off my heels or dropping my peace offering. I started to have second thoughts en route. *Rudy hates yummy food.* Queero didn't know that when he'd made the suggestion. He'd been thinking like a normal Polean. Rudy would never be wooed by pastry. He'd probably scoff at me and I'd be left to share the pie with Snowflake and Silentnight and all my friends, which would be fun and delicious, but I still wouldn't have Rudy.

No, I told myself, the pie wasn't the point. I could throw away the pie if I wanted to. The point was to tell Rudy once and for all that I had feelings for him and that I thought he did too, and if that was the case then we shouldn't let anything else matter, not even my father.

Still debating what to do with the pie, I rounded the corner. "I don't believe it," I said out loud.

There was Rudy, strutting into the Cotton Candy Lounge, a warm smile plastered across his stupid face—and his arm nestled cozily around Vixen.

twenty

Okay, I admit it. It's been brought to my attention on more than one occasion. I sometimes have a tendency to overreact. Like the first time I visited Daddy's office. You know, the Workshop.

I must have been two years old, just barely walking, and didn't quite grasp what my father did for a living. We passed a cubicle with pictures of me taped up all over the walls and on the computer screens and everywhere. If I saw something like that now, it would creep me out. But like I said, I was two, and I guess I just giggled curiously.

Silly the Elf somersaulted into his cube and smiled and tugged on my cheeks. Then he showed me a doll fresh off the floor of Doll Wing A, where only the most important dolls are handmade, night and day. It was like looking into a miniaturizing mirror. The doll was me! The brand new Baby Candycane doll, designed and manufactured exclusively by Silly the Elf, T.S.Q., Santa's Workshop, The North Pole.

She had my big brown eyes and wore a candy-cane-striped bonnet. She suckled a candy-cane pacifier (which I had outgrown in real life by then), and was draped in a plush velvety red coat like my dad's, but with candy-striped fur trim that looked like it had been skinned off a lollipuss—a rare species of red-and-white-striped kitten indigenous to the Arctic region. No actual lollipusses were harmed; the elf union guarantees only fake fur is used in the manufacture of all toys.

Technicolor the Photographer Elf came to get a picture of me holding Baby Candycane for the box. I held onto her so tightly, she nearly suffocated. Mom says I wouldn't even loosen my grip for Silly to position the doll's face toward the camera. When the photo session ended, they tried to pry the toy from my itty-bitty fingers. I screamed so loudly, every elf in the Workshop stopped what he was doing and rushed over to see if I was all right.

"Honey, that doll is already spoken for," Daddy said in his most soothing, gentlest voice. "It's going to Ashlee Litowsky of Indianapolis, Indiana. Silly's going to make a special one just for you."

I backed away from Daddy and shouted, "My doll! My doll!" over and over at the top of my lungs. Then I threw the biggest kicking and screaming tantrum Daddy had ever seen—and believe me, he's seen plenty in his line of work. I didn't know who this Ashlee Litowsky was, or where the heck this Indianapolis, Indiana was for that matter, but nobody was getting my doll! I didn't understand that Silly hadn't perfected the design yet and wanted to get it just right before presenting me with my own Baby Candycane. All that mattered to me was, I had that doll—Ashlee Litowsky's doll—in my hot little hands. It was *me*, for goodness sake!

With a thousand tiny elf-eyes upon him, Daddy had no choice but to relent. He instructed Silly to assign the next one on the line to Ashlee Litowsky, then swiped his hands together twice as if the crisis were all done and over with. I could keep my doll and hadn't he adjudicated that beautifully, thank you very much. But when it dawned on my tiny toddler brain that there were going to be more Baby Candycane dolls... well, Mom likes to joke that I singlehandedly invented the terrible twos in that moment. I didn't care. I would not have this *Ashlee Litowsky*, or any other Ashlee Litowskys, playing with a me-doll in that Indianapolis, Indiana, or any other Indianapolises,

Indianas. I guess I was supposed to be flattered by the whole thing, but this simply would not do!

I continued my tantrum all the way home and all through the night and into the next day and for three more days, according to the way my mother tells the story. I, of course, have little recollection of any of it. Yet I've been told that was the reason the prettiest dollies ever to come out of an elf's cubicle never made it to Indianapolis, Indiana, or to any other lands between the Poles. Sorry, girls.

In all, about fifty were made and stored in the Warehouse of Unsuitable Toys. Rumor has it that a few elves sneaked some out to the occasional super-duper good little girl over the years. Maybe even to Ashlee Litowsky. If you're lucky, you might be able to find one on eBay.

So why did I go off on this tangent? I act out sometimes. There. I admit it. I'm not apologizing for my irrational behavior. And I'm not making excuses. Or maybe I am. Maybe I'm putting the blame square on my parents. If you said it was my fault and sent me to a shrink, any therapist worth her cookies would eventually conclude it was all my parents' fault anyway, because, well, that's what they always say. So why not cut out the middleman and go ahead and call me a spoiled brat and agree it's because my parents spoiled me and that's what makes me impulsive? Whatever. I accept that.

This was different. I could have handled it if Rudy really had asked Snowflake to the Snow Ball. I would have been sad, but I would have eventually come around and said, hey, they were meant to be, right?

But Vixen?

Let me tell you something about Vixen. She strips off her coat and scarf the minute she enters a building like she's on a fashion runway, and no matter how freezing it is, she's always wearing short skirts and tight belly shirts and, please, who still dresses like that after seeing how it worked out for Britney Spears? Hopefully one day Vixen will shave her head too.

And guess who was the first girl in our class to develop? That's right. Vixen. DDs. *In middle school.* You wouldn't believe the letters Daddy got that year. I'm not supposed to see any of that stuff, but I happened to be snooping around my mother's office one day and found them. The Letters. From just about every girl in North Pole Jr. High. Asking for boobs. Apparently he gets letters like that every year, tons of them, from flat-chested girls all over the world.

Daddy's always had a wee bit of an issue with children outgrowing him. When he first started getting those letters, like in the ancient 1950s I think, his initial response was denial; he'd write back and say he didn't really exist. So that's how *that* myth got started. Ever since then, the mail-room elves have been careful to route those letters to my mother, even though it's technically not part of her job description. That was also about the time Daddy began his lifelong jelly-bean habit.

One other thing about Vixen—and, now this part my publisher's lawyers want me to stress is all "conjecture" and I can't prove it and stuff and blah, blah, blah—but all the boys have *supposedly* gone on many a sleigh ride with her, if you know what I mean.

Not that I was jelly of her. But she was soooo not right for Rudy. If all he cared about were boobs, then I had sorely misjudged him. And when I misjudge someone, I consider it their fault for pretending to be someone they're not.

So when I saw Rudy with his arm around Vixen's waist, I did what I always do. I acted impulsively.

I went macadamia.

I bawled my way straight to the nursery, a burning hatred

toward our so-called work of art festering within me. Our tree had suddenly become one big fat tall green lie. I kicked it, beat it, tore it to shreds and pelted it with wads of Rice Krispies Treats pie. I stood back and watched as the gummy worms burrowed into its trunk, sucking its nutrients dry. Our beautiful creation could wither and die, for all I cared. I pretended the escaping sap was Rudy's blood dripping out of its severed limbs. Rudy liked dark? Ha. Wait till he saw my new design.

By the time he swaggered into the lab, I'd lost sight of everything I had ever known about the purpose of Christmas trees, not to mention how important this project was to my GPA. Rudy glanced over my shoulder as I drew a new sketch: a tree made of fireballs and rats and cockroaches and Rudy's severed head stuck on top where the star should be.

"Change your mind about the color scheme?" he said, as if he could just show up after ditching for two days—to go play with *her*—and then try to make a joke of my pain.

"No." I slammed my pencil down hard. It tumbled across the workstation. "I changed my mind about *you*!" I could barely bring myself to look at him, much less talk to him. "Go work on your own tree!"

He shrugged and headed for the adjacent nursery. I followed as he approached the mangled pile of rotting twigs caked in messy globs of Rice Krispies Treats pie—our wounded baby. It may have had both our DNA, but let's face it, I was the one who carried it, birthed it, nourished it, loved it, virtually on my own. He didn't deserve even the remnants for salvage.

I scooped it into my arms and dragged it outside, grabbing a blowtorch from the lab on the way. I didn't stop to put on a coat, my boiling blood masking the subzero temperatures from my bones. I steamed around to the ice fields along the east side of the schoolhouse, my breath rising in wisps of smoke into the pitch-black midday sky.

"Stop following me!" I shouted when I noticed Rudy about ten paces behind me. "I don't want to have anything to do with this tree and you can't either."

I reached the edge of the slick ice, my anger propelling me forward, step by precarious step, in my stupid heels that I'd worn for his benefit. I nearly lost my balance every third or fourth step, but managed to stay vertical through sheer will power; no way would I let him have the satisfaction of helping me up if I fell.

I dumped my topiary hostage in the middle of the field and fired up the blowtorch. "You'll have to start a new one all on your own," I said. "If you even care, that is."

"I don't," he admitted. "I couldn't care less. You're the one who's all, 'What's more important than Christmas, and Christmas trees, and Christmas Spirit, and Christmas cards, and Christmas boogers?' Go ahead. Torch it. See if I care." He folded his arms in front of him and watched, as if I were acting out some dumb TV sitcom for his amusement.

I held the flame to a cluster of pine needles. The tree wasn't dry enough to go up in the blaze of glory I had hoped for. The cold wind kept blowing out the droplets of fire that did manage to catch, slowing its spread to a snail's pace. Frustrated, I switched off the blowtorch and pulled at the skull-shaped ornaments, smashing them against the ice one by one. I'd made over a dozen in the two days Rudy had ditched class. Would *she* have done that for him?

"Why don't you make Vixen your new tree partner?" I shouted.

"Vixen is a poo-head. What does she have to do with any of this?" He took a step toward me.

I hurled a skull at him. "What were you doing with her

156

in the Cotton Candy Lounge?" It bounced harmlessly off his shoulder, his approach unhindered.

"That's none of your business." He took a couple more steps, closing in on me, unafraid. "Did I ask you why you were having dinner with Hanukkah the Outcast Elf?"

So that was his game plan. Blame me. Wouldn't he have to admit he liked me before he could claim to be peanut-butter-and-jelly? "That was my father's idea," I said. "He's deranged. And why am I explaining any of this to you?"

"That's right. I forgot." Another step closer. "You belong to Tinsel. Or is it Silentnight? It's hard to keep track."

The nerve! He was close enough to touch me now. Half of me wanted to blab all about what I was doing with Silentnight and why. The other half wanted to scream. If I'd had a third half, it might have wanted to slap him.

"You stop talking to me, Rudy Tutti!" I stomped my feet, still the impetuous two-year-old girl clutching Ashlee Litowsky's Baby Candycane doll in Silly the Elf's cubicle. The mistake this time, however—besides that I was sixteen now and no longer a baby—was that I was wearing stilettos, one of which snapped off. So that sucked. That, and we were standing on a sheet of ice that happened to be right in the middle of a thin patch.

twenty-one

The telltale crackling sound ripped closer with each pounding of my boots. I paid it no mind and kept right on ranting. "I wouldn't care if you were the last boy on earth! I never want to see you aga-a-ahh—"

The ground literally opened up. Painfully cold water swallowed me whole. I sloshed and screamed and groped for the edge of the ice. I grabbed hold of a corner and started to pull myself up. It broke off. I started to sink again. The cold pressed on my face like a vice. My hair floated up above my head. Rudy's fingers clutched at my wrist. He tugged on my arm until my head broke the surface.

"Rudy!" I gasped, spraying him with the cold mouthful of water I had almost swallowed.

"Hold on, Candy! I got you!"

As he strained to pull me out, the chunk of ice under his feet gave way. He slid into the water, on top of me. My body blocked his from falling all the way in. His rear end came to a rest on a sizable shelf, his legs dangling in the pool like he was sitting on a pier, ice fishing for Candy. He'd hooked me, but still had to reel me in.

"Hurry, I'm freezing!" I cried. I hugged his legs, nearly pulling him down with me as I crawled up them like a frozen lobster.

His muscles tightened as he helped me scrape my way up his rugged torso until my left ear rested on his chest and I could feel his heartbeat thumping louder and faster than mine.

"Are you all right?" he asked.

For a moment I felt safe. Then his face went ashen. He squeezed me hard, flipping me off of him, onto my side. He scrambled the rest of the way out of the hole shouting, "Run!"

We were not alone. A howling, snorting leopard seal, ten feet long, had emerged from the opening. It flung its twelve-hundred-pound mass onto the hard surface with a thud that splintered the ice further. The ferocious creature kept coming at us, slithering along like an ice-breaking steamship plowing its way through the frozen Arctic seas.

Rudy wrenched me away from the monster's wide open jaws just inches from me becoming seafood and I slid halfway across the field on my butt. He lunged at the slimy gray animal and a second later they were engaged in a slippery, slobbery rumble. I confess I tingled a little at the thought of Rudy defending my honor from this marauding intruder. But mostly I worried about the well-being of the seal.

"Rudy, wait! Stop! Don't hurt him!" I shouted, even though he was fighting a losing battle. "Otter, off!" I commanded.

The furry, spotted blob wriggled away from his opponent and sat like an obedient puppy.

Rudy clambered to his feet, scratching his head. "I guess I showed him," he said, dazed and out of breath, as Otter barked at him playfully.

"That's Otter," I explained with a chuckle as I made my way back to them. "He's a leopard seal. You can tell by the spots on his throat. We call him Otter because he's as gentle as an otter. Aren't ya, boy?" Otter rolled over and clapped his flippers. I rubbed his belly and he sprang up and licked my face. "He's a friend of Chefy's. He came up with him from the South Pole. He must have sensed I was in danger when I went through the ice and swam over to rescue me."

Rudy's face flushed pink before he turned away.

My wet clothes began to stiffen. I ached all over and my joints locked up. I felt like the Tin Man in *The Wizard of Oz* when they found him all rusted out and unable to move. Still not ready to forgive Rudy, I wondered if I, too, were missing a heart. Otter had scared the chocolate out of him, yet he'd thrown himself in harm's way for me.

"Not that you didn't do a commendable job yourself," I finally said. "You were very brave, Rudy."

"Yeah, right. I protected you from that." He pointed at Otter, who was clumsily attempting a headstand, his heavy tail tipping him over again and again.

"You didn't know he was harmless," I said. I'd never played the damsel in distress before. I thought we were supposed to fall into each other's arms next, then iris out and fade to black. It didn't happen that way. "I'm sorry I got mad at you," I added.

"Yeah, well, I'm gonna smell like blubber all day now." He noticed I was shivering. My lips must have been as blue as his piercing eyes. "We'd better get you inside," he said as he wrapped his warm leather jacket around me.

Otter barked his goodbyes and dove back into the hole, his wake causing the last vestige of our smoldering tree to sink into oblivion. Weeks of hard work gone without a trace. I frowned. A tear rolled down my cheek and froze solid at the corner of my mouth. I desperately wanted to swim after the dying remnants of our joint Christmas Spirit.

"Don't even think about it," Rudy said. He put his arm around me to start me heading back to the schoolhouse where I could thaw out.

"Rudy, just so you know, Silentnight asked Snowflake to the Snow Ball." I stopped and waited for a response. He nudged me to keep me moving. "I was helping him practice to get his courage up to ask her, that's all."

"It doesn't matter. Forget about it."

"Seriously. He's shy."

"Silentnight?" Rudy howled. "That guy is not shy. He's annoying. He's annoying *because* he's not shy. Those two nutcakes are perfect for each other."

"They are not nutcakes. They're my friends. And I had to help him so he'd ask her... before you could."

There, I said it.

Rudy laughed so hard he snorted. "The girl who's been on me like an Eskimo tracker all week? Why would I take her, of all people, to some lame school dance?"

"It is not lame. It's like the hugest celebration of the year. Everybody goes. The whole town."

"Ahh. Another Christmas celebration."

"Actually, by that time we're all Christmassed out. That's why we do our Christmas in April. The Snow Ball is our time to unwind after all our hard work for the year is over. It gets super wild. You wouldn't believe it." We kept walking. Wet braids of my hair whacked against my jaw like a dozen tiny sharp icicles. "You should ask Vixen to go with you," I said with a swallow.

Rudy stopped and faced me. "Candy, it wasn't what it looked like."

"It doesn't matter." I kept going.

"I swear, I wouldn't be caught dead taking someone like Vixen to the Snow Ball."

This time I stopped. I peeled a frozen strand of hair off my cheek. "Oh? Who would you be caught dead taking to the Snow Ball?"

He flashed his once-a-year smile at me. "I suppose if I were going, there's someone I might ask... if she didn't already have a boyfriend."

"You should ask her anyway," I said, playing along, trying

my best to act casual. "Maybe she doesn't anymore."

"Oh, yeah?" He arched one eyebrow. "Well, her father would never let her go with me."

"That's stupid, Rudy. The Snow Ball is on Christmas Eve. Her father might be out of town making some—I don't know—important deliveries?"

"Good point. Maybe I'll give it a shot, then. I'll let you know what she says."

I no longer felt the cold and the wetness. The slush on the ground swayed like clouds under my feet as we finished our trek to the cozy red schoolhouse. A minute later we were back indoors, out of the frigid, dark dampness, away from the harsh, bitter wind that had battered our skin so relentlessly for what seemed like hours. And yet, I could have stayed outside and rolled myself up into the happiest snowgirl in town. We never said it out loud, but we both understood it the same way. I officially had a date for the Snow Ball with Rudy Tutti!

We headed for the locker rooms. I planned on a long hot shower before changing into my nice dry gym clothes. But Mr. Polar Bear pounced on us the second we passed his classroom. He curled his heavy bear claws around me and dried me off with his fur until I stopped shivering, then dragged the two of us into his office. And by the way, what we call a "bear hug" doesn't even compare to the real thing. It's quite indescribable.

Mr. Polar Bear looked down his flattened olive of a nose at Rudy. "I am officially not allowed to encourage my students to drop out of North Pole High, but..." He shook his head. His glassy eyes shifted in my direction.

I was too afraid to say anything. I wanted to step up and remind him that he was the one who had paired us together in the first place, but I didn't want to piss him off any more than he already was. Polar bears are known more for their tempers than their compassion. On the playground, we always used to say it was only a matter of time before a teacher mauled one of us to death and ate us for not doing our homework.

So I ducked behind his computer monitor, which did nothing to hide me from those giant bear eyes.

"As for you, young lady, how do you think this reflects on me?" His voice had much less of a growl when he addressed me.

In the version of the story I gave him about our tree accidentally plunging through the ice, I'd nearly drowned trying to save it when Rudy heroically rescued me. Close enough, huh? I left out the part about how I'd willfully destroyed the thing first. It didn't matter, though. We were never supposed to remove the trees from the building.

"We're real sorry, Mr. Polar Bear. We'll work extra hard on a new one." I spoke for both of us, knowing Rudy would never kowtow to authority.

"You'd better, Miss Claus." It looked like he bared a little fang there. "Your prototype shows promise, but it's not your best work." Ouch. "You might want to rethink the concept."

I glanced over at Rudy, slouched low in his chair, brushing his fingers through his thick hair with an uncaring look of defiance that made me want to make a rude gesture to Mr. Polar Bear and run off with Rudy into the wilderness. Maybe we'd join an Inuit tribe and learn to live off the land and build igloos and never have to deal with school and Christmas again.

"Don't forget," Mr. Polar Bear said, "artificial trees are not eligible for a grade in this school." *Duh. Who does he think I am?* "If your tree is not at least ten feet tall and completed by the due date, you will both fail this class. And"—wait for it— "no student who fails this class will be admitted to the Snow Ball."

Chicken schnitzel with meringue! Just when it looked like I'd gotten the only thing I wanted for Christmas. Right then and there I vowed I would get a new tree made if I had to kidnap a hundred tree faeries from the Snickerdoodle Forest and use their magic to make one grow. Nobody was going to take away my date with Rudy after all I'd gone through to get it!

The polar-bear meanie then handed us each a sealed envelope and said, "Your parents will need to sign these before I can let you back in class."

My heart stopped.

When Daddy reads that note, there won't be any Candy *left* for Rudy to take to the Snow Ball!

twenty-two

The Workshop should have been humming with the sound of busy elves making hippity hops and pogo sticks and baseball mitts and Sit 'n Spins and Spirographs and yo-yos and xylophones and basketballs. Instead, a strange quietude greeted me. I checked the giant gauges on the wall. Just a little more than a month till Christmas, the top gauge noted, while the Toys-Completed gauge sat at only sixty-five percent. That couldn't be right.

Half the cubicles in the main office were empty. Jellydonut was asleep at his desk, on an elf-imposed break. I peeked onto the floor of the cavernous manufacturing room. A supervisor elf approved a batch of trapezoidal hula hoops that didn't look like they would be any fun to hula with, and scratched his head over a tricycle whose handlebars were where the pedals should be and vice versa.

"I guess they're okay," the supervisor elf said. "I'm sure Santa won't notice."

The hula-hoop elf and the tricycle-maker both shrugged, then tossed their products onto the Completed Toys conveyor belt, which whooshed them to the QA department.

A few other elves loitering in a corner noticed me and snapped to attention as if they were afraid I'd tell Daddy what they were up to—or not up to. I simply waved a cheerful hello.

"Candycane! How delightful to see you," Lolly the Elf said as her colleagues blew me tiny kisses. The entire workforce livened up as though a film projector had been switched from slow motion to normal speed.

"I'm afraid I don't know where your father is," the supervisor elf said.

"He's hardly ever here anymore," another elf added.

"But if there's anything we can do for you," the supervisor offered, "just name a toy. Any toy. It'll be our pleasure to whip it up for you."

"Actually, I'm here to see my mother," I said, glad to hear of my father's absence. Only one parent needed to sign the note from Mr. Polar Bear, Rudy had pointed out, so I could bypass Daddy entirely and take my chances with Mom. I liked the way Rudy thought. Finally he had something to teach me in exchange for all the Christmas enlightenment I'd given him.

"She's in her office," the supervisor elf informed me.

I climbed the stairs to the second floor. A glimpse through the gap in the partially open door to my mom's office revealed a heated, crowded group-therapy session in progress. There must have been twenty-five elves stuffed like Cracker Jacks on her faux deerskin couch, with another thirty or forty in the corners, on the floor, on the coffee table, under the coffee table. Not wanting to interrupt, I stood outside the doorway and waited quietly. I recognized Angry the Elf's complaining voice right away.

"I'm bustin' my butter makin' this toy, see, and I'm thinkin', what if the kid who gets it doesn't want it? What if he gets tired of it and stops playin' with it after a week, see?"

The other elves grumbled in agreement.

"Now you all know Santa goes to tremendous effort to find out exactly what every little boy and girl wants for Christmas. Why, your toys will be played with for ages," my mother assured them.

"Then why do we make new ones every year?" asked an elfin voice I didn't recognize.

"Yeah," said Angry the Elf. "Soon as those runts get their mitts on a new toy, they'll take the ones we made 'em last year and toss 'em into landfills."

"It's all such a waste of time," Pudding the Elf added.

If anyone could sympathize with having to live up to Daddy's illogical standards, it was me. It made me giggle.

"Is somebody there?" my mother called out.

"Sorry, I didn't know you were busy," I said, leaning my head into the small space of the doorframe.

Her face was aged with worry lines. "Not at all, dear." She waved me in for a welcome respite from the overwhelming volume of troubled elves griping and sniping all over her furniture. "We were just wrapping up, like a nice present! Isn't that right?"

One by one, the little helpers untucked their legs and stretched their backs and bounced to their feet as if the office had become an enormous package of Jiffy Pop. They filed past me, each one saluting me with a smile or a wink or a backflip or a magic trick, all their cares and woes seeming to fall from their pockets like so much loose change.

"Come by my cubicle later," Silly the Elf whispered to me. "I'm making a tea set out of genuine Fijian candy cane coral."

"Cool! I will!"

"You got so tall," said Wizard the Elf. He raised his tiny hand in the air and played got-your-nose like he did when I was still his size. "Makes you an even bigger inspiration."

I'd been a muse to the elves for as long as I could remember. Every time one of them dreamed up a new toy with me in mind, it filled my heart with elation, humility, honor, serenity, and about a thousand other incredible emotions I can't even name. You never get used to that. By the time my mother shut the door on the last elf out, I'd almost forgotten why I came.

"Elves," she said with a frazzled sigh. "They always have such trouble adjusting to the heavier workload this time of year. It gets worse every Christmas." She pushed a loose strand of silver hair behind her ear, then smoothed a wrinkle on her rose-colored blouse, slipping effortlessly back into her Mom character. "So what brings you here, darling?"

I frowned. "You have to sign this," I said, holding out the letter from school.

Her shoulders slumped like sandbags. She took the note to her desk and put on her reading glasses.

"Do we have to tell Daddy?" I asked before she even reached the second paragraph.

Silence. She kept reading. Another sigh. She looked up. "How did this happen?"

"I don't know," I sputtered. I welled up from the disappointment written in her unblinking gaze. The thought of hurting my loving, caring mother with my thoughtless misdeeds made me so ashamed, a wave a nausea threatened to spill my lunch on her antique desk.

She sighed again. "I don't understand. You worked so hard on that project."

I launched into a much more sanitized version of the story than the one I'd given Mr. Polar Bear. Like I needed her worrying about how I almost died from my foolishness. As usual, her magical intuition honed in on the part I'd tried to keep the most hidden.

"Do you have feelings for this boy?" she asked, peering over her wire-rimmed bifocals.

"Mom, this has nothing to do with that." I could almost feel my nose grow.

"Maybe so." She waited.

"I think so," I finally said. "Look, I promise I won't let it

168

get in the way of my schoolwork ever again. I'll work really hard and I'll fix my grades and I'll make you so proud."

"I'm always proud of you," she said. She studied my face for a long time, her blue eyes crinkling at the edges. She had this uncanny way of making me open up when I least expected it.

"He wants to take me to the Snow Ball," I told her. "And I really, really, really want to go with him and I promise I'll never do anything bad again."

Her tender smile reappeared. "When I was sixteen, I thought I could solve my problems by myself too. All I ask is that you remember I'm here for you." And just like that, she hunched down over her desk and scratched her quill pen across the bottom of the page.

"He's really not as bad as Daddy says, you know."

"It's between us. You just worry about your grades. Christmas is getting dangerously close. Your father has plenty of other things he'd better start worrying about."

I hugged and kissed her and was still thanking her and promising to be a good girl from now on when her office door swung open.

"Hi, princess," Daddy said. "I figured you were here when I saw Angry Elf smiling."

"Hi, Daddy!"

"As long as you're here, I want to show you something." He whipped out his phone and displayed a picture of Randolph Bush collecting nuts. "This is Rupert's nephew. He said he can have dinner with us next Tuesday."

I rolled my eyes. Daddy must have been off on the internet somewhere looking for more "suitable" dates for me.

"Uh, Dad? Randy's a squirrel."

He looked at the picture again. The puffy cheeks and bushy

tail didn't seem to bother him one bit. "Of course he is. He works at the bank with his uncle. He's a good catch, this one."

"Dad, I am not attracted to rodents."

"Okay, enough." My mother grabbed the phone out of his hand. "If Candy wants your help with boys, she'll ask you. Right now, you need to pay more attention to this…" She shoved a computer printout under his nose and tapped at a series of pie charts. "Nearly thirty cases of elf truancy in the last two weeks."

Daddy gave the data a cursory glance and put it back on Mom's desk. "It's nothing. I'll give the little guys a pep talk."

"Have you seen the production levels lately? Do you realize how late in the season it is? Have you seen the defect reports from QA? Your little helpers have become so apathetic—"

"Relax. It's the same thing every year. We always say, 'It'll take a miracle to get all those toys done in time.' And they always pull through. I'm telling you, I have it covered. What's this?"

He'd been poking through the papers on Mom's desk the whole time, and of course he stopped when he came across the handwritten note from my teacher.

"It's a letter," Mom said as she hastily folded and stuffed it under her arm. "To me."

"If that's from little Kenny Walton complaining about the video game he got last year, it won't do him any good going around me." He tugged at a corner of the letter. Mom twisted away from him.

"It's one of those girl letters, Daddy," I blurted. "You know, the ones you don't like to know about."

I probably shouldn't have said anything. His eyes narrowed into suspicious slits. "That wasn't a girl's handwriting," he said. "You think I can't tell the difference? It looked like it was written by a polar bear." He watched my reaction carefully, my lips pressing together, my knuckles whitening from balling my fists so tight. "Come to think of it, that looked like North Pole High letterhead. Hand it over."

My mother caved. Daddy's critical gaze sawed across the pawwritten words. Amidst the nervous silence, a lump rose in my throat and I heard Rudy's voice bubble up in my head: *You're old enough to do what you want, Candy. Stand up to him. Tell him what's on your mind.* Against my better judgment, I listened. I swallowed hard when my father looked up, his jaw set tight beneath his pillowy beard.

"Daddy, I'm growing up now. You have to let me make my own mistakes. So I can learn from them." I thought saying that would make me feel incredible, but I trembled, waiting for an answer.

"That so?" he said rhetorically, then paused. "Okay, you've made a mistake. Now what?"

I hadn't expected him to lob the ball back to me like that. I raised my eyebrows and said meekly, "I won't make it again?"

Good answer, kid. Go suck on your candy-cane pacifier while you're at it if you're gonna act like a baby.

Shut up. He's my father.

"Fair enough. And while you're not making the same mistake, you can take over your brother's chores for a week." *Thus spaketh the Claus.*

To be honest, it wasn't the worst punishment he could have given me. I knew that. Maybe what I'd said to him had actually worked in my favor in some small way. But still, what girl wants to spend her Friday night in a barn shoveling reindeer chocolate? Besides, did he ever stop to think that maybe the reason I fell behind in botany was because he had ordered me to stop doing my homework? So I didn't exactly take my lumps

171

with grace.

"'I understand, princess,'" I said, mimicking Daddy as I fed and brushed the girls that night. "'Everybody makes mistakes. I trust you. You'll learn so much more by feeding the stupid reindeer!'"

Dasher started to fly out of her stall. I promised her I didn't mean it as I nudged her back to the ground. I refilled her bucket of magic cocoa beans and commiserated with her being stuck there like nothing more than one of Daddy's possessions. "I don't blame you for wanting to get out of this place."

Prancer, Donner, and Blitzen kicked up their hooves too.

"Well, I am your keeper this week," I said with a mischievous laugh. "And it is my duty to keep you in shape, isn't it?"

Now, I know I promised my mother I would never do anything bad again, but I itched to do *something* to warrant my unjust sentence. So I harnessed together eight co-conspirators as I hatched an impetuous scheme to prove to Daddy he'd overreacted. His daughter could be so much badder than a little slip in grades.

Even Mr. Tough Guy Rudy hesitated to go along with my larceny when I showed up unexpectedly at his doorstep.

"Hey," he said, surprised to see me. "Your old man's letting us work here again?"

"I'm not here to do homework, Rudy."

I stepped aside so he could see the doe all lined up at the curb, two by two, Daddy's one and only sleigh in tow. It had been around the world, one night a year for over a hundred years, never without my dad at the reins. And now it stood at the ready outside the humble Tutti abode, waiting to take two teenagers on a weekend joyride.

"Is that what I think it is?"

I nodded. "Wanna go for a spin?"

He approached the vehicle in a cautious reverence, tapping the runner with his toe, tracing his fingers across the satin lining of the seat. "Are you sure you know what you're doing? I mean, this is Santa's ride we're talking about."

"Don't be such an L7," I said, laughing at him. I made an L and a seven with my fingers, then brought them together to form a square. Then I climbed into the sleigh ahead of Rudy and picked up the reins. "What are you waiting for? Let's go touch the sky."

I couldn't figure out how Daddy managed to squeeze his colossal tush into that cramped passenger compartment and still have room for a couple of elves, but it fit two normal-sized teenagers rather cozily. Rudy wedged himself in right beside me. Even better, the closeness inspired him to drape an arm around me. I can't tell you how nervous that made me.

You know how many times I'd driven Daddy's sleigh before? Daddy's *stolen* sleigh? Once. On the way over to Rudy's. That was it. I mean, I'd taken Mushers Ed in middle school; the mechanics weren't that much different. But still, this thing traveled on thin air! And all I wanted was to concentrate on Rudy's wonderfully firm body pressed tight against mine. Without letting him see the sweat stains forming in my armpits. While I tried to focus on my flying.

I gave the lift-off command and the carriage arose with a jolt that jerked Rudy backward. His hand came off my shoulder and found purchase on the sturdy ledge of the dashboard. Seeing his childlike fear somehow helped put me more at ease as the sleigh rocked over invisible air currents. Ascending higher into the eternal night, the reindeer adjusted to a load far lighter than the billions of toys they were used to carrying. Once they'd taken us beyond the tallest green trees, the flight became breathtakingly smooth.

The moon was full and blueish green, low on the horizon. I put both reins in my right hand, Rudy's hand in my left. I squeezed it gently and he squeezed back. Every care I'd ever had in the world washed away except for one: If only I could capture that moment, live in it forever, and still have enough left over to use as a bow to wrap around every Christmas present in the Workshop. Then I could truly make the world a happier place.

twenty-three

Remember the end of *Grease*? When Danny and Sandy drive away in the fantasy version of Greased Lightning and it sails off into the clouds? That's what it felt like flying through the starlit sky with Rudy. So how perfect was it that *Grease* was playing that night at the North Pole Drive-In? Dream dates in actual dreams never get that dreamy.

Rudy thought I'd planned it all, but I hadn't. The drive-in had merely been a serendipitously spontaneous destination. We parked in the rear of the sloped viewing area, across a row of open spaces wide enough to accommodate our herd without their twisty, knobby antlers blocking anyone's view. The entire N.P.H. student body dotted the hillside in their snowmobiles, or lying in the snow beside their snow scooters, gazing up at the flickering images that danced across the immense white wall of the Great Glacier.

Our craft now grounded and motionless, Rudy felt safe enough to wrap his arm around me again. I leaned into his embrace and sang "We Go Together" softly in his ear. He gave me a blank stare and wondered aloud why they weren't showing something like *It's a Wonderful Life*.

"Not everything here is Christmas," I said.

Especially when it came to movies. Daddy headed up the North Pole Motion Picture Board, carefully selecting which movies could be projected onto the ice at the town's only movie theatre. Not many Christmas movies made the cut, mainly because Daddy found most of them insulting. Like that one with the alcoholic Santa who robbed department stores.

Of course, the minute Daddy banned it everyone in school downloaded it to see what the fuss was. Now I watch it in my room whenever I'm really mad at Daddy. It's sooo funny.

I fed Rudy a fresh piece of enchanted chocolate. I'd never seen him that relaxed. I would almost say he glowed. "You look happy," I said, as Danny and Sandy mirrored our tranquil drive-in experience up on the widescreen surface of the frozen mass.

"What, I enjoy a good musical," he said defensively.

I laughed. "You're not even watching the movie." Not that I was complaining. I'd caught more than a few stolen glances during *o-oh, those su-u-mmer nights!* I brushed a curly lock from his eyes and my hand landed momentarily on his bicep. Not too rippled like someone obsessed with trying to impress people, but definitely sculpted. Afraid to leave it there too long, I searched for something to say so he wouldn't notice my lingering touch. "I think you're starting to like it here," I teased.

"Don't make me laugh, ha, ha, ha," he quoted Danny Zuko, perhaps to prove he'd been watching. Or that he'd seen the picture before.

I pushed out my tongue, then smiled. "Before you know it, mister, you'll be roasting chestnuts o'er an open fire."

"O'er?"

"It's a word."

"You think you got me pegged, don't you?"

Not in the slightest. "Pretty much."

In the distance, Snowflake cuddled with Silentnight in his Snow Pod. I couldn't tell if they were making out like all the horny teens in their Chevies and Oldsmobiles at the make-believe drive-in on the movie screen. I hoped they were. I wondered if I would be anytime soon.

I fed Rudy another piece of reindeer poop. He savored it,

spreading the taste all over his tongue. He nodded toward the girls and asked, "Which one of them was that from?"

"Vixen," I said, a cloud of awkwardness floating out with the answer like a thought bubble in a comic strip. But hey, he was the one who asked, right?

"About that," he said. "She was trying to get me to score her some 'toe."

Again, the lawyers insisted I point out that this is only "hearsay." That is, the part about Vixen wanting to buy high-grade, uncut mistletoe, better known on the street as megatoe or just plain *toe*. I have no idea if Vixen is a 'toehead and I don't care. The part about why Rudy would be mistaken for a supplier, on the other hand, turned out to be a matter of public record.

I scooched away as far as the confining interior allowed, which wasn't a lot, while I let him explain.

"It's why I was expelled from my last school," he said.

"You?" I pictured Rudy bleary-eyed from doing foots all day with guys like the greasers in the movie, stealing cars to support his habit, getting into fights where nobody got tickled.

"I walked in on a deal going down in the bathroom," he went on. "The lookout spotted the principal coming. They all scattered, you know, the way roaches do when the light goes on. But not before tossing a sack of their junk in my lap. I didn't have time to dump it. As the principal put it, I was caught green-handed."

Lords a-leaping! For a minute I wished this had been the part of the book where my too-perfect boyfriend revealed he was a werewolf or a goblin or something a girl could get used to. But a convicted 'toe dealer?

"It wasn't mine," he said, as if he could read my mind. "You believe me?"

I bit my lip. *Did I?* I wanted to. "Maybe," I said.

"That's more than I got from my father. I don't blame him, either. I've been in trouble before. That's why we ended up here. There weren't any schools left where we lived that would take me." He squirmed into the extra inch of space on his side of the bench. "Well, there you go, Candycane. You got your man to open up. Bet you don't wanna be seen at that Snow Prom thing with a guy like me now, huh?"

I had this icky feeling, like maybe he'd made up the whole 'toe story to scare me away, to get out of taking me to the Snow Ball. But why would he do that? Did he like me or not? Then I remembered my father saying something about him being in trouble at his last school—that night in the barn, that incredible, awful night that was so confusing I'd chosen to ignore the parts that scared me the most. Maybe it was all true. Maybe my father had been right about him all along.

"Look, Rudy…" I started to say. "If you don't want to go…" I was afraid to finish my thought. Afraid if I gave him a way out, he'd take it. And maybe a little more afraid he wouldn't.

Then out of nowhere, he leaned forward and the next thing I knew, his mouth was on mine. I didn't have time to prepare, to think about which way to tilt my head or how much to part my lips or how long I'd waited for this. Our lips just slid against each other, back and forth, melting like warm, sweet butter, and I never wanted it to end.

I was still lost in that kiss long after he'd pulled away. When I opened my eyes, he was staring at me. I wanted to shout, "That was incredible! Give me more!" but instead I just stared back, waiting for him to say something first.

He did.

"Your turn to tell me something. What do you want with me, really?"

How could he expect me to talk after having been caught off guard like that, after having been kissed like that, and not sound like a blubbering idiot? "I, uhhh, I. You…" Like that. "I don't know."

Sandy slammed the car door on Danny, but Rudy and I were still very close inside our intimate little cabin.

"Look, I know who you are," he said. "I gave up roasting chestnuts a long time ago. That open fire burned itself out. Now it's just a pile of ashes." His eyes locked intently on mine, haunted, swimming in anger and—*despair*? "I won't ever change," he added. "I'll only bring you trouble."

"Mom says… people don't outgrow Christmas. Sometimes they set it aside and forget. But it always comes back." I wanted to drop the subject and get back to the one that didn't use words because it involved our lips being stuck together.

He dangled his arm out his side of the sleigh, turning so he wouldn't have to face me. I must have sounded like a stupid child to him.

I moved closer; he stayed facing forward.

"Daddy says—"

Rudy shook his head. "Don't you get it?" Then something took over him. Something deep and too painful for him to remember. After a long silence, he drooped his head over the side, watching the snow melt, his thoughts falling out of him so softly I had to lean over to hear him, my hand smoothing his back in small, reassuring circles.

"The last present your father ever gave me," he said, "I never even opened it. Christmas was always her. She made it sing for us. I strung popcorn and cranberries with her. She told my dad what decorations to put up outside, and every year she made us all go take a new portrait for the family Christmas cards. You can surround me in all the ho-ho-hos and Merry

179

Everydays you have up here, but it won't come back. Not for me."

I took his hand and caressed it. I wished he would cry—he needed to—but I knew he would never grant himself that noblest of vulnerabilities. So many things started to make sense, though. "The electric train set," I guessed. The one he'd said could never make up for suffering.

He turned and looked at me. A slight nod. "She died that Christmas Day."

I dug my head into his chest, enveloping him in my arms. He hugged me back, tight as a drum. I tried to imagine what it would feel like, such a tremendous loss, all that sorrow, on the one day set aside for giving, for joy, for peace.

"I'm doing fine without Christmas," he whispered, and I believed he meant it. No magic could fix that.

The rest of the events of our date that night have been exhaustively documented on gossipy blogs and in all the tabloids. As we told the police, neither of us saw what spooked the reindeer.

They just took off.

twenty-four

One minute we were sitting there bonding, really bonding, and the next we were catapulted across the sky without warning.

"No, Dasher! No, Dancer!" I cried out.

The reins out of reach, tangled around the yoke, we had no way to control the crazed deer. I had no choice. I climbed up on the seat, clenching my fingers around the curve of the dash with one hand, grasping for the reins with the other.

"I don't think that's a good idea!" Rudy shouted, trying to pull me back into the cab.

"Hold me!" I shouted back. "I have to get the reins."

"Let me. I'm taller."

We started to switch places. The sleigh made a sharp turn, flinging me over the side. At fifty feet up, I'd have been snow soup in a matter of seconds, but Rudy's strong grip caught my wrist in the nick of time. I dangled like that, legs flailing in the wind, as we flew wide circles over the North Pole Drive-In.

Rudy pulled and pulled. Inch by terrifying inch. I made the mistake of looking down once. The white-blanketed mountain rushed by, far too far below me. I screamed, even knowing Rudy would never let me fall.

My classmates stopped whatever they were doing. No more kissing, no more groping, passions frozen, replaced by panic. They leaped off their snowmobiles and pointed and gasped each time we buzzed by. We whooshed past Silent and Snowflake in their Snow Pod and for just a blurry moment, I could make out the worried looks on their faces.

Rudy tugged hard, straining to pull me to safety, making too little progress. My arm felt like it was in a taffy pull. Had I been able to let go when we dipped low enough, I would have made a nice soft landing in the snow. But Rudy held tight, too determined for my own good to save me himself.

He finally managed to wrestle me back into the sleigh. I latched onto him for dear life. We zipped past the image on the silver ice-wall—Danny belting out his misery over losing Sandy—while I held Rudy more snugly than a true bear hug, relief flowing through my veins, safe in his embrace.

But only for a second.

We felt a bump, heard a clink. The sleigh's runners had clipped a chunk of ice off the movie screen. Rugged cubes bounced down the side of the glacier, crashing at its base like glass. If Rudy hadn't pulled me in when he did, those shattered ice fragments would be mixed with sprinkles of crushed Candycane bits.

"The reins, Rudy!"

I buckled myself in and hugged his legs as he climbed up the dash to retrieve our only brakes. The sleigh circled back toward the face of the glacier. The looming ice block sped at us head-on. The deer climbed. They would easily clear it, but not by enough for the heavy runaway chariot they dragged behind them.

We were about to be smashed to ribbons when Rudy untwisted the reins. He yanked hard aport on my command. A little too hard. The girls steered us away from certain doom, but we whiplashed wide out to starboard.

Sideswiped for a second time, the berg took it out on the sleigh's fragile runners, crippling them beyond repair. Great. Now even if we were lucky enough to survive, Daddy would kill me.

I helped Rudy slide back onto the bench, reins now securely in his possession. Then came a loud, sickening rumble. I turned to look at the animated wall of ice.

Danny Zuko was pointing at a cartoon hot dog flipping itself into a bun, while large cracks snaked rapidly across the movie-screen-on-the-movie-screen, as if the fictitious drive-in were experiencing an earthquake. The cracks continued creeping down the real screen, our screen, the one made of ice. Giant boulders tumbled down its face. This was no polar quake, though. Nor a Hollywood special effect. It was much worse.

A giant, furry-knuckled fist punched through John Travolta's anguished mug, followed by a furious roar. Our minor collisions awoke the beast that had slumbered undisturbed inside the glacier for decades. Now, old Yeti plowed his way out of his cavern. And he was *pissed*.

I'd never actually seen him before, but his features were unmistakable. Imagine a pizzly bear. The girth, strength, and stamina of a grizzly; the height, speed, and cunning hunting ability of a polar bear. Matted white Wookie-like fur with yellowish brown patches. Now imagine that creature crossed with King Kong.

That was the Abominable Snowman, muscling through the falling ice, shaking the ground with each footfall. Moviegoers below abandoned their vehicles and scurried in all directions for fear of being crushed.

"Now that's what I call 3-D," Rudy quipped inappropriately.

"Rudy, do something!"

He thrust the reins in my face. "I don't know how to drive this thing."

I took over and got the reindeer flying straight, then started looking for a place to land. Yeti swatted at us like we were a fly. He missed, but the current sent us reeling, spinning, tumbling.

"We have to stop him!" I yelled.

"You mean he's not another one of your friends? Like that Otter seal?"

"Not this time. He's the Abominable Snowman. He lives in the glacier. We must have woke him up."

"That's not good, right?"

"Who said you were slow?"

Instead of helping, Rudy planted a succinct but tingly kiss on my lips.

"What was that for?" I asked.

"I already saved your life twice today. I'm out of ideas."

Boys! It was up to me to fix this disaster.

I flew us over the chaos to survey the damage, keeping our distance from the monster. Yeti stomped on abandoned snowmobiles, flattening them like blueberry pancakes that reminded me of being home at the breakfast table with my mommy, who I might never see again, eating Chefy's unbelievable blueberry pancakes with strawberry syrup and whipped cream and chocolate shavings and a tall glass of freshly squeezed key-lime marmalade juice. How I wished I were there and not in a hard-to-handle, flying sleigh with a gigantic hairy beast threatening to destroy my town.

Yeti's forceful paw stopped a speeding Snow Pod from its escape. He picked it up, with Silentnight and Snowflake trapped inside, and toyed with it like a plaything, trying to jam his big stubby fingers through the cage to see what Silent-and-Snowflake dip might taste like. Unable to get at them, and tiring of the effort, he tossed the machine aside. It landed on top of a snow bank, immobile.

He decided to try for the sleigh again. He seemed to prefer

moving objects. He took another swipe at the air, just missing us. I got Dasher and Dancer to pull faster, but Yeti needed only a few giant footsteps to catch up to us. He pinched the runners of the sleigh between his thumb and forefinger and laughed. The doe struggled to keep flying, frustrated they weren't getting anywhere. But they didn't give up.

Neither did Rudy. He reached into the back of the sleigh and picked up a small bundle of Christmas presents.

"Where did those come from?" I asked.

"How should I know? It's your sleigh. The old man must have missed a few deliveries."

"Daddy never forgets anyone!"

"What's a few out of a billion? It's still a good record."

Rudy lobbed one of the presents at Yeti's nose.

"What are you doing!"

"Pissing him off."

He threw another, hitting the target's lower lip.

"Rudy, don't. He *started* at pissed off!"

The third one almost took out Yeti's eye, making him yelp like a puppy dog. He let go of us, which I supposed was Rudy's plan. Except the sudden movement made Rudy lose his balance. He plunged out of the sleigh, sailing through the air until Yeti reached out and caught him.

I squeezed my eyes shut as Abominable brought Rudy to his mouth. A bloodthirsty growl filled the air. In the empty silence that followed, I forced my eyelids open, convinced I'd lost my new boyfriend forever. But for some reason, the giant had placed Rudy gently on a jagged ridge at the mouth of his busted ice cave. Could Yeti be a vegetarian?

I didn't have time to find out. He was after me again. I mushed the reindeer faster. The snowmonster was gaining.

Behind him, Rudy waved his arms like a freak, shouting,

"Hey, fur-butt!"

Yeti slowed, staring daggers at him.

"Yeah, I'm talking to you, you Abominable Biyotch!"

The creature howled at him. And I gotta say, I wasn't too fond of that move either. Sure, it got the beast off my tail for a minute. But now I had to one-eighty the sleigh and stop Big Abe from serving up a Rudy-Tutti-fresh-and-fruity breakfast special!

I swooped past Yeti's head, then lurched the sleigh into a steep climb to avoid the wild swinging of his filthy mitts. Rudy slid off his perch, down the ice, dashing through the snow surprisingly fast. He must have had a lot of practice outrunning truant officers back home.

He vaulted up the snow bank where Silentnight's Snow Pod lay stuck in a drift, its two passengers still trapped inside. Rudy had to pry open the dented hatch to get them out. I kept up my flybys to distract the Goliath, buying my friends extra time.

I started to get the hang of controlling the sleigh in a trial-by-fire sort of way. But the girls became dizzy flying around in circles. Blitzen threw up at one point. Dasher and Dancer, the team leaders, fought my directions and attempted to land us on Yeti's head! They came pretty close once. Yeti banged his fist into his temple trying to crush us, angering himself even more.

"Hey, Snowchump! Over here!"

The furry behemoth trampled toward Rudy, who taunted him from atop the summit. Snowflake and Silentnight, freed from the Snow Pod, shimmied down the other side of the embankment. Remembering all he'd mastered on Butterscotch Hills, Rudy heaved the Snow Pod out of the dip, planking it as it took off down the powdery slope. Even hanging on from the outside, he Podded more expertly than Tinsel ever could.

He whipped the Snow Pod between the beast's sequoian legs. Yeti nearly toppled over trying to nab him.

The distraught reindeer, no longer heeding my commands, flew right into the danger zone. Yeti straightened up, bumping his head against the hovering carriage. He took another swing at me as I tried to recover from the rough jolt.

Rudy spun back around in his Pod. He streaked over the big animal's nasty yellow toenails.

Yeti didn't like that at all. He pounded his fists into the snow in a crazed tantrum that put my historic act in Silly the Elf's cube to shame. He thumped the ground so hard I thought the stars would fall out of the sky.

Rudy careened back toward his opponent, picking up speeds never before attained in a Snow Pod, swooshing by so fast his movement created a high-pitched whistle that sounded like a screaming ghost.

Then he let go.

The cage barreled forward without him, like a guided missile. It ripped through the fleshy tendon in the Abominable Snowman's ankle like a shot from a cannon.

Now, you may have heard the whole Achilles' heel thing is a myth, but one thing's for certain: Yeti hadn't heard that. His hairy butt plunged into the snow as he cradled his wounded foot, letting out a wail that could probably be heard as far away as the South Pole.

His reign of terror for the night had ended.

The rest of the kids emerged from their hiding places, pointing and laughing at the poor injured monster crying like a big baby. They called him a wuss and a sissy. Some even lobbed snowballs at him.

Maybe Abominable deserved to be made fun of. His behavior certainly had lived up to his well-known moniker.

But these were the same kids who had scattered and fled like vampires at daybreak when the big scary ape-bear-baby-thing first hit the fan. They were hardly in a position to see every little thing that had transpired while cowering in the nooks and crannies of the drive-in. I'm not saying my friends would lie, but you can't believe everything you hear.

What I've just written is *my* version of the story, the facts as I witnessed them, the details as I remember them. No matter what you read in the papers, that's what really went down the night my hero landed in the North Pole Jail.

twenty-five

Curled up into cute little fuzzballs, the reindeer were already fast asleep in the snow when Officer Brownbear and his cubs arrived on the scene. I tried to explain how it was all my fault, but what bear in his right mind would lock up Santa's little princess? So I went downtown with them to the police station, where they booked Rudy on grand-theft sleigh, reckless endangerment, and corrupting a Kringle.

Super. Now I'd turned my boyfriend into a sleighjacker. I wouldn't blame him if he hated me.

"But Rudy was so brave," I whined to the arresting bear. "He deserves a parade."

"Then I'll parade him to his cell," the brown bear replied.

He fingerprinted Rudy and took his picture, then shoved him into a cage made of black bars as thick as licorice. The smell was horrid, but I promised Rudy I would stick with him no matter what.

An inebriated elf got up from the metal bunk and circled his new cellmate like a finicky cub inspecting a fish. He wore a dark, wrinkled trench coat that went down to the floor even though it was a child's size. The points of his ears were crooked and he burped and scratched himself a lot. "Hey kid, what're you in for?"

"Nothing," Rudy snapped.

"They sure are cracking down on that these days," the puny lush said with a cackle. Then to me he said, "Hey, cutie. I'm Flasher. Wanna see me do a cartwheel?"

"Not especially," I said.

"Then tell me what your loverboy did."

"I didn't do anything," Rudy barked at Flasher the Degenerate Elf.

"No, my son never does anything."

The three of us turned to see Dr. Tutti stride through the precinct house with Sugar Plum flitting in his shadow. His lips drew a thin line; the disappointment seemed to fit him like a comfortable old shoe he'd gotten used to. As he neared the cage, he blinked and said quietly, "You know what surprised me the most when my son came home with a note from his teacher today? That it took this long. We've been in this frozen tundra for, what, almost four months now."

"Yeah, about that note," I said sheepishly. "You see, that was sort of my naughty. I'm the one who ruined our homework."

"Oh, yeah? What about the fire in middle school? Was that somebody else's fault? And the cherry bomb incident? Don't look at Rudy, he's innocent. He's always innocent. How about those grades that got erased from the school's computers?"

Sufferin' snowballs! What else had Rudy been up to— melting the polar ice cap with a magnifying glass? With a list of priors like that, nobody would believe *I* was the one who'd been the bad influence on *him*. Any minute now, there'd be villagers gathered outside with pitchforks and torches demanding he be tarred and feathered. And Chefy would be there to prepare a Tarring and Feathering Feast.

"I got an A in that class," Rudy said. "The teacher confirmed it. Why would I delete that?"

"Poor Rudy. Always in the wrong place at the wrong time, but never doing anything wrong."

"That's right, Pops," Flasher gurgled, inserting himself into the conversation.

Rudy's father sneered coldly at him.

190

"Hi, Flasher!" Sugar Plum chirped. "I hope you've been flossing."

"Hey, I know you two." Flasher scratched behind his malformed ear until their identities came to him. "The dentist and the, uh, dentistette. I didn't recognize you'se all without yer fingers jammed in my chompers. Lady, what're ya doing with Pops here? Jingling his bells?"

Sugar Plum flushed. "We were just having dinner. Right, Tony? I mean, Dr. Tutti? Or can I call you Tony? But only when we're not at work, Tony. Okay, Tony? Haha. Tony. That sounds right, doesn't it? Am I talking too much? I should shut up. I can make a toothbrush out of a carrot. Wanna see?"

The dentist opened his mouth to respond but thought better of it and turned back to Rudy. By then, he'd forgotten what he wanted to say and his gaze darted back to his hygienist. Sugar Plum shifted back and forth on her feet and smiled nervously.

Wouldn't they be a cute couple?

Apparently Rudy saw the same picture. "Wait a minute," he said. "Are you two dating?"

"Never you mind about that," his father said, wagging a stern finger.

"Well, I wouldn't call it a date," Sugar Plum said, revving up her motormouth again. "Just a man and a woman having a simple dinner together that the woman spent a week preparing in the copious spare time she has after spending ten hours a day working in close quarters with the man laughing at his jokes or at least planning to if he ever makes any and you know getting to know each other outside of work where all they ever talk about is teeth while she's wondering stuff about him like how many Christmas carols does he know by heart and what's his favorite raspberry." Sugar Plum tended to speak without

191

commas.

Dr. Tutti scratched his head. "There's more than one kind of raspberry?"

"Well, sure, *Tony*, tee-hee," she said, still tickled by the simple pleasure of trying on her boss's first name. "There's red, golden, purple, black, Meeker, Munger, Malahat, and even Ripley, believe it or not."

"I don't eat raspberries. The seeds get stuck in my teeth."

"There you go again! Errrr! What's it gonna take to get you to open up, Doc, an 'Ahh' stick?"

"Can we stick to the subject, please?"

Sugar Plum raised her penciled eyebrows and stage-whispered to Rudy, "Nope. Your father and I are definitely not dating."

Haha. I so knew what she was going through. I couldn't wait to get her alone to give her some pointers I'd picked up on the Tutti men.

"That is *not* the subject!" A piece of spittle flew out of *Tony's* mouth as he hollered. "Am I the only one who sees where we're standing? Ladies and gentlemen, we are gathered here tonight to bail my perfectly innocent boy out of jail for his latest and greatest escapade—stealing Santa's sleigh."

"Wow!" Flasher poked Rudy in the ribs and smiled wide, like he'd found his new BFF. "That thing at the drive-in? You did that? I'm impressed."

"I didn't steal the sleigh," Rudy said, glaring my way.

I wanted to say something, but by that point I didn't think it would do any good.

His father paced in front of the bars as he mocked his son. "I suppose Santa Claus is also in on this vast North Pole conspiracy to frame poor, misunderstood Rudy Tutti."

"Maybe he is," Rudy said.

They weren't that far from the truth. Daddy had been suspicious of Rudy from day one. So had I, for that matter.

"The fat dude does have a record of breaking and entering," the degenerate elf pointed out.

"Do you mind!" Dr. Tutti shouted, a thick vein bulging down the center of his forehead.

"Suck it!" The little fellow lewdly flashed open his raincoat, exposing a giant all-day sucker hanging from his neck.

I had to chuckle at that.

Dr. Tutti didn't find it amusing at all. He threatened to leave Rudy in that stinky cell overnight to teach him a lesson. But when Flasher rejoiced at the prospect of what he referred to as their "sleepover," Dr. T relented and limped over to Officer Brownbear's desk to take care of Rudy's bail, grumbling all the way—*I don't know what you were thinking. First megatoe, now this. Cookies don't grow on trees, you know.* (Technically, some do, but not the ones we use for currency.)

I reached into the cell and stroked Rudy's soft, dark tangles while we waited for him to be sprung. In a way, we were kindred spirits. Neither of our fathers got us. I couldn't attest to the laundry list of pranks he'd supposedly pulled when he lived in the land between the Poles, but I knew for a fact he hadn't demolished our tree or stolen Daddy's sleigh or spooked the reindeer. And if the boy who hadn't done any of those awful things I'd gotten him blamed for said the 'toe wasn't his, then I had to believe him, even if I was the only one.

I promised Rudy I'd figure out a way to get Daddy to drop the charges. I doubt he believed me. I know I sure didn't.

Luckily Daddy was still at the scene of the crime, dealing with his precious sleigh. I guess no one had told him how close his daughter had come to being stomped into candy-cane pancakes, because he sure as Christmas didn't rush over to see if I was all right. Which, as I said, was just as well. I mean, I wasn't out of the blizzard yet. There would still be a symphony of music to face for this fiasco, and I'd have to face it one note at a time.

Officer Brownbear gave me a lift home. My brother was waiting for me at the top of the stairs to wag his finger and steal Mom's line: "Just wait till your father gets home." Then he ducked into his room before I could so much as stick my tongue out at him.

Chefy made some delicious cocoa—creamier than I'd ever deserved—while I told Mom everything. She took it surprisingly well. She was relieved I was okay and disappointed by my decisions, in that order. But Frostbite was right. When Daddy got home, it would definitely not be a silent night.

twenty-six

Thirty-two tiny hooves clippity-clopped up the walkway alongside two heavy boots. My whole body quivered. I'd been waiting alone in the dark, empty stable for over an hour, sitting in front of the storage space under the sink where I sometimes used to hide when I was little, wishing I could still fit—my father might be making me live out here from now on.

I shuffled outside to help unhook the reindeer's harnesses and guide them into their stalls. The pits of Daddy's coat were stained with perspiration from walking the girls home. Neither of us said a word. I waited for him to break the silence, then decided an apology would sound more sincere if offered before being demanded.

"I'm really, super-duper sorry, Daddy."

He kept tending to the animals as if he hadn't heard me. Then he made a heavy sigh and, without looking at me, as if he were talking to Cupid instead, said, "In over a hundred years, I have never had to pick up my reindeer from an impound lot."

He went back to filling Cupid's water bowl.

I'd never felt so small.

"Look at Blitzen!" Daddy's face turned purple. His eyes widened as if they had a mind to shoot out of his head and spank me. "She's shaking! These deer need to be in tip-top shape! I have a mall tour coming up."

I deserved to be scolded, even though it seemed kind of pointless since the things he was yelling at me were not things I didn't know. As he bellowed about my foolish irresponsibility, I couldn't help but remember how proud I'd been of my dad the first time I got to go with him on a mall tour—his annual visit to every department store in the world, where he finds out what you all want for Christmas. My father, at his best. He so loves getting out there in front of all the good little children, it shines from him as if his soul were composed on a Lite-Brite set.

I sometimes envied the attention he lavished on all those kids during all those business trips. Kids he barely knew. Then this one time, at the Millenia Mall, a little girl named Kimberly told me how lucky I was to have the coolest guy for a dad all year round. To her, he was a rock star, and it was easy to see why.

"It was so stupid of me to take the sleigh," I told him. "I don't blame you for being mad at me."

Daddy tore off his gloves and whipped them to the ground so fast it made me shudder, along with half the reindeer. "That right there is what angers me the most. That you want to protect that miscreant sleigh thief. He has dragged you down so low you don't even know which way is Christmas anymore."

"But Daddy, I'm the one who took the sleigh. Rudy had nothing to do with it."

"It won't do you any good covering for the scalawag."

"I'm not covering for him. Honest. It was my idea."

"Don't you lie to me. I am still your father. It's not too late for you to wind up on the Naughty List too, young lady."

Sweet Nicholas! He'd never threatened to N-List me before. He'd never even joked about it. Nobody born in the North Pole, let alone of Claus blood, had ever come close to making the List. It just didn't happen. And did he say "too"?

"You can't put Rudy on the N-List!"

"Oh no? For this he goes straight to the top. Over the

top. The double-top. Why, he's the whole Top Ten wrapped up in one slimy son of a—"

"But, but, Daddy, I'm the one who should be punished. He just came along for the ride. Because *I* invited him. Because I *like* him."

"Ho-ho-ho. Who said I wasn't going to punish you?"

Gulp.

My father circled around me like a lion challenging its tamer. "This was not your doing, Candycane. I know that. But still, you should have known better than to go along with his heinous crime."

"For the last time..." I started to repeat myself, then decided it wasn't worth it. Instead, I took a deep breath and said, "I'm ready to accept any punishment you think is fair. As long as you drop the charges against Rudy."

Daddy folded his arms across his chest. "Just like that. You think you can exchange a punishment like some oversized sweater. What do I look like, the customer-service department at Macy's?"

"I'm just saying, he didn't do anything wrong." At least not in this case, I added to myself.

Daddy parked his jumbo butt on a wooden stool and ran his fingers through his beard to make it look like he was weighing my pleas. But he had his mind made up the entire time.

"Your mother thought I was being too hard on you over the incident with your grades," he said. "She thinks I should butt out of your 'private affairs'." He made air quotes and sneered like the words were choking him. "*Boys*, she meant. Well, look where *boys* have gotten you so far."

I looked hard at his shiny nose, his wrinkly forehead. What was behind it that made him think the way he did?

He meant well. He wanted me to be safe and happy and perfect forever. Making kids happy came easy to him. But it was like he'd never had to deal with a teenager before. We're not perfect. We're works in progress. He once made a doll that blossomed from prepubescent child to full adulthood simply by rotating her arm. No muss, no fuss. Did he think there'd come some magic day when he finally decided I was ready to be a grown-up and he could throw a switch on the back of my neck and—POOF? We don't work that way.

I forced myself to pay attention to the rest of his speech as if I cared.

He popped a handful of jelly beans in his mouth and kept lecturing while he chewed. "…No, in truth it appears you require even more discipline. I was prepared to let you come with me on my mall tour this year, but now," he blinked for dramatic effect, "I'm afraid that can't happen."

My reaction was the last thing either of us expected. It started with a laugh, but that didn't hurt his ego enough. "Good!" I shouted. "It's *boring* going to malls with you. You only pay attention to those brats who line up begging you for toys. You think they idolize you, but you're just buying their love, and I don't want any part of that. I'm sick of being a Claus!" What had once come out of me as a crying and kicking tantrum when I was two had now emerged as words; sharp, angry, hurtful words.

I stomped my foot and swallowed hard. I didn't honestly believe any of those terrible things I'd said about my father, but then I couldn't exactly invalidate them either. Would a billion strangers care about him if he didn't bribe them with toys? Did that make my father unlovable as a person?

And then it dawned on us both at the same time—those weren't my thoughts at all. It may have been my mouth moving, but those were Rudy's thoughts spilling out of it. How could a trick like that have been pulled off by someone who didn't even believe in magic?

"What has he done to my princess? I don't even recognize you anymore." He reached out to me with the same hands that had cradled me as a baby, and I backed away from them. "Are you on 'toe?"

That stung. "No, *Daddy*. Rudy let me see who he truly is. He thinks differently than we do, but he's not the troublemaker his father thinks he is. He's not the delinquent I thought he was. He's a real person. He hurts, he dreams. He cares about me. And I think he's hot chocolate."

Daddy got up to wrap a blanket around Blitzen, who was licking a sore forepaw.

"The megatoe wasn't his," I said. "I can't prove that. I just know it. And, no, he hasn't broken my cookie, if that's what you were going to ask next."

Daddy tried to get Blitzen to eat a cocoa bean. She spit it out. "You are not to see him again. At all. For anything."

"You can't stop me."

"Wanna bet? As of this moment, there will be no more study sessions with boys, no more drive-ins with boys, no more Snow Pod races or fruitcake pizzas. No more leaving this house after dark for any reason."

"It's dark for six months."

"*Exactly*," he said as if wielding a sword. "You are grounded. Fully grounded. All the way. Grounded for the rest of the season. I have too much to do without worrying about you and that, that... You will be homeschooled by Chefy. Do we understand each other?"

I grimaced and tried to calculate how much time he might need to calm down and relent, just by a little, just by enough so that I could maybe still go to the Snow Ball with Rudy.

"Do we understand each other?" he repeated.

How much time if I stayed on my extra-good behavior?

"Do you hear me?" he prodded. "Candace Jane Kringle, I am talking to you!"

He hadn't used my full name in that tone since the time Snowflake dared me to put cherry-flavored hair-removal cream on half his beard while he was napping. I thought I'd never hear the end of it. He had to wear fake whiskers that year. A lot of kids noticed, reviving the tired old rumor that he wasn't real.

"I'm going to the Snow Ball with Rudy and there's nothing you can do about it. You have toys to deliver!"

Oh, way to start that good behavior, Candy!

"Just try me." He glowered. "I'd sooner cancel Christmas!"

So, making me miserable had just taken precedence over making the rest of the world happy. That hurt more than a slap in the face. I burst into tears and ran to my room.

And I didn't come out for a week and a half.

twenty-seven

I'd never been grounded before. Ever. It sucked so bad. A bunch of little groundings spread out over my lifetime would have been so much better than this one apocalyptic detention.

Daddy still hadn't given me back the keys to the Range Rover. Now he took away my phone and computer too. Not that I didn't deserve it, but come on! I bet all of you got away with buckets of naughtiness while Daddy was busy watching over me like a partridge.

He allowed Snowflake a ten-minute visit each school day when she brought me my assignments. The rest of my life was straight out of some non-Christmassy Dickens novel—homework and chores.

I missed Rudy so much it made me sick, especially whenever Snowflake told me what a good kisser Silentnight was. I used her as a carrier pigeon to exchange notes with Rudy. Once, with her help, I managed to get a Candy-gram to him— gummy hummingbirds that spelled out "I MISS U" in mid-air while singing and dancing clowns performed a gushy poem I'd written just for him.

> Once upon a time
> There was a boy named Rudy.
> At the N.P.
> We all found him super moody.

I took time to get to know him
And he wasn't half bad.
But my dad won't let me see him.
Now I'm very, very sad.

I always think about you, Rudy,
Every time I dream.
I want you more than peppermint
And strawberry ice cream.

My heart is aching for you.
You know I'll find a way
For us to be together.
You're my hero every day.

Okay, so I'm no Clement Moore. But Rudy got the message and that was all that mattered.

Heavy snowfall piled crystalline mounds practically up to my bedroom window. My brother teased me mercilessly about how much fun he was having outdoors, sledding and snow scootering and building snowpeople and snowfortresses, while I remained locked inside under house arrest. My giant walk-in closet held one of every toy ever made, but I couldn't find the fun in any of them.

Mom said she'd try to work on Dad to shorten my sentence, but I shouldn't hold out for miracles. I heard them yelling at each other in their bedroom. Frostbite said it was mostly about work—apparently problems were piling up at the Workshop even higher than the snow—but it sounded an awful lot like they were arguing about me.

The reindeer proved to be super hardy, bouncing back into shape and ready to take on the challenge of another rigorous mall tour. When the day finally came for Daddy to leave, I watched from my window as my mother pinned an ALL-ACCESS badge to his neatly pressed red velvet suit and tucked an itinerary into his inside pocket. His newly repaired sleigh awaited him at the curb on shiny new runners—just between you and me, it needed them anyway—and Mom gave him a kiss as he boarded with Angry the Elf and the rest of his pocket-sized road crew.

Settling into the musher's seat, he glanced up in my direction, his gaze still scolding me from afar. I snapped the curtains shut to hide from his stare. Still, I couldn't escape it—I moped on my bed and there he was, watching me disapprovingly from an old framed photograph on my dresser. In the picture, he wore a super-jolly grin, with a younger me all smiles in his lap. But all I saw now was the cruel disciplinarian hidden behind a bearded mask of joy he put on for the rest of the world.

Funny thing is, Daddy's punishment did nothing to curb my mischievous streak. Throughout my incarceration I patiently counted down the days, secretly plotting my escape into Rudy's arms once Fatty Claus left town.

As luck would have it, my mother had her hands full down at the Workshop. Her elfin problems had expanded like Daddy's waist while he'd kept himself busy at home playing jailer. And Frostbite was always out who-knows-where, frolicking in the snow with Flip and Flop. That left Chefy, my closest ally in life, as my sole guard.

We were alone in the kitchen, the only ones home, when he swept a plate of uneaten food away from me. He'd been making all my favorite milkshakes and pie crusts for days on end, trying to cheer me up, but it never worked. I hardly touched any of it.

"Hibernation time." Chefy froze, his eyes shut tight.

I gazed at the statuesque penguin for a full minute, curiously baffled. "Penguins don't hibernate," I said.

"Are you sure?" he murmured out of the corner of his beak.

Well, no, I wasn't sure. I used to think bears hibernated until I found out differently freshman year, when Cookiejar failed a pop quiz on *Rumpelstiltskin*. It had only one question: What was Rumpelstiltskin's name. And he got it wrong. He complained to Miss Pandabaker that it was a trick question and told her to go hibernate. The petite panda pointed out that bears don't really hibernate. They simply like to sleep late during the winter. Unless they have jobs teaching high school, in which case they sleep the normal amount, just like people.

So just because I'd never seen a penguin hibernate didn't mean they couldn't. For all I knew, it might have been one of those once-every-sixteen-years things. I'd only been alive for sixteen years and Chefy was the only penguin I knew.

"Chefy?" I poked his tummy. Tickle, tickle, tickle. I jabbed at his chest. Jib, jib, jab. Nothing. Behind him, through the mudroom, the side door invited an easy exit. I waved a hand in front of the motionless bird's face. I snapped my fingers. Not a hint of a flinch.

"If one were to sneak out," he squawked, still out of the side of his beak, "to see whomever it is who's got her so lovesick she's turning down my deep-fried s'mores, a hibernating penguin would have no way of knowing, now would he?"

Sweet! Daddy probably hadn't cleared Iceland yet and I'd already found my reprieve. "Do you mean it?" I said.

No answer.

I got all goosebumpy over the possibility of being close

to Rudy again. I wished Chefy would have opened his eyes for just one second to see my lips split into the widest smile I'd worn in ages. But then his ruse would be ruined and he might end up in the puffinhouse along with me.

"Chefy, you're the greatest!" I stretched onto my tippy-toes to kiss him, then dashed into the mudroom, throwing on my boots and outerwear as fast as I could, before he "woke up"— LOL. I threw open the side door to a wonderful blast of cold air and stepped outside.

I was free!

twenty-eight

I hugged the beautiful snow. I danced with my lovely snow scooter. I wanted to leap a hundred thousand miles and spin the moon where it hung, pink and rosy-cheeked, in the starry, starry sky.

I plowed over hill and dale so fast I left a geyser of snow-wake ten feet high trailing my snow scooter. I must have broken several land-speed records racing to Rudy's condo in Noël Valley.

I didn't know what kind of hot water he might be in with his father after all the trouble I'd brought him. What if Dr. Tutti turned my one and only chance at a romantic outing into a curt "get lost" over the intercom? So I carefully broke the rounded tips off several icicles and flung the snowpebbles at Rudy's window.

To my delight, Rudy's square jaw forged a half-moon smile when he saw me. My knees nearly buckled from the flutter in my heart as his cute behind wriggled down the drain pipe.

I had my guy back and had no intention of wasting our precious alone time with small talk about school or arraignments or stuff like that. I jumped on my snow scooter, instructing Rudy to hang on, then whisked him away to the most fantastic spot in the North Pole. In the whole world, if you ask me.

I weaved in and out of the foreboding snickertrees of the Snickerdoodle Forest, dodging the formidable strudel bushes and sticky, ropy taffy plants, zooming along like Ms. Pac-Man on megatoe. Rudy's stout limbs curved snugly around my waist made me feel invincible.

We emerged in the clearing on the other side of the forest. I skidded the snow scooter to a clean, slow stop and we dismounted under the brilliant dancing colors of the aurora borealis—the Northern Lights. Indescribable waves of emerald light beams swirled and crashed over our heads. Magnetic currents pulsed through our spines.

The magic took even Rudy's breath away. "What *is* this place?"

"Wait, we're not there yet."

I tugged his hand and ran with him up a small hill, to a level plain as big as a fishball field. I used the stars to guide me to the exact spot I was looking for.

Behind us, beyond the forest we had just navigated, the blinking lights of The Village of the North Pole twinkled like stars. That village, where we lived, was not the actual North Pole.

I took about a dozen more steps, then one Neil Armstrong leap. We had arrived.

I turned to Rudy and proclaimed, "You're on top of the world!"

"You mean...?" He let it sink in a minute, then stood closer to me, close enough to dance, and surveyed the dazzling show in the sky. Polaris, the bright and mighty North Star, lit our faces like an intense spotlight from hundreds of light years directly overhead.

"True North," I told him. "The physical, geographical North Pole."

"The earth's axis of rotation. I get it." He tried to be nonchalant.

"You know what else?" I said. He shook his head. I spun him around as if we were playing Pin the Tail on the Woolly Mammoth. "From right here, no matter what direction you look, you're always facing south. Isn't that weird?"

He laughed and completed the circle on his own power, taking in the infinite souths before him. Then he planted his boots on either side of mine and faced me, standing closer than he'd ever been. I trembled. Our noses were almost touching. He looked deep into my eyes and said, "There's only one direction I want to look."

I melted right there, so flushed and hot with excitement I thought I might literally melt the ice beneath us and sink into the center of the earth. We pressed our palms together. He rested his forehead on mine. I laced my fingers through his. We stayed like that for the longest time and let the planet rotate us as if we were on the world's largest carousel.

Then he breathed my name. "Candy." Like an angel.

I closed the narrow gap that separated his lips from mine. I devoured his mouth as if chewing on the warmest, chewiest cookie. He kissed me back with equal hunger. Prickly passions shot up and down every part of me, traveling to him through our melded mouths, then journeying all over his body and back to me as our tongues met and played tag.

I ran my fingers through his unruly hair. His hands caressed my back. He pulled me tight to his chest. I wanted more, so much more. I let go of his luscious lips and fell backward, lying in the snow over the very engine that makes the earth move, then reached out and drew him down with me.

He rested on one elbow and leaned over me. Again with that angel's breath, he whispered, "You're beautiful."

"You know what I want to do now?"

He shook his head and asked with a cheesy grin, "What do you want to do now?"

"I want to make... snow angels with you!" I shoved him onto his back so we were side by side. Our inside hands latched together. We flapped our arms and legs with wild abandon, laughing hysterically as we cut angelic impressions deep into the powder.

I couldn't believe this was the same Rudy Tutti who'd shown up a few months ago so closed-off and detached, hating the winsome allure of his new surroundings, now giving in so completely to the silly whims of the dorkiest little girl at North Pole High.

He let himself shout at the top of his lungs, "I'M ON TOP OF THE WORLD!" like a total dork. A totally handsome dork. My handsome dork. My new boyfriend.

I was still in stitches when he stopped flapping and rolled onto his side so he could kiss me again. My breaths came faster and shorter as his kisses intensified. I groped his tight chest with my free hand, then walked my fingers down his outside arm to pull him on top of me.

The entire weight of his body pressed down on me. I maneuvered his arms and legs, rhythmically, in sync with mine, as our two angels became one, and kissed him so hard I thought I might break his teeth. Our kisses became sloppy. We moved up and down against each other, our arms and legs swinging furiously, faster, until a liberating breeze washed over us and all at once we were lighter than air!

Literally.

As in no longer on the ground.

"Rudy, what's happening to us?"

"How should I know?"

"Hang on, kids." The voice came from somewhere else. From behind my head, beneath the frosted wings beating hypnotically around us as we soared through the glowing aurora.

Our Snow Angel had come to life!

We were on her back, swooping across thin air, three stories high. Rudy and I disentangled ourselves from each other. We scrambled to grab hold of her shoulders as she dipped toward the ground and climbed into an unexpected loop. The next thing I knew, I was tumbling down to earth, my fists full of the angel feathers I'd been using to keep my grip on our celestial pilot.

Rudy plopped into the softly packed snow seconds after my own bumpy landing, more loose feathers trailing him. We dusted each other off, then looked back up into the night in puzzled wonderment.

There she was. A faint dot that grew brighter like the approaching light of a train in the distance. A shimmering white robe flowed down her body like a blanket of snow. Cold blue phosphorescent beams emanated from her golden, cascading hair. Her beautiful, other-worldly features gradually came into focus as she neared us. She had the smile of a happy baby playing with its favorite toy and the grace of a ballerina as she drifted to the landscape, one leg extended, *en pointe*, the other bent at the knee.

She sank smoothly into the snow a few feet away from us and giggled. "Oops. Sorry about the drop."

"No, we're sorry. I hope we didn't hurt you." I curtsied and held out the clump of feathers she had lost.

She giggled again. "That always happens. Are you two all right?"

"What are you?" Rudy asked.

She spoke only to me. "You will come to know of my power in time. Be good, Candycane Claus." And with that she waved her arms and shot back into the sky, leaving nothing but a puff of stardust floating over two freaked-out teenagers.

Rudy and I stared at each other, our mouths wide open.

"Was that a good witch or a bad witch?" he wisecracked, trying to bring us back to some sense of normalcy.

The dissipating stardust bunched itself into a shape that landed about fifty feet away. "She dropped something," I said, and we raced to the glowing object.

I dug into the snow and extracted a bright, gleaming star, just a little bigger than my hand, both hot and cold to the touch in a weird, neutralizing way. It cast watery shadows across our faces in a rainbow of colors that drew my lips back to his like a powerful magnet. This kiss had an entirely different kind of passion, like Christmas times ten.

"I'm keeping this," I said, as I stuffed the star into the pocket of my parka.

I smiled dreamily all the way back to Noël Valley, where I dropped Rudy off, then sang the rest of the way home, joyful and triumphant, hang a shining star and sleep in heavenly peace on earth and mercy mild, a thrill of hope with the angelic host proclaim, let it snow! Let it snow! Let it snow!

twenty-nine

His kisses left an amaaazing Rudy aftertaste, soured only by the mystery pounding on my skull, nagging me unendingly: Who was she? I'd made snow angels with boys lots of times and nothing like that had ever happened.

Mom was at the Workshop round the clock now, so I couldn't ask her. I tried beating around the tinselbush about it with Chefy, but he abruptly remembered something that needed immediate basting, then something that needed serious thawing, followed by something that needed careful mincing. You'd have thought I'd asked him where babies came from. Maybe he was having second thoughts about his complicity in my midnight rendezvous and I'd seriously blown my chances for the repeat performance I so ached for every second of the day.

Frostbite was acting weird too—weirder than the usual little-brother-weird—asking me all sorts of questions about Daddy's work. How did I think Daddy would handle an elfpox epidemic? What would he do if there weren't enough toys for Christmas? "Just asking," my screwy sibling would say. "No reason."

I figured some polar bear at school had gotten to him with the what-do-you-want-to-be-when-you-grow-up routine and he suddenly decided he'd better start learning the family trade if he were going to fill Daddy's boots. Whatever, right? But if this new Santa Jr. were to get wind of my recent extracurricular excursion, no telling what he might do with that information. So far he didn't seem to have the sees-me-when-I'm-sleeping gene.

Without Daddy around to breathe down our necks, my daily visits from Snowflake became much more gossipy. The kids at school couldn't stop talking about what a rebel I'd turned into. Rumors of my exploits mushroomed. The silliest was from Walter the Asthmatic Walrus, who heard from a reliable source that I'd burned down the schoolhouse. He was in the school when he repeated that, and yet the building's unscorched walls could do nothing to persuade him he might be mistaken.

Things between Snowflake and Silent had gotten hot enough to burn down the whole town. She told me they'd made snow angels and I got all tingly, my cheeks burning up. But she only mentioned it as part of a long list of snowgames they'd played; their angel didn't appear to have bonded with her the way mine did. I told her about me and Rudy kissing at True North and watching the Northern Lights, but decided to keep the part about our visitor strictly between me and him.

Every day, Snowflake brought me a new love letter. Of course Rudy never called them that because he's a boy and boys all think that's a stupid word. But he did use plenty of mushier ones. He called me "radiant," "unforgettable," and "better than pudding." And he said he missed me like a hundred thousand times.

An unspoken rule kept us from writing about our mysterious encounter, almost as if she'd never happened. I hid her star away in a drawer, resisting the urge to bask in its luminescence every five seconds. I was less successful stopping myself from replaying the other sensations of that night over and over in my head: Rudy's lips on mine, his body held tight against me, the scent of coconut in his hair, my hands caressing his muscles feverishly.

I may have been stuck in the house, and deservedly so, but

I was living on a cloud—until my father came home from his business trip with a big fat sack of cloudkill.

As Daddy's road manager, it fell upon Angry the Elf to oversee the enforcement of his four-page rider. The malls were required to provide, among other things, a plate of cookies containing no less than thirteen chocolate chips per cookie, a rooftop landing pad for the sleigh, swag "of the highest quality" for his helpers[1], and above all, lots and lots of jelly beans.

It was this last item that had supposedly brought Daddy home in the foulest of moods. He claimed he'd cut the whole trip short because the Mall of America had skimped on the beans. But that wasn't how Angry told the story.

A formidable elf, Angry was used to handling mall managers who tried to squeeze extra hours out of Daddy—messing up Mom's meticulous whirlwind schedule—and department-store owners who stuck their own nieces and nephews in front of the line expecting Daddy to grant them special toy requests. So none of that type of nonsense had been slowing them down. And reports of those jelly bean shortages were greatly exaggerated. According to Angry, the tour started out perfectly.

Thousands of tykes queued up to meet Daddy at Harrods in London, politely requesting gumball machines, Easy-Bake Ovens, and assorted whatnottery. One little boy, who had never seen Daddy in person, got so nervous he peed in his pants and left a big stain on the knee of Daddy's trousers. Daddy took it all in stride with a hearty "Ho-ho-ho," and quickly changed into one of the spare pair he travels with for just such occasions.

---

[1] According to Hershey Barr, attorney for Mr. Claus, his client brings all swag items back to the North Pole, whereupon his diminutives make significant improvements, then re-gift them to orphans.

He wore shorts and shades at Horton Plaza in San Diego where he took orders for the latest video games and smart phones. At Waikiki's Royal Hawaiian Center, the kids asked for surfboards and bodyboards. Daddy bundled up again for more normal weather at the Gateway in Salt Lake City where he presided over a new toy store's dedication. Snowboards and ski accessories were popular wants at Cherry Creek Mall in Denver, while the children at Chicago's Water Tower Place favored classic games like Monopoly, Simon, KerPlunk, and Gnip Gnop.

Things didn't go grinch until Daddy arrived in the Twin Cities, where little Minnesotans converged on the Megamall with their, shall we say, inappropriate Christmas demands. It was Daddy's worst nightmare. Sally Fitzsimmons asked him to make Johnny Dorman like her because Johnny liked Lisa but Lisa kissed Timmy so Johnny was wasting his time with Lisa.

"Aren't you a little young to be thinking about boys?" he said, dipping his hand deep into the requisite jelly-bean jar at his side.

Hello? Sally was *eight*! *I* liked boys when I was eight. Granted, I never asked Santa Claus to do anything about it, but that's only because he's my dad. ;-)

Another little girl asked for the latest cosmetics from M·A·C—stylish lip glosses, glamorous eye liners, fancy nail polishes. Daddy wasn't too keen on that either. *Why didn't she want a teddy bear?* he wanted to know, fully aware her old one had fallen apart two months ago.

The Santaland jelly bean supply diminished rapidly.

When Brittany Henderson came straight out and asked for boobs, Daddy calmly recited his stock answer: "Ho-ho-ho. That's not something Santa can put in a stocking." To which Brittany bratted back that, *duh*, she knew she had to wait for her own to grow, but she thought he could maybe bring some fake ones in the meantime. Or at least a water-filled training bra.

It wasn't just the girls, Angry said. Billy McKendrick asked for a certain kind of balloon, but didn't know what they were called. Daddy inhaled the last of the jelly beans when he realized the boy meant those rolled-up balloons his older brother Michael carried around in his wallet.

The final straw came from ten-year-old Virginia Reinheit, who made the audacious mistake of asking Daddy to please hurry up and bring her her first period. LOL! I would have gladly figured out a way to give her mine just to have been there to see Daddy lose it. He was said to have sprung up out of his throne so fast that the poor little darling slid off his lap, bruised her tiny butt on the fake-snow-covered tile floor, and bawled like a girl who was nowhere near ready for that special gift she thought she wanted.

Angry the Elf couldn't stop snickering as he recounted the details of Daddy's melt-down. True to his name, Angry has been known to fly off the handle himself from time to time, so he got a perverse pleasure whenever he witnessed someone else go ballistic. Wheezing until the chocolate milk he was drinking spouted from his nose, Angry went on to describe how my father, all out of beans now, had stomped past the long line of adoring fans, pointing his stubby index finger at each and every girl who had dared to wear makeup or even fix her hair with a pretty bow to look nice for her Christmas portrait with him. *They were all naughty!* he howled, damning every single child in both Minneapolis and St. Paul to receive nothing but lumps of coal this Christmas.

Parents stared in horror as the real live Santa Claus made their children cry. A couple of outraged fathers yelled and shook their fists at Daddy while security guards rushed in to keep them from hitting him. The manager swore that next year they would hire one of those fake Santas like they have at Southdale.

Yes, Virginia, there is a Santa Claus, and he's completely macadamia.

Daddy bellyached to Angry the whole ride home: This was all Angry's fault. This would absolutely be their last year. They'd have to fax some ground rules to the malls next year in advance, listing requests that were off-limits. And what was wrong with these kids anyway? All they wanted to do was grow up. And why did they have to be in such a big fat hurry to do it? They're supposed to want toys, only toys, toys that are appropriate for kids, while they still are kids. And boy was his tooth killing him.

Angry humorously reenacted Daddy holding his mouth and crying out in pain when the real thing erupted from the den. A deep, long, loud bloodcurdling scream like a beluga whale passing a kidney stone.

We were in the kitchen with Chefy. The three of us looked at each other and feigned deafness. Anyone who'd spent a significant amount of time at Number Sixteen Gingerbread Lane over the past couple years had grown accustomed to that primal noise echoing out of my father whenever he bit down on a jelly bean with one of his impacted molars. It was usually best not to get in his way.

Hearing my jailer's misery, however, was not the cloudkill I spoke of that dampened the bliss that had stayed wrapped around me like a Snuggie ever since my nocturnal encounter at True North. 'Twas the second scream, two minutes later, that made me quake in my slippers.

"Candycane! Get in here! Now!"

217

thirty

I crossed the threshold into his private lair.

He'd come home with an agenda. He must have sensed I was happy and wanted to make me sad—so I could love him again when he gave me a stupid toy. At least that was how my boyfriend might have put it. Daddy had a lot to learn about me.

He stood behind his desk waiting for me, leaning forward, the whole left side of his face swollen, inflamed. The plum pudding Chefy had brought him a half hour ago sat uneaten beside the stack of gift lists he'd brought back from the malls. Jelly beans littered the room. A haphazard trail of them led to his trophy case, its glass door hanging wide open. In addition to the numerous keys to the cities and other awards he'd collected over the centuries, the cabinet held about a year's supply of his most favorite beans in a secret compartment. Though always locked, we all knew he kept the key in the right-hand pocket of his very first Santa suit adorning the wax replica of himself he proudly displayed beside his custom frozen yogurt bar.

"Are you okay, Daddy?"

"You haven't left this house, have you?"

Sugarcubes! He knew. He knows everything. Or was he just sniffing?

"Why do you ask?" I tried my best to hide my fear behind a cheesy, innocent smile.

"Who else has been here? In my den?"

A tightness grabbed my chest. It had to be a trick question. But Rudy hadn't been to the house. I had nothing to fear. "Other than family? Just Snowflake. To bring me my homework. But we never came in here. Honest."

"No boys?"

"Boys?" I trembled.

"Has *he* been here?"

"I would never do that!" *I might sneak out and go to True North with him, but you didn't ask that.*

Daddy sized me up for a tense moment. My feet started to sweat. He rolled aside his ostentatious leather chair, then tilted his computer monitor till it faced us both.

"I want you see something," he said. He had that look in his eyes like he was about to remind me not to try to fit a whole candy cane in my mouth all at once because of that time I'd almost choked on one when I was three.

I leaned in and held my breath, feeling lightheaded. I noted how far the guest chair was from my butt. Whatever he wanted to show me, I had a feeling I might need to sit.

Daddy clicked open the official Naughty List. There at the top, just as Daddy had threatened, my boyfriend's sullen but handsome mug scowled at us, his name in bold lettering, his N-rating in the high nineties like some common school bully. It made me queasy.

It could have been worse. For a second I thought I might see myself up there.

"Daddy, this isn't fair. You N-Listed Rudy yourself because you don't like him and you don't want me to see him. But that doesn't count. I didn't lie about what happened at the drive-in."

He double-clicked Rudy's profile and waited for it to come up. "I may not have given the boy a fair shake, but to be honest, I never believed he was *this* bad."

Harsh blinking red text in the Naughtiness This Year box spelled out all the allegations I already knew about: the sleigh, the 'toe, the Pod race, the unleashing of the Abominable

Snowman on the Village of the North Pole. I could have argued till next Christmas that all of that was circumstantial, unsubstantiated, and had no business being used to factor into his N-rating until proven in a court of law. But what I saw when Daddy brought up his History List would have been tough for even Atticus Finch to defend.

"This has to be a mistake," I whimpered.

"If it was one or two years, maybe. But, Candy, my goodness, look at this."

All at once, my world turned upside down. The tone in my father's voice—not gloating, not argumentative. He actually sounded like he cared, like a real caring father, which made the gravity of the evidence all the more heartbreaking.

"He really is naughty?" I said.

"Angel, he was *born* on the Naughty List."

Age 1: Stole a pacifier from another baby.
Naughty 46.33%

Age 2: Threw things and didn't listen to his parents.
Naughty 47.55%

Age 3: Used naughty words fourteen times.
Naughty 65.81%

It went on and on like that, every year of his life. He bit a babysitter for no good reason, long before he'd come to NoPo. He broke into a drugstore and got into fights, way before Daddy could have disliked him for my sake because it all took place before I knew he existed.

Age 6: Ditched school, wished his mother dead when she found out.
Naughty 91.19%

Age 7: Hit a teacher, refused to apologize.
Naughty 78.49%

Age 8: Defaced Christmas decorations.
Naughty 94.65%

This didn't sound anything like the Rudy I knew, the Rudy who risked his life for me, the Rudy who felt so warm and tender in my arms. It did sound like the Rudy his father knew. And the sad thing was, it didn't even cover all the terrible misdeeds Dr. Tutti had cataloged at the jailhouse. If those were missing, who knew how many other bad things had escaped Daddy's List elves?

Age 11: Bullied a boy online until the boy cried, didn't care.
Lied to his parents seven times.
Naughty 97.00%

Age 12: Stole best friend's bicycle, sold it for money to buy junk food, never told his friend and didn't share the food.
Naughty 93.27%

"Now do you see that I was only looking out for you, sweetheart?" He gently placed a hand on my head, combing his fingers through my hair like he did when I was little. "I sense these things. We're just lucky I have the List to check twice."

I drew away from him, not wanting to be touched. Then I seized control of the mouse and scrolled to bring the rest of the long list of offenses into view, unable to let go of the button even when his infractions had finally stopped drifting up the screen.

There, at the very bottom, the worst one of all. From just last year.

Age 15: Cheated on girlfriend. Bragged about it to his friends.
Naughty 74.55%

Cheated on girlfriend.
Cheated on girlfriend.
CHEATED. ON. GIRLFRIEND.

That should have had a way higher N-rating than seventy-four! Daddy had been right about Rudy all along. That boy was truly rotten to the core. No wonder Yeti wouldn't eat him. Yuk! I clicked the mouse and annihilated that awful profile from the screen. "I don't ever want to see Rudy Tutti again," I said.

I ran straight to my room and locked the door. I cried into my pillow for twenty minutes, then, before my tears dried, I hastily composed a new Candy-gram for my mean ex-boyfriend.

Once upon a time
There was a boy named Rudy.
At the N.P.
We all found him super moody.

I took time to get to know him
And he wasn't half bad.
But he's a fake and a phony
And it really makes me mad.

Now I know all about you, Rudy.
I know you're not nice.
If you ever try to speak to me
I'll bury you in ice.

I didn't have the energy to think of another rhyme so I ended it with a curt "bye now." Then I placed the order with the singing and dancing Candy-gram clowns before I had time to wonder if maybe his incredible kisses really did mean something. They didn't. They couldn't.

He was Naughty with a capital N and that rhymes with men and all men stink. On ice.

CHRISTMASTIME!

"For yonder breaks a new and glorious morn."
- John Sullivan Dwight

thirty-one

I made myself forget all about the Bad Times. I told myself I'd been put under some kind of spell, like a sickness that made me bad, drew me toward bad people, clouded my judgment with badness and made me think and do and say bad, bad things. That sickness had a name and I would no longer utter it as long as I lived.

I learned my lesson.

Having spent all that time around the Dark One, I must have confused the familiarity with actually liking him, when really he'd been poisoning me like a vampire draining me of my sweet, cherry-peppermint blood, turning me into some acrid zombie who needed to get her naughty on to survive.

Daddy had no trouble believing I'd been possessed. Sure, I could be tricky and get away with a little tomfoolery here and there, which of course he always knew about because of who he was. But inherently, *Candycane Claus was a good girl.* Put my profile side-by-side with a real baddie's and you'll see the difference plain as Christmas lights.

Daddy trusted me to go back to school, now that I was cured. I still had to come right home after, but I didn't mind. Having a dad with a superpower to know who to protect you from was the best thing a sixteen-year-old could have in her back pocket.

Tinsel's injuries had healed and he'd returned to class while I was gone. With Daddy's approval, we worked together on a new Christmas tree for Mr. Polar Bear's class. Considering how badly I'd been infected with the evil disease by the one who shall not be named, I couldn't blame Tinsel for how badly he'd treated me. For we had all been affected by the intruder, each in our own way.

Perhaps my own history had blinded me too. After all, I first fell for Tinsel while working with him on a school project. Clearly that was different. Tinsel was a stand-up guy. Tinsel wasn't a cheater. Tinsel didn't sell 'toe. Tinsel didn't wreak havoc wherever he went. Tinsel's Naughty scores were non-existent.

The time had come for things to get back to normal. We fashioned a new tree entirely out of bright, shiny tinsel. We hung large candy canes all over it as ornaments, in every color imaginable. I even found a few colors that couldn't be imagined. With our combined skills, we'd be able to whip up a functional tree tall enough to deserve more than a passing grade, but we certainly wouldn't have time to create another award winner. Not this year.

On my second day back, Mr. Polar Bear praised our progress, patting me on the head with his giant paw and gently pinching my cheek between his claws. Tinsel and I were so wrapped up in our handiwork, we didn't hear the door open. Our furry teacher gazed past us, shaking his head and sighing like a sad, disappointed polar bear. "Rudy Tutti. Oh, Rudy."

I froze.

"I got your message," Rudy grunted behind my back.

I forced myself not to look, not to make eye contact, not to say a word. He wouldn't dare go to my house to confront me about the Candy-gram, not with Daddy on guard duty. But I always knew I'd have to face him at school. I even prepared for it at home by having Flip and Flop take turns pretending to be him, trying everything to get my attention, while I practiced ignoring him.

Now I weakened.

But Mr. Polar Bear had my back. "Class time is not social time, Mr. Tutti."

"Get your freezing paws off me, polar bear!"

I could see their reflection in the window: PB trying to escort Rudy to the door, Rudy sticking out his chest, PB letting go to avoid a lawsuit but still blocking him from coming any closer to me.

"Since you and Miss Claus have made so little progress on your tree, I have taken the liberty to make some reassignments. You may work with Walter, if you like."

Walter stopped working on his feeble Popsicle-stick Christmas tree and clapped his flippers. The excitement made him wheeze. A portion of his tree toppled over into a puddle of his slobber.

An asthmatic walrus was too good for Rudy.

"*Look* at me, Candy," he demanded.

I stayed focused on my new tinsel-and-candy-cane tree. Tinsel placed his warm hand on top of mine and curled his fingers into my palm.

"Did your father have something to do with this?" Rudy said.

So what if he did?

Tinsel tensed up.

I couldn't hold back my glare any longer. I spun around to face my enemy. Rudy had to poke his head around Mr. Polar Bear's hulking, carpeted torso to meet my gaze. The anger and hurt bounced off us both as though we were peering into some special funhouse mirror that only reflected raw emotions. A shudder traveled through me. I'd forgotten how handsome he was. His nostrils flared. He blinked.

I slowly turned back to my work.

"I'm outta here." His heavy footsteps carried him away.

The door slammed.

Mr. Polar Bear told the class to get back to work.

Tinsel joked about where he'd like to stick the next candy cane—and it wasn't on our tree.

I'd made a deal with Daddy that I would tell him everything that happened at school. So as soon as I got home, I told him all about how I'd gotten my solo back in Caroling class. I told him I got an A-super-duper-plus on a pop quiz in Inuktitut. I told him I had lunch with Snowflake and she told a joke that made Silentnight spray apple cider out his nose.

And I told him what happened in Tree class. But not about how it made me feel—how it made my insides twist into painful knots because I'd hurt Rudy, and no matter how naughty someone was, I didn't like to be the one to hurt them.

I passed the test. The one where Daddy compared my story against the report he'd persuaded Mr. Polar Bear to email him.

To my surprise, my reward for ignoring Rudy and telling the truth about the confrontation was that I got to go on a date with Tinsel. A real honest-to-goodness, out-in-the-open, Daddy-approved date. Of course he made up a lot of ground rules first. Tinsel had to come over so Daddy could talk to him. Then, after passing an initial inspection, my dad told him where he'd be allowed to take me, places that were off-limits, and how late I could stay out. Eight-thirty!

I didn't have it in me to argue. I was lucky he was letting me go out at all.

After my second bite of pizza at T.G.I. Fruitcake, I realized why I hadn't fought Daddy's ridiculous curfew. I didn't really need to spend that much time with Tinsel. He was day-after-Christmas boring.

He spent most of our date trying to convince me how

right the two of us were. He'd stare at me all googly-eyed and say, "You're so hot chocolate, Candy."

"Thank you," I'd answer dutifully. Yawn.

"I can't believe we were apart for so long." He slurped up the last of his banana-candy-cane milkshake and played with the fruitcake toppings on his slice of pizza. "This is where you belong. Not in some icky bar in Eggnog Alley."

"I guess."

"Hey, look!" He pointed out the window, his elfin eyes alit. "A fresh snowfall."

He knew the snow would cheer me up. He flagged down a seal to have the leftovers boxed, then hurriedly dropped a couple cookies on the table and whisked me outside. I let a dozen flakes fall on my tongue as my first smile of the night crept up on me.

Tinsel ran toward an acre of untouched snow and dived into it head first. He twirled over, face up, and started flapping his limbs. "Come on, babe. You love making snow angels."

Tinsel knew me inside and out. He cared about making me happy. That had to count for something. I fell in beside him and held his hand while we carved our seraph into the glistening white ground cover. He yowled merrily. I tried to enjoy it with him because that's what I would normally do. But it was no use. My heart wasn't in it. His arms kept flapping like a hummingbird, while mine wound down like a neglected cuckoo clock.

"Isn't this fun?" Tinsel asked, propping himself up on one elbow as I scanned the stars. "Whatcha looking for?"

"Nothing."

I hated myself for letting my mind wander back to that night. Why couldn't it be that way with Tinsel? I got up and kept looking for nothing, which I found in abundance. Nothing in the sky but the moon and the stars; nothing in the snow but my own depression.

I helped Tinsel up, reminding him what time I had to be home. When he dropped me off, I was secretly relieved to have Daddy spying on us. No tickling. No peck on the cheek. Thank you. Goodnight. See you in school. You have a lovely home, Mrs. Cleaver.

I climbed onto Daddy's lap and thanked him for being my dad, for staying home to watch out for me even with Christmas less than a week away. I begged him not to let his work suffer over all the trouble I'd been. I understood how important his job was and I couldn't bear the responsibility of letting down so many children.

He smiled warmly and told me not to fret. He had everything under control. He kissed me goodnight and sent me skedaddling up to bed. But I just lay there feeling nothing. Not anxious. Not sleepy. Just blah.

After a while, I turned on the lights and paced back and forth across my carpet. I must have put in enough miles to circle the Arctic twice by the time Mom came home, shortly after two in the morning. She saw the light in my room and knocked.

"Is everything all right?"

I opened the door and sighed. "I don't know."

"Anything you want to talk about?"

I shrugged. "Not really."

"Oh." Dark circles ringed her tired, button eyes. She turned and started to leave, walking stiffly.

"Mom?"

"Yes?" She came back.

I stepped aside so she could come all the way in. "How are things at work?"

"The truth? I've never seen it this bad." She leaned against my desk and removed her glasses, letting them dangle from her thin neck on their silver chain. "The elves took a vote. They decided to go green. They think the children should recycle the toys we gave them last year. A lot of them are blowing off steam down at Eggnog Alley." She must have seen the panic wash across me, because she added, "I know it sounds serious, but your father will eventually get on the ball and see us through it. He always does. And besides, maybe the elfnip will make them work faster." She let out a polite giggle as if it were no big deal, but I sensed the lingering worry lurking behind that laugh.

"I'm starting to get afraid for Christmas," I said.

She stroked my chin lovingly. "Oh, honey, it's not your job to make Christmas happen. It's your father's." I fell into her warm embrace. "Is that all that's bothering you?"

I sat down on my bed, then lay back on my side, groaning as though I had the worst stomachache ever. I closed my eyes for a moment. When I opened them, I lifted my head and studied the embroidered children playing their reindeer games on the front of my mother's sweater. "Have you ever... Did you like to play in the snow when you were little?"

"All children like to play in the snow. Even way back when I was a girl."

"With boys?" I sat up. Millions of tiny pins and needles scraped against the inside of my skin. Did I really want to bring any of this up with my mother?

"What's on your mind?" she said.

"Well, you see... I've made snow angels with boys before. It's like the funnest thing to do in the snow..."

She put a hand in front of her mouth. She already knew what I was getting at. I crossed over to my dresser and dug deep into my sweater drawer. I took out the still-twinkling star—a question I couldn't quite put into words.

As expected, she showed not a trace of surprise. Only a slight nod. She put her arm around me and brought me back to the bed where she sat down right beside me, keeping me enveloped in a comforting cuddle.

"We should talk," she whispered. She gave me a little squeeze. "No gingerbread cookies this time. I promise. There's something you need to know."

thirty-two

"I was your age when I met your father," my mother began. "He was a much different man then. His name was Kris Kringle. He was seventeen, very generous. He loved to shower me with gifts. Little trinkets, you know. Things he made himself."

She beamed and rubbed her cheek with her free hand, dusting off a hazy memory inside her head.

"My father didn't like him at all. He accused Kris of trying to buy my affection." A small chuckle escaped her throat. "He thought your dad would never amount to anything because he had no head for business. Even then, your father's greatest joy was to give things away without asking for anything in return. It was a radical idea for its time.

"But that's not really part of this story," she said as she swatted the tangent away. "The thing is, your grandfather wouldn't let me see your father at first."

"Grandpa Goody?" That was Mom's maiden name.

"That's right. It didn't change how your father felt about me. He kept sending me gifts every day. Grandpa kept sending them right back. So your dad would end up giving them away to other children."

I wondered how come I'd never heard this story before, but I let Mom continue, listening intently to every word.

"One day I made it known to your father that I was open to being courted by him. I suggested that maybe he would have more success appealing to my father if he expressed how deeply he felt about me.

"Do you know what your father said?"

I shook my head.

"I'll never forget. He puffed out his chest and said, 'Whatever do you mean, m'lady? I like to give gifts. 'Tis what I do.'" Mom laughed. "You see, he was afraid to admit his feelings for me."

"You mean, boys were always like that?"

"Oh, yes. Do you know what made him change?"

I shook my head again. "What?"

"I think you do." She pointed at the star in my lap.

"I don't understand."

She drew a deep breath while she thought of how to explain it. "Sometimes playing in the snow is just playing in the snow. It's fun and everybody laughs and has a wonderful time. But other times, under certain, very rare conditions, it's been known to mean... something else."

She paused, suddenly taking on the guise of a teacher waiting for me to solve some tricky math problem on my own. It was my turn to tell her.

"We were at True North." I looked away, afraid she would be mad at me, and said to my pajamas, "It was while Daddy was out of town." My heart beat faster.

"I had to sneak out too," my mother confided. I thrust my head up to face her again. "Your father took me there in his one-horse open sleigh."

"And you saw her?" Blood rushed through me as though a relief valve had opened in my heart.

My mother's gaze bounced from the ceiling to the window and back again. "Saw who?" she said.

Huh? The room started spinning. We had to have been talking about the same thing. "The Snow Angel!"

"It's getting late, dear." She smoothed the pleats on her skirt and started to get up.

"Wait!" I tugged on her elbow. "You know what I'm talking about. I can tell."

She lifted the top corner of the bedcovers and blankets for me to crawl under. "You need to get some sleep, young lady. It's almost 3 a.m."

"But, Mom!" I reluctantly slid between the flannel candy-cane-striped sheets, letting her tuck me in snugly.

She lay the star back in my sweater drawer, pushing it shut, but not all the way. "I've told you everything you need to know. Don't forget what makes you special." She kissed me and switched off my bedside lamp. "Goodnight, sweetheart."

When the door closed behind her, the room glowed faintly from the star shining through the crack in the partially open drawer. I still couldn't sleep—now because of the million new thoughts buzzing through my head. The shadowy, pale yellow light spilled across the ceiling as I tried to sort through the mishmash. I was more confused than ever.

The Snow Angel was real. I figured that much out. *She had something to do with Mom and Dad falling in love.* Did that mean Rudy loved me? That I loved him? But I didn't, did I? Was she meant to bring us together? Didn't she know how awful Rudy was? Did I make a mistake giving up on him? Did *she* make a mistake? Had I already lost my one true love? Would she find someone else for me? Was that how it worked? She didn't seem interested in Tinsel, that's for sure.

I fought sleep with all my might, desperate to reach the elusive conclusions that would tell me what to do next, no more successful in finding those answers than in keeping myself from drifting in and out of restless fits of slumber, dreams mixing with unanswered questions, adding to the blur of perplexity that made my toes twitch and my stomach knot.

When my alarm clock jangled the familiar strains of

"Jingle Bell Rock," the unchanging blackness of our cold, cold winter shone outside, as it would all day, every day, for a long, long time.

thirty-three

Mom and Dad were already gone by the time I came down for breakfast. A good sign. The Workshop needed Daddy. Since returning from his trip, I don't think he'd checked in more than once, for about an hour, to drop off his mall reports. He'd been using his toothache as an excuse to monitor things remotely from home, but really he'd been standing guard over me. Hopefully that was all over with now.

I walked to school, still trying to interpret my mother's unfinished stories, the careful hints that convinced me the Snow Angel had been summoned by True Love. My Claus intuition, however, reminded me that Rudy Tutti lied, cheated, hit, bit, fought, defaced, stole, teased, bullyragged, harassed, tormented, heckled, persecuted, irked, vexed, pestered, nettled, and provoked.

Snowflake tried to help. She prattled on about how lucky I was that Tinsel was giving me a second chance and what a perfect couple we were and how she had always been rooting for us to get back together. She didn't stop until she noticed I was breathing funny and I told her I was going to throw up.

Contrary to popular belief, my vomit does not come out striped or flavored like candy canes. That rumor started in the second grade when I ate too many caramel-corn-dogs at the school carnival, but I swear they mostly came up the color of caramel-corn-dogs, not candy canes. The joke has dogged me ever since. In fifth grade, Cookiejar made a bet with Silentnight that the rumor was true and they spent the rest of the year trying to come up with creative ways to make me puke.

Now I sat on a pile of snow. Snowflake made me put my head between my knees. That didn't ease the nausea or cold sweats, but it got Snowflake to change the subject. As long as she wasn't gushing about Tinsel the Terrific or grousing about Rudy the Rotten, I would be okay.

I barely said two words to Tinsel in Tree class. I wasn't mad at him or anything. It's just that every time I formed a sentence in my head that I considered saying out loud, it seemed too unimportant to be worth the bother. So instead of gabbing, we focused on our tree.

With precision teamwork honed over years of collaboration, we'd made enough progress to earn back the admiration of our ursine teacher. "I'm thinking of giving you both an A-super-duper-plus just for the effort," he said. "Given the circumstances, you could have chosen to give up, like Rudy, but you persevered. Good work. I'm proud of you."

Then the door flew open and Walter the Asthmatic Walrus slimed himself across the linoleum, nearly crashing into the opposite wall. He barked and sneezed excitedly, evidently trying to tell us something. He wouldn't stop. We all gathered round.

"What is it, Walter," Mr. Polar Bear said. "Did Timmy fall down the well?"

Walter shook his head and waddled back out the door, disappearing for a second. He flopped back in, pushing himself backward with his tail, thwack, thwack, thwack against the floor, inch by inch, a bright red Radio Flyer in tow, its handle looped around one tusk.

I couldn't believe it. There in the wagon—a Christmas tree, a little baby one, about half the size of the one I'd made in kindergarten, but so beautiful and intricate that size didn't matter. This tree was stylin'! In a style that certainly hadn't come from any walrus. It was *my* dream style.

Hundreds of tiny, feathery red and white flowers fastidiously arranged in candy-cane stripes, curved at the top, adorned with elegant, glistening ornaments. My original design, realized in living color. A bona-fide work of art.

If I were a snowgirl, I'd have been a big sopping puddle by then because my heart melted, my palms became sweaty, my face felt like hot cider, and my ears radiated with a buzzing that overpowered the sound of the other kids going "ooh" and "ahh."

"Did your partner help you with this?" Mr. Polar Bear asked.

Walter nodded and barked, but I already knew the answer.

He must have been up all night. A message meant just for me. What was he trying to prove anyway? That he really cared about me? Okay, he really cared about me. I'd rubbed off on him. Big deal. Snow Angels could be wrong sometimes, couldn't they? He was still super naughty. Daddy proved that.

"Look!" Silentnight said, pointing at the tree.

The buzzing wasn't in my head after all. A whistle sounded. Then a chug-a-chug-a, chug-a-chug-a as the tree revealed the secret of its maker's soul. Out of a winding tunnel that burrowed through its branches emerged the cutest little electric train set you ever did see. A bright blue engine car, a little yellow caboose, wobbly Weeble engineers at the controls, tiny red and green freight cars in between that overflowed with toy Christmas presents, running along an itty-bitty track woven up and down and inside and all around that sublimely beautiful tree.

As if an electric train set could make up for all his misery.

He had successfully merged his most cherished—and at the same time, traumatic—memory of Christmas with my ideal design without overwhelming either concept. I'd taught him well!

"Who ever heard of a train on a Christmas tree?" Tinsel cackled. "Not even Walter would come up with a dopey idea like that."

Tinsel and the other kids laughed. To them, it may have been merely a gorgeous baby Christmas tree with an electric train set cleverly incorporated into it. But to me, there was something more, something that mattered somehow, something that nagged at me and wouldn't go away.

As the train came around the bend again, passing over the side of the tree that faced me, I saw the familiar stamp on the side of one of the cars: MADE IN THE NORTH POLE.

Of course it was. Toymakers from between the Poles would never think to make a toy train that carried more toys. This was the very train that Rudy had gotten for Christmas the year his mother died. The one he never opened. Until now. For me. And it came from the North Pole. Which meant my father delivered it to him six years ago on Christmas Eve. Which meant Rudy could not have been on the Naughty List that year. Which meant the List my father showed me had to be a lie!

This changed everything.

"Rudy really is nice," I said out loud, feeling a little faint.

Walter sneezed and wiped his nose with his flipper, then rolled over. Footsteps echoed outside the door, hurriedly receding from the classroom.

"Rudy?" My heart skipped a beat. I had to go after him. But a bundle of long, tickly fingers stopped me. In a flash my head went back to that crowded ice bar, reliving the moment when Tinsel had so thoughtlessly shoved me aside. "Let me go!" I snapped at him now.

He smirked. "Candy, baby, forget about him. He's a loser. We have work to do."

"He's not a loser!" I twisted Tinsel's disgusting ticklers off my shoulder, hard enough to make him scream his high-pitched elf scream, and headed in the direction of those fading footsteps.

"If you go out that door, you won't get credit for our tree. Isn't that right, Mr. Polar Bear?" He fluttered the undamaged ticklers of his other hand under the teacher's nose menacingly.

Despite his enormous size advantage, Mr. Polar Bear didn't seem willing to chance the devastation of a tickling from an elfman. "I'm afraid your partner here is correct, Candycane."

"Oh, yeah?" I said, glaring at Tinsel. I went over to our workstation and, for the second time that semester, took out my anger on an innocent Christmas tree, knocking our redemption to the floor and jumping up and down on it until it was flat as a Peppermint Pattie. "Go tickle yourself!" I screamed at Tinsel.

Laughter erupted, some of it probably at me as much as at him, but I didn't care. I was already out the door, speeding down the hall, turning the corner, seeing just a clip of Rudy slipping out the front door as it clanked shut and blocked him from my sight. I ran faster and called out his name even though I knew he couldn't hear me on the other side of that steel barricade.

I reached the exit, banged the metal push-bar, and swung it wide open, almost smashing the heavy door into my little brother, who happened to be running up the front steps of the high school at that exact moment.

He zipped past me, then doubled back and shouted, "Candy, you gotta help me!"

He wore an approximation of Daddy's suit. He must have stitched it together himself out of the old ones Daddy stowed in the attic. The cap hung over his eyes, the sleeves drooped to his knees, the pant legs were uneven, and the wide belt looped around his waist three times.

"Not now, Frostbite."

A gap of no more than twenty yards separated me and Rudy. "Come back, Rudy, pleeeeeease!" I shouted. He had to have heard me this time, but still he tromped through the snow, each step carrying him further away.

Frostbite tugged on my sleeve. "It's important!" he cried, with a sense of desperation I should not have been ignoring.

Rudy's slouching frame grew smaller in the distance. *I never should have doubted him. I never should have doubted him.*

"It's the elves," Frostbite persisted. "They're breaking all the presents."

"Ruuuuu-dyyyyyy!" No use. My shoulders slumped. The apology I owed him would have to wait. I'd catch up with him another time. He would forgive me. He had to. We'd make up and everyone would see we were meant to be together, forever and always, and I'd just die if that didn't happen, if I had ruined that by listening to my father instead of my heart, and maybe I should have been listening to my brother too because his words finally caught up to me. "What did you say?"

"We can't let Dad find out. I'll get in trouble."

"Why would *you* get in trouble?"

Frostbite stared at the tops of his boots. "I was only trying to help," he mumbled.

I lifted his face by its little round chin. "Frostbite, what did you do?"

thirty-four

Tinsel explained it to me once. The old fairies' tale that elves worked slower every year. In reality, the more children born each year, the more toys they needed to produce. Basic supply and demand. But the elf population grows at a slower rate, proportionally, because of their longer life spans, so...

Well, this isn't an elf-history book. Suffice it to say the increase in demand had always been worked into their schedule gradually so as to be virtually unnoticeable. Sometimes they'd forget and gauge their progress based on the previous year's less-demanding performance, then they'd have to adjust with a mad spurt of productivity in the last few weeks before Christmas. But it always worked out.

This was different. Even accounting for the expected fluctuations, the elves were way off their game.

I should have been more alarmed by their laziness when I visited Mom at the Workshop, but I had my own problems to worry about. Mom had properly pegged the elves' crankiness as an early warning sign, but she always had blind faith in Daddy when it came to his official duties. Of course, Daddy should have been the first to notice, but his priority seemed to be making up hurtful lies to keep his only daughter from having a life.

Only Frostbite showed the appropriate Claus level of concern when the T-C gauge slipped backward, dipping below fifty percent, while the Days-Until-Christmas gauge inched closer and closer to T-minus zero. He should have said something sooner, but decided instead to play Santa himself.

Together with Flip and Flop, he concocted a plan.

When a ten-year-old comes up with a plan and asks two puffins what they think, look for a margin for error as big as the solar system.

While the elves were out at Rocks getting juiced on elfnip, my brother and his co-conspirators slipped into the elf breakroom and dosed their hot chocolate with even more elfnip. In theory, it should have helped twice as much. But like I said, we're talking about a kid, two birds, and Murphy's immutable Commandment.

I knew a way home that was all downhill, so I borrowed Queero's sled from the sled rack in front of the school. Hot pink with rainbow-colored candy sprinkles painted on it. I knew he wouldn't mind. I threw Frostbite on my back and we tore down Winterborough Way.

We were on our driveway in less than three minutes, strapped into my Range Rover half a minute after that. I started her up for the first time in a month. Now that I'd discovered Daddy's Big Lie, I felt it only fair to usurp the authority to commute all punishments. Besides, this was an emergency for Christmas' sake—literally. As I darted onto the icy road, I asked Frostbite what on earth Mom and Dad could be doing while this crisis was snowballing.

"They had another emergency," he replied.

"*What!*" I almost skidded off the road.

"Uh... a fake Santa promised a little girl he'd give her mother her voice back in time to sing in the Christmas choir... I think."

Oh. That kind of emergency. By tradition, Daddy liked to make time to perform one last-minute Christmas miracle in the betweenlands every year. Lucky break for Frostbite, assuming we could resolve the elf problem before they got back.

We weren't too far from the Workshop, but the Range Rover couldn't go faster than 30 m.p.h. with snow chains on. Light snow flurries stuck to the windshield. I switched on the wipers in time to catch the gray nose of a fluffy white arctic hare hop in front of us. I swerved to miss it, nearly tipping the car over. After I got us going in a straight line again, I had time to process Frostbite's story.

"Hey, wait a minute," I said. "That's an episode of *The Brady Bunch*." I glanced over at my brother squirming in his seat, then quickly fixed my gaze back on the road.

"It's all I could think of," he said. "I panicked."

"*You* called in the emergency miracle?"

"Well, duh. I disguised my voice and everything. I told you, I didn't want Dad to find out what I did to his elves. Swans a-swimming, Candy, I thought you were on my side."

"I am. But that was such a lame story."

"Flip and Flop bought it," he argued.

"They're puffins. They'd believe goldfish were made of real gold if you told them so."

I pulled the Range Rover into my reserved parking space, the one Daddy had candy-striped for me when I got my license, and cut off the engine. I already had one foot on the wet gravel when I realized Frostbite's door hadn't opened. He sat in the passenger seat, biting his lip and choking back tears.

Here the lad had come to me to avoid getting yelled at by our father and I ended up treating him just as harshly as Daddy might have. What kind of big sister was I? Despite my recent disciplinary history, it was still my job to show him the ropes in How to Get out of Trouble Behind Daddy's Back if he ever wanted to grow up to be like me.

"Let's go see how bad you messed up, kiddo," I said as I reached inside the car and mussed his hair. "I'm sure we can figure something out."

I held his hand as we snaked through the maze of cubicles toward the manufacturing area. Flip and Flop stood guard in front of the large double doors, right where Frostbite had left them. We could hear them rehearsing excuses they might use to keep Daddy off the toy floor, were he to show up unexpectedly.

Flop lowered his voice as much as a puffin could and went, "Ho-ho-ho, Flip. Make way. I'm Santa Claus and I wish to enter."

"Oh, you don't want to go in there, Flop—I mean Santy Boss. Psst. I'm not supposed to tell you this, big guy, but the little guys are planning a surprise party for you in there."

Flop lit up, breaking character. "Sweet! I never knew they cared."

They swapped places with a hokey square-dance move and Flip said, "Okay, now it's my turn to be Santa. Ho-ho-ho. I'm Santa Claus. Out of my way, Flop."

"Guys, guys, guys!" Frostbite ripped his hand from mine and ran ahead of me. "I brought Candy."

"Yay! I love candy," said Flip.

"I love ice cream," said Flop.

"Ooh, me too. With candy on top!" The puffins raised their wings and high-fived their feathers.

The enormous door to the main work area behind them, sealed tight like a vault, muffled what sounded like a chipmunk party coming from inside.

"Guys, the elves?" I bent over and shook Flop out of his drooling, giddy mis-anticipation of ice cream *a la sucrerie*.

"Quite right," said Flip. "We hypothesized the elfnip would speed 'em up."

"It shouldn't not speed them up," said Flop.

"Isn't that not a double negative?" said Flip.

I navigated around the pair of auks as they debated their grammar, and slid aside the heavy latch to open the gateway to untold elf chaos.

A familiar odor overwhelmed me the moment the door's seal cracked. A pleasant odor. A sweet, sweet sugary pink smell that reminded me of—

"Bubblegum," I said out loud.

"I smell it too," one of the puffins agreed.

"I love the smell of bubblegum," the other one said.

"You know what smells like bubblegum?" the first puffin asked.

I knew what was coming before they both answered in unison: "Elf farts."

Frostbite, Flip, and Flop began to giggle uncontrollably. They drew big whiffs into their nostrils, then broke up even more. Frostbite put the heel of his hand to his fat lips and made loud farting noises. The puffins fell over and laughed their heads off.

I wrenched Frostbite's hand away from his mouth. "Where did you get that elfnip?"

"Some dude behind the school."

"That wasn't elfnip," I informed him. "Elfnip doesn't make elves fart."

"It doesn't?"

I shook my head. "No. You know what does?" He shrugged his dorky little shoulders. "You got Daddy's elves booted up on megatoe!"

I swung the doors wide open to reveal thousands of elves run completely amok. Everywhere you looked, amorous elves rolled indiscriminately about the toymaking machinery, hooting and caterwauling, sharp squeaky chirping noises emanating from their puny bungholes. Half-wrapped toys lay in heaps on stuck conveyor belts. Jack-in-the-boxes escaped their boxes left and right and went on insane missions to beat up rocking horses with wiffleball bats.

"Leapin' lollipops!" I said. I never imagined little people could make such a big mess.

"This doesn't look good," said Flip.

"In point of fact, it looks quite bad," his counterpart added.

"What are we gonna do?" Frostbite bit his lip, his pleading eyes waiting for my answer. I didn't have one. "Christmas is right around the corner."

"And on the ceiling," said Flop.

"And in the air. And on the floor. Hoohoo."

"No, guys. Christmas is on the wall." I pointed to the giant Toys-Completed gauge. The needle clicked, as if my finger had magically tapped it from across the football-field-length warehouse, dropping from forty percent to thirty-nine.

"There it goes again," Flip whispered to Flop. "How did she do that?"

"She didn't do it, Flip."

"Well, it's not supposed to do that."

"I don't think it knows that because it just did."

"Guys, this is serious." I couldn't think with the two of them blabbering.

"It's hopeless!" Frostbite cried. "We'll have to cancel Christmas and it's all my fault. Not even Daddy has the power to fix this. He's gonna kill me."

Flip and Flop broke down and sobbed loudly, waterworks sprinkling out of the corners of their eyes.

I hated to admit it, but it did seem bigger than I could ever hope to handle. I braced the wall with my hand to keep myself from curling up on the floor in defeat. Frostbite's problem had become my problem as much as it was now the world's problem.

I pictured children everywhere waking up Christmas morning to trees with no presents underneath. Or broken presents at best. The devastation Rudy must have felt, was still feeling all these years later, when he lost Christmas—I multiplied that by a billion. The world would surely stop turning under the weight of all that sadness.

And yet I couldn't help flushing with warm memories in Rudy's sturdy arms under the Northern Lights. What was it she said? *You will come to know of my power in time.* Yes—the power to save Christmas!

"I've got an idea," I announced to the boys.

"And I've got a bunion," said Flip.

"And I've got an ointment," said Flop.

"Oh, bliss!"

"I think I know who can help," I said. "You three stay here."

If my instincts were right, the one person on Earth who could help me summon the very power that Christmas now needed was the boy who hated Christmas the most. Our only hope was for me to find Rudy and make him forgive me, so together we could bring back the Snow Angel.

thirty-five

So I'm driving all over the North Pole on this monumentally important quest to save Christmas, and I have to admit, all I could fixate on was how incredibly romantic it would feel to be next to my Rudy again. Side by side, the touch of his hand, twice as big as mine, our fingers interlaced, our legs scissoring rhythmically through the cold, wet snow, waiting for that sweet dose of magic to lift us into the sky. And all the while, a fist twisted inside my chest and clenched around my heart, a pair of mice dancing in my stomach. How would I ever convince him I was sorry for abandoning him? For being just like everyone else in his life who had lost faith in him?

And yes, it did occur to me that maybe I had come up with this particular plan for *me* more than for Christmas. Maybe the Snow Angel was nothing more than a silly little fairy whose only power was to illuminate True Love. In truth, I did desperately want to test that part of my theory too. But my plan was not born of selfish intent, the Snow Angel's role a trivial afterthought. She would know what to do. That was my honest, gut instinct. The chance—no, requirement—to reunite with Rudy was the icing on the carrot cake.

I didn't bother to call him. He wouldn't have answered. Or if he did, he'd probably hang up, refusing to help, and that would be that. End of Christmas. So first, I tried his condo. Nobody home. Next, I checked his father's office. Dr. Tutti told me to spit, but when I did, he said that he meant for Snappy, the elf in his chair, to spit. Then he said about Rudy, "Who knows where that boy goes. Did you try the jail?"

I went to the high school and looked under his favorite gumdrop tree. I asked Walter if he knew anything, because he'd seen him last, but he wouldn't talk, the stupid walrus. I even drove by Eggnog Alley. Too afraid to get out of the car, I rolled down the window and offered the homeless polar bear a cookie to go poke his head inside Rocks and tell me if Rudy was there. The bear never came back.

I needed a bloodhound. For that I knew just where to look. The nearest ice fields were at Yuletide Park. I drove there as fast as I could and ran out into the middle of the first frozen pond I came to. I found a large tree branch and used it to chip a hole in the thin, watery ground, reminding myself over and over, *try not to fall in this time—Rudy's not here to rescue you.* When the opening was just large enough, I took off one boot and one sock. Teetering on the edge of the hole, I wiggled a naked toe into the numbing waters.

Otter caught my scent and skyrocketed to me under the ice. In one cacophonous burst, he crashed through the hole and leaped on top of me, licking my face with his tickly, sandpapery tongue.

"Down, boy. Down." He rolled over and listened intently as I explained how important it was that he help me find Rudy. With the memory of an elephant, the obedient leopard seal knew exactly who I was talking about and took off straight away—without me. I raced back to my Range Rover and headed in the direction Otter had gone.

Due North.

Of course! A silly grin stuck to my lips as I traveled longitudinally to 90° N. He'd gone to "our place"—a sign. Of all the places in the Arctic Circle an angsty teenager could hide out, he picked that one. The spot where the magic had happened. At the top of the world. *Wherefore art thou, Rudy? I am on my way to thee.*

I had to ditch the SUV at the edge of the thick Snickerdoodle Forest and hike the rest of the way on foot. Otter had located Rudy by then, as evidenced by his loud, continuous roar echoing through the woods like a sick, broken foghorn.

The signal stopped the instant I came into Otter's view. In the distance, I could only make out silhouettes as Otter slithered up to Rudy, nudging his elbow with his wet, bulbous nose, begging to be petted.

They weren't alone. Rudy had built himself another companion out of three badly misshapen spheres of tightly packed snow. As he worked on the snowperson, I took a moment to engrave the idyllic image into my brain—a future Rudy molding a junior moppet one day, coddling it, nurturing it, coaxing a smile out of it by tracing one across its face, with Otter, the beloved family pet, at his master's feet. The moment was all mine.

I continued my northward climb. Dead ahead, he faced south—technically in my direction—but would have needed the ability to see all the way around the globe to spot me coming. For a second, I imagined he had such a power, that his eyes could always find me whenever he wanted, and I wondered if our Polar position had anything to do with how my dad was able to see all the children of the world and know all at once if they'd been bad or good.

I almost called out to Rudy, until he began to put on a curious performance. The first hit made me flinch, only because moments before, I had imagined his victim as a symbol of the child we might one day produce. Thank goodness this was only a snowbaby. His fist connected with its lopsided head again and again as he took out all his frustrations on the poor inanimate creature.

He pummeled its nose, socked it in the stomach, shoved a boot hard into its snowballs. He pounded it repeatedly in the side of its head until the block of mush came clean off. He'd bloodlessly decapitated his opponent like a slippery Rock 'Em Sock 'Em Robot.

"I had my money on you the whole time," I said. "Not exactly a fair fight."

He looked up, noticing me for the first time, then gathered more snow to rebuild his punching bag. Otter stretched and mewled, wanting to play.

"If you sent him to attack me," Rudy said, "it didn't work."

Had he meant his injured snowman to be me? I wanted to run into his arms and tell him how sorry I was, and that the snowman, by rights, ought to have been my father. If he made it fatter and put a beard on it, I would gladly help him destroy it again.

"The tree was beautiful," I squeaked.

"Can't you see I want to be alone?"

"You picked a nice spot for that." Stars shot across the sky. The Northern Lights glimmered and glowed, casting shimmering shadows of violet and pink across his stoic face. A cool breeze pulsated around us, ruffling the faraway trees. And millions of toys that would soon need to travel to their own faraway trees sat miles away being slaughtered by 'toed-up elves while we admired the heavenly scenery in silence. "I really liked the train, Rudy."

"Candy…"

My heart raced. I half-expected the wind to carry me away like a thousand heart-shaped snowflakes that could swirl around his oval head and get stuck in his thick, dark hair, then melt and run down his soft neck, trickling into his mouth before turning back into me inside his hungry, hungry kiss.

He backed away from me, saying my name again, *Candy*, and I realized I was moving toward him, my legs acting on their own accord, a determination I didn't know I had. As if I were being puppeteered by the Ghost of Christmas Yet to Come, my mouth opened and words tumbled out of it, unfiltered by any known process of thought. "I'm sorry I hurt you," they said, "and I will find a way to make you believe me. But right now, I need your help and I don't have time to explain."

I charged at him. He tumbled backward over Otter, like the old schoolyard prank where one boy sneaks behind another on his hands and knees. I vaulted over the blubbery sea creature and connected with my paramour, lips-first. He resisted the force of my arms dragging his in the flapping motion of snow-angel-making, even as his mouth involuntarily consumed me. His resolve weakened as his tongue responded to the deep, delicious probes I sent him.

"What are you doing?" His words slid down my throat, heard more by my heart than my ears.

I removed my lips from his long enough to answer, "Trust me." The light show in the sky made his blue eyes purple, then orange, then gold. I nudged his feet aside with mine, rapidly parting and closing our legs like fairy wings. Snow flew furiously around us, a private blizzard kicked up by our wild motions.

Otter squealed as if he'd been stepped on, freaked out at the sight of the snow rising beneath us, forming a new life before his eyes, floating above him with us on her back.

We stopped our thrashing. I almost jumped for joy at the sight of the fairy's golden hair flowing beneath us, her wings fluttering on either side, but stopped myself when I realized how high we'd already soared.

"Are you going to hold on this time?" the Snow Angel said.

I crawled off Rudy and wrapped my arm around her neck.

"Grab hold of her!" I yelled.

Rudy rolled himself over, clutching at feathers. "I don't understand you, Candy. You like me, you don't like me, you kiss me, you stop talking to me. What did I ever do to you?" The plumage slipped through his fingers, causing him to ratchet down the spirit's back. He reached around her midsection and squeezed.

"You have to hold on!" I shouted, then tapped our driver on the shoulder and said, "We have to hurry. Please."

"Where to?" Her echoey voice floated all around us.

"My father's Workshop."

"Here we go." She kicked her hidden thrusters into gear and the earth sped by below in a blur of snow-covered trees. Clouds of stardust blew into my eyes, nose, and mouth, making it difficult to breathe.

We came out of warp-speed only a moment later. The unmistakable outline of the Workshop lit up before us in a majestic array of beautiful flashing colors. Daddy's face appeared in lights and blinked across the side of the building. The words "SANTA'S WORKSHOP" strobed above it in a bright neon glow.

We spiraled like a shooting star toward a tiny window on the top floor. I held my breath and ducked, waiting for the glass to shatter around us. But somehow we passed through unharmed, landing safely in the very spot where I had left my brother only a short while ago.

thirty-six

"Took ya long enough." Frostbite stood in front of the double doors, arms folded across his chest. "Who's she?"

"I brought help," I said.

Flip and Flop snickered, their wings tucked behind their heads as if they were snoozing in a hammock on some tropical beach along that equator thing where they say it's always warm.

Flip flopped to his feet and boasted, "Have no fear, fair princess."

Flop flipped over to the steel-gray doors. "We called for reinforcements." He undid the latch then tried to pull the doors open, straining against their weight.

"No offense, Candy," Frostbite scoffed, "but what do you think *she* can do? One girl? Flip and Flop brought *hundreds* of friends."

"Thousands," said Flip.

"Millions," said Flop.

"Nobody likes an exaggerating puffin," Flip admonished Flop.

"Be that as it may, Flip, we have saved day."

"Not just any day. Christmas Day!"

"We rock!"

Flip joined Flop in his quest to pry the doors apart. Frostbite pitched in too. He guessed it must be all the new toys piling up on the other side that were blocking those tenacious doors. I enlisted Rudy to help.

"Not by the hair of my chinny-chin-chin," he said. "Not until someone tells me what's going on."

Why did I have to have such strong feelings for someone so stubborn? I stomped a foot and whined, "Rudy! We're running out of time."

"How do I know this isn't some kind of set up to get me in more trouble with your old man?"

"Is that what you think?" My eyes stung, but I willed my tears to stay at bay.

The Snow Angel glided forward, gently tapping Rudy's head three times with her glittery wand. "Listen to what I say to you, Rudy Tutti. You must stop questioning everything if you wish to see a genuine Christmas miracle."

A crease formed between his eyes, then a strange calm washed over him. I blinked a double take. Another moment later, a more cooperative Rudy was sizing up the barrier that stood between us and the work area. He heaved it with all his might. It opened. An inch at first. Then another. The sounds of toymaking seeped out the small opening: tools clackity-clacking, squeezy toys squeaking, machines whirring and humming.

The rest of us leaned forward, anxious to see all the beautiful toys being packaged and shipped to the delivery area. Rudy gave the doors one final yank and they slid wide open.

The problem stared us in the face. The doors had been stuck on a mountain of discarded toy parts: doll limbs, sunken Battleships, punctured soccer balls, totaled Matchbox cars, buckets of Monopoly thimbles, misshapen Lego blocks, crashed smartphone apps, overly serious Silly Putty, and all-too-sensible Silly String, all piled clear to the ceiling.

The pieces avalanched toward our feet like waves crashing against the shore.

Beyond the debris, thousands upon thousands of feathery puffins cooed and squawked like squeaky toys. They fluttered their wings and clickety-clacked their beaks at each other—with nary a finished toy in sight. Many were trying in earnest but were even more clumsy than elves on 'toe. And any toy that approached some semblance of usability would go to a segregated flock who would play with it instead of packaging it.

Some of the elves still rolled about, laughing and farting. Others picked violent fights with the puffins to reclaim their jobs as their footsiness began to wear off.

"What have we done?" exclaimed Flip.

"We made things worse," said Flop.

"We didn't make them better."

"If we made them worse, at least we accomplished something."

The Toys-Completed gauge disagreed, dropping its needle below ten percent, into the Red Zone, triggering site-wide sirens to blare ear-shattering wails loud enough to be heard in outer space. The noise attacked my head like a jackhammer and made my bones rattle inside my skin.

Frostbite became as pale as snow. "We are so dead."

Yep. Daddy would get a distress signal on the sleigh no matter where he was. By now he'd probably forgotten his fruitless search for a Carol Brady with laryngitis and was already hightailing it straight over Canada. If the Workshop had a chimney, he would be sliding down it any second.

The clanging bells and piercing buzzers made me shake like a pair of dice in a Parcheesi player's hands. I turned to the Snow Angel and begged, "Can you fix this?"

She tittered and replied, "In my sleep, my child. Stay back now. All of you."

She levitated above our heads and floated through the entryway, over the mound of broken dreams, crisscrossing each section of the enormous toymaking plant. Everywhere she flew, she sprinkled her special blend of moonbeams, starlight, and fairy dust over the chaos below. The room brightened like the summer solstice, the glare almost burning our eyes.

Frostbite stared, not bothered by the intensity, but I had to squint. Rudy shielded his eyes, like a wanderer lost in a brutal snowstorm. Then he was at my side, his other arm enveloping me protectively, an unexpected gesture that moved me almost enough to ignore the miraculous beauty of the Snow Angel's work.

An ominous rumble replaced the blare of the alarms. Then, before our very eyes, the toys stirred as if awakening from a winter-long slumber and began to put themselves back together again. If only Humpty Dumpty could have seen it.

Marbles grouped themselves into sets and rolled into cloth pouches with drawstrings that drew themselves closed. Tinkertoy pieces assembled in their containers. Nutcracker dolls marched into gift boxes that wrapped themselves in colorful bows. Crayons mixed to form brilliant, never-before-seen colors. A clearing sprang up along one wall and became a parking lot for rows and rows of bicycles, tricycles, unicycles, and Big Wheels.

The T-C meter rose. Twenty-five percent and climbing. The magical dust made the elves sleepy. They started to nod off. So did Flip and Flop's so-called helpers. Thirty-five percent. Conveyor belts started to convey again. Finished packages journeyed to the Distribution Center. Fifty-five percent of the year's Christmas presents were ready to be loaded onto Daddy's sleigh.

Music filled the air from out of nowhere. Nobody questioned it. It reminded me of the sound of children all over the globe, laughing and playing with new toys in a not-too-distant future.

Rudy and I huddled with Frostbite before the rapidly dissolving heap of toy parts that had once barricaded the entrance. We wore smiles bigger than any child's would be come Christmas morning, children who would have no idea what we'd gone through to get their toys made on time.

Eighty-five percent.

The Snow Angel flew by and waved us in with a wink. I took a cautious step forward. A euphoric feeling spread through me, as if my insides were being gently massaged by Peace itself. Rudy and Frostbite followed close behind as a team of Slinkys sprang past us like a group of marathon runners toward some distant child's stocking hung at each of their finish lines.

Eighty-eight percent and still climbing. I was so overjoyed that the rattle of the door to the loading dock rolling up on its tracks behind us barely registered.

"What the fa-la-la is *he* doing in here!" a voice bellowed.

The music stopped.

I spun on my heels with a nervous shudder. Standing there in front of the sleigh were my parents, back from the world, in response, as I had feared, to the five-alarm fire we had managed to put out.

We may have saved Christmas in time—but not soon enough to save our own hides.

thirty-seven

"**Y**ou!"

Daddy pointed the angriest finger I'd ever seen in my life. At Rudy. As if thunderbolts might shoot out of it and burn him to a crisp. "How did *you* get in here?"

"Daddy, please!" I wedged myself between Rudy and The Finger. "I can explain everything."

"Don't you say a word to me. Look at this mess!"

The toys continued their quiet rally as the Snow Angel merrily went about her business, blissfully tuning out the Mad Santa below her. I wished I could do that.

Elves and puffins lay on the cold cement, snoring and wheezing, still knocked out from the fairy dust. Flip and Flop, quaking with fear, hopped into a gaggle of their kind and played dead to cloak themselves from my father's wrath.

My mother urged Daddy to calm down and eat some jelly beans for fear he might give himself an attack of apoplexy.

Daddy lifted a comatose elf. He nudged open an eyelid, then scowled at Rudy. "These elves are on 'toe! And *you* brought it in here, into *my* Workshop!" He gesticulated wildly as he hollered, swinging Dizzy the Elf so hard that something rattled loudly inside his grapefruit-sized head.

"You've got it all wrong, Daddy. You have to stop picking on Rudy. If it weren't for him—"

"What? If it weren't for him then *what*? You wouldn't have nearly flunked out of school? You wouldn't have come this close to becoming Abominable sushi? Do you want to ruin your life? Because that's what's going to happen if you keep defending this... this... nogoodnik." Daddy squeezed Dizzy, and a high-pitched fart squeaked out. "He's dragging you down with him, Candycane. Can't you see that? You saw his rap sheet with your own brown eyes."

That List was a lie and I could prove it! And Rudy didn't cause all those bad things that happened to me—things that admittedly had never happened before I knew him. Then for the tiniest fraction of a second, Daddy's angry words succeeded in twisting my convictions back into doubts. Was I sliding into some dark chasm where I might one day no longer be able to look out and recognize Christmas?

If it weren't for Rudy, Tinsel never would have turned into the jealous oaf I could no longer stand. If it weren't for Rudy, I never would have known the pain of having my heart stomped on all those times I'd lost him, no matter that it usually wasn't his fault.

If it weren't for Rudy, my life would have stayed exactly as it was before, no better, no worse, no more exciting, yet possibly duller. Would I have stolen Daddy's sleigh for a date with Tinsel? Never. Or experienced the thrill of learning to fly it on-the-fly, or the danger of battling a vicious monster in the sky? Whatever happiness I'd had in my old life with Tinsel was just there, in the air, not at all like the happiness I had to work for, to fight for with a passion that I, at last, was passionate about.

I turned to Rudy and saw a man who could make me look forward to every day like Christmas morning with a cherry on top.

"What rap sheet, fat man?" Rudy said, as always unafraid of my father. "You think you know me? The only record I have is from when you came along with your trumped-up charges. Sleigh theft!" He spit on the floor, just missing a neon pink and purple Play-Doh dinosaur on its way to turn itself into a Christmas present for a child in Naperville, Illinois.

"Ho-ho-ho," my father replied. "The rap sheet I use goes much deeper than arrest warrants. Tell him, Candy. Go ahead." Again, he didn't wait for me to answer. "Lying to your parents. Not listening to your parents. That's what you brought to this village. That's what you brought to my little girl."

The shook-up elf in Daddy's big hands started to come to. A lopsided frown wriggled across his pallid, purplish-gray face and he probably had whiplash by now, but he kept quiet while his boss continued to rant and rave.

"You think I need the N.P.P.D. to read you your rights? I'm *Santa Claus*! I know who's been good or bad! *I'm* the judge and jury in this town. And I want you and your father on the next ice floe out of here!"

Banishment.

Now, I love my father and my whole family dearly. Even Flip and Flop. But if it came down to a choice, if Rudy were forced to leave the Pole because of me, I'd go with him in a heartbeat.

If he'd have me.

I cried out for my mommy and ran over to her, my eyes puffed up from damming back my tears. I needed her help the same way Christmas had needed the Snow Angel's.

"I can't talk to him when he gets like this," my mother whispered. "He's being stubborn and unreasonable, but he *is* Santa Claus."

My heart sank into my stomach. My own mother. Advising me to give up. To walk away from True Love. After encouraging me to believe in it—I mean, wasn't that the message behind her midnight anecdote?

She kept talking, not making sense anymore. "You know

your father. It's the stress of the holidays talking. He'll calm down in a month or so and we can send for the Tuttis to come back then."

"Don't bet on it," Daddy said.

"Whatever." Rudy punted a stray soccer ball over Daddy's head, demolishing a magnificent doll house with an ugly crash. The Snow Angel zoomed over to fix it. "What makes you think I'd come back to a backwards place like this anyway?"

"Please, Daddy!" I begged. "You can't banish him."

"Too late. The Tuttis are *banished*." And with that pronouncement, he bounced poor Dizzy on his tiny butt. The bruised elf limped away as the jolly dictator proclaimed, "Our long Christmas nightmare is over."

"Good riddance," Rudy said. He waved us off as if he were shooing away a fly, as if we had been the nuisance to him instead of the other way around. As if he thought his presence had had no impact on our community whatsoever.

But I knew better. As Rudy started toward those large double doors, now almost completely cleared of all the chaos that had been wreaked, I summoned up the courage to plead my case one last time.

"Freeze!" I commanded.

Rudy stopped and turned back to me, his arms slowly folding in front of him, his mouth widening into a scornful half-smirk, challenging me—daring me—to dig my own grave. His expectations were low. I'd let him down before.

"Look around you, Daddy. Don't you see what's happening?" I pointed to the Snow Angel buzzing overhead like a kite. "This isn't a Christmas nightmare you walked in on. This is Christmas waking up from a nightmare. Christmas *was* almost destroyed. But Rudy didn't do that. You know who did?"

Frostbite tiptoed over to my mother and hid behind the hem of her skirt.

"I may have fallen behind in school this year, but I learned an awful lot. I learned that Christmas toys are not made by elves. The elves assemble them, but it takes Christmas Spirit to turn those toys into gifts of wonder. And that was *your* job, Daddy. Wasn't it?"

My father stared at me, stone-faced. The more he let me talk, the more I felt my knees knock together. I imagined steam building up under that pointy red hat of his, ready to blow at any second, but I kept cranking the boiler anyway.

"You're supposed to embody the Christmas Spirit," I said. "You're the one who makes this all happen, year after year. The elves put in the elbow grease. All you have to do is walk this floor once a day with a 'Ho-ho-ho,' and your Christmas Spirit rubs off on them.

"But where were you this year? Obsessing over who I was dating. News flash, Daddy: I'm not a little girl anymore. That doesn't mean I'm not still *your* little girl. It just means I'm growing up. The more energy you expend trying to stop me, trying to do the impossible, the less Christmas Spirit you have for the elves and the rest of the world.

"Rudy didn't nearly destroy Christmas. *You did.* And if it wasn't for him, there wouldn't be a Christmas this year."

I came up for air and waited.

Now I have to prepare you for this next part, okay? This is not coming from the lawyers or anything. I mean, it happened. There's witnesses. The workers filed a grievance with their union, a settlement was reached, and all was forgiven and blah, blah, blah. I'm just saying, if you've been thinking to yourself there's two sides to every story and Candycane is this spoiled little teenage drama queen and she must be exaggerating 'cause

267

her father could never really be as pigheaded as she's been describing, well, maybe you're right. Maybe he was just being an appropriately protective parent all along and I chose to see things differently because, well, I'm a kid and I don't know any better and I was experiencing all kinds of feelings and powerful emotions and stuff that I didn't understand. Fair enough.

But I'm telling you, you might want to brace yourself for what comes next. It's gonna be graphic. If you want to preserve what's left of your image of my dad being all saintly and jolly and benevolent all the time, then you'd better skip the rest of this chapter. He does have that side of him. I'm not disputing that. I'm just saying he has his good days and his bad days, just like anyone else. This was one of his off-the-charts days.

I'd be lying if I told you no elves were harmed.

You've been warned. Okay?

So after this long, excruciating silence, my father reached down and scooped Stuffy the Elf into his big palm, stuffing the sleeping dwarf's little head and legs into a tight elfball, then delivered his response to my impudent sermon in a ghostly, guttural voice. "That's not the way I see it." He reeled the folded elf over his shoulder and heaved him like a shot put.

He's not exactly proud of it, but he did have excellent aim. Stuffy came out of his fairy-dust stupor mid-flight and screamed like a siren, his eyes bugging out just before hitting his target. He dropped Rudy clean off his feet as if an elf-shaped anvil had fallen from the sky.

"Strike!" said Flop.

Stuffy shook himself off and staggered away, dazed. Mom threw her hand over her mouth; even she never expected Daddy to react like that. As soon as the shock wore off, I ran over to help Rudy up.

Daddy found a fresh pile of elves and picked up another

to lob at Rudy. I had to duck to avoid getting tagged myself as Giddy the Elf flew past my ear. Rudy managed to catch him and set him on his feet. Frivolous came next. Rudy caught him the same way.

"I want you out of here!" Daddy shouted, loading his arms with more elf ammunition. One by one he torpedoed the diminutive toymakers at us like a fat, red-coated, out-of-control pitching machine.

I caught Woozy. Rudy got Flippant, then jumped to snag Jingle out of a wild pitch, saving him from breaking his bells against the back wall. Next came Twinkle and Sparkle, as Rudy and I continued our compassionate defense against the barrage of incoming elf missiles.

Then Angry...

"And no..."

...then Zany...

"...more..."

...then Nipper...

"...boys..."

...and Jiffy...

"...for you..."

...and Wizard...

"...EVER!"

Mom, Frostbite, Flip and Flop, and fifteen recently revived puffins rushed at Daddy to stop his assault. Three puffins latched their beaks onto his throwing arm, only to be pitched off in all directions as Daddy launched a final attack before being overpowered.

Nimble the Elf, the last elf thrown, sailed ten feet high, somersaulting through a wide arc as if high-jumping a rainbow. He spiraled downward, his tumbling little body making a whistling noise as it cut through the air. Rudy got into position, hands raised for the pop fly, when the falling elf's trajectory was unexpectedly offset.

A mid-air collision, accompanied by an angelic "Oof," dropped Nimble into a stack of plush teddy bears—but the Snow Angel was not so fortunate. She came down hard on the cement with a sickening crunch. As her lights went out, so did the ethereal brightness that had bathed the Workshop ever since her magic had begun.

The room plunged into a drab dimness. The toys froze, then fell apart. Skateboards cracked into pieces. Jigsaw puzzles, already in pieces, simply disintegrated. Giant bubble-wand bubbles burst into thin air.

Toys moaned in agony, dying painful, horrible deaths all over the Workshop. They needed Christmas Spirit the way life needed oxygen. And with the Snow Angel out cold, the emergency backup supply her magic provided was irrevocably cut off. The Toys-Completed gauge plummeted to zero. Alarms came back to life. Sirens. Buzzers. Bells. Whistles.

Toys choking… gasping… slowly suffocating…

There really wasn't going to be a Christmas this year.

thirty-eight

Mom slammed a fist on the large circular button that flashed urgently on the green wall of the Workshop's grand toy room. The pounding, blaring, screaming, ear-splitting alarms fell silent once again.

"Well, isn't this a merry mess?" she said, as if nothing more had happened than someone spilling tea. She kneeled over the unconscious Snow Angel and called for a stretcher, then hurried off with Jiffy and Nimble as they carried the inert fairy to the second-floor elfirmary.

Daddy slouched and poked through the damage as if sifting through the ashes of all his worldly possessions after a long-lived-in house had burned to the ground. Defeated like never before, his helplessness gave me the shivers. He kept his back to us as if he were too ashamed to show his face.

Warbly, stinging echoes of the now-dormant sirens gave way to the deadest silence I'd ever heard in my life. Then a loud click shot out. The Days-Until-Christmas gauge had just shifted its ornate arrow by one notch, now pointing menacingly at a big, bold numeral 2.

The closest we'd ever come to missing Christmas, I'd heard, was the year of the pinniped flu outbreak. Over three hundred people and elves were infected—a sizable portion of the North Pole population. Luckily Chefy had concocted a home remedy consisting of two turtle-dove eggs, lime phosphate, and octopus secretions. That kept most of the workforce going. Some Aussies may have received slightly smaller presents that year, but no good boy or girl had ever been missed.

The idea of every toy breaking just two days before Christmas was so inconceivable, no contingency plan had ever been devised. We were all of us helpless.

So when Rudy walked up to my father, I didn't know what to expect. Were he to laugh in Daddy's face, he would not have been out of line. Yet there he stood, toe-to-toe with the icon of a tradition he claimed he had no use for, and asked "Where do we start?"

"Start what?" my father scoffed sullenly.

"The way I see it, Pillsbury, is we all got a lot of work to do and not a lot of time to do it."

Daddy studied Rudy's paradoxically contemptuous yet earnest expression. He might have suspected Rudy of plotting some diabolical prank to make things worse—if it were possible for things to get any worse. "It's too late, kid. Go home. The party's over."

"With all due respect, pork belly, the Santa Claus I once believed in would never give up."

"That so?" He tried to stare Rudy down.

Rudy ignored him and crouched in front of my little brother. "Hey, Frost-breath. Run down to the school. Tell all the kids we need their help. Tell everyone in town." He stood up again and spoke louder for my father's benefit. "We're gonna pull an all-nighter."

Frostbite lit up, saluting Rudy like a G.I. Joe. "You can count on me!"

"I'm going, too," said Flip.

"I'm going three!" said Flop.

"I'm going infinity."

"I'm going infinity plus one."

"Get it? We're counting on thee, tee-hee... Frostbite?" Their master had already left. They rushed after him, flipping and flopping all the way to the front door.

"That's rich." Daddy adjusted his belt to let out some sarcasm. "You've been here, what, four months? And now you're gonna pull off Christmas in a night? Ho-ho-ho." He patted his enormous belly. "Look around you, son. We're talking a year's worth of toy making for millions of children. It can't be done."

"You got a better idea, blubber-butt? Let's hear it."

"Rudy!" I wasn't sure anymore if he was trying to help Daddy or provoke him. I put a hand on his shoulder. "Face it. You can't fix this."

"What do you know, Candy?" He thrust my arm away, obviously still hurt over how I had so abruptly shut him out of my life.

"I know you don't believe in Christmas miracles, Rudy. But take it from someone who does because she's seen them up close."

"Where I come from, we don't use magic and we still manage to get things done." He rummaged through the rubble and found a paddle, then a ball on a string, and hooked them up. He scrounged up a golden ribbon and affixed it to his newly assembled toy. He carefully placed it in a clean area of the floor, anointing it his holding area for finished products, then moved on to find another knicknack to put together, stopping only to shoot me an angry *so-there* glance.

The Toys-Completed gauge didn't budge. Not even a gazillimeter.

Rudy rounded up a group of toy soldiers and found a nice box for them. He set it down next to the paddle ball.

Rinse and repeat.

My father shook his head. "At that rate, you could be here ten years and you won't have enough toys to get me past Nova Scotia."

273

"You know what? People have been blaming me for stuff I didn't do for a long time now. There's no way I'm taking the heat for Christmas not happening. I know what it feels like for a little kid to lose that. Believe me. If one of these toys makes one kid happy, I'll have done more than you."

So there *was* more to Rudy Tutti than met the eye. When he first told me of his sad Christmas loss, I sympathized with him turning his back on the profound joy of giving. But in all his Scroogery, he never really hated Christmas to begin with. He didn't want it for himself anymore, but he wasn't ready to see others deprived of it. I'm convinced he would have put on Daddy's red suit and grown a beard if he thought it would help.

If Rudy and Christmas could inhabit the same world, maybe Daddy could see what I saw in Rudy.

"What makes you think I'd ever deliver a toy made by you?" Daddy shot back coldly.

"What's your plan B? Gift cards for the whole world?"

I turned my back on both of them and fished a fragile Barbie from a sea of plastic figurines. Rudy and my dad tracked my every move as I found her a nice ensemble and combed her hair, then introduced her to Rudy's toy soldiers.

Rudy and I exchanged a glance of truce and went to work.

Daddy shuffled to his office, calling back to us, "You kids have fun. I think I'll look into that gift-card idea. Ho-ho-ho."

It didn't take us long to discover how right he was to think us ridiculous. If the world could fit in a football stadium, we wouldn't have ended up with enough presents to give to just one of the teams, let alone all the spectators in the stands. Not in two days. Not with just the two of us.

But, as the cleverest amongst you have already deduced— since Daddy never missed your house, not in that or any other year—we did get help.

thirty-nine

From T.G.I. Fruitcake to North Pole High, not a creature was stirring, and I'll tell you why. Within an hour, all over the land, the Poleans gathered to lend us a hand. First, Chefy arrived to help and assist. "No more rhyming, my child," he had to insist.

But seriously, even thinking about it now, my Christmas Spirit rejuvenates so. Frostbite had spread the word and the whole town shut down to pitch in. While you were all busy preparing to travel home to be with your families, or dressing your goose for your Christmas feast, or luring your pretty co-worker to the mistletoe at your Secret Santa office party, every man, woman, and bear in the Arctic Circle was filing into the greatest toy-making plant in the world, which until then had been the exclusive province of Elves' Equity, Local 1225.

Believe it or not, even though we lived it 25/7, we sometimes took Christmas for granted. As if it happened all by itself—the elves took care of this, Daddy took care of that, and we never had to worry about any of it. We'd sing and play and enjoy it all.

Not this time.

And without the slightest bit of grousing or finger-pointing, everyone merrily chipped in. I nominated Rudy to direct us, and who would argue with a Claus at a time like this? Mr. Polar Bear took a giant push broom and swept the elves to one corner, the puffins to another, getting the useless helpers out of our way. Snowflake and Silentnight let their love flow onto an assembly line of pretty little dollies and movie-star doll houses. The Toboggan brothers made tricked-out race cars for boys. Frostbite led a team of his fifth-grade classmates in manufacturing Nerf balls and weapons.

Everybody had a job to do. Delicious made board games. Sugarcookie made trampolines and slides. Cookiejar made jacks and model-airplane kits. Chefy made snacks and distributed them every time the T-C meter rose a full percentage, which kept us super motivated through those long and arduous hours.

Kanye North snapped together a toy drum kit and started beating out a pa-rum-pa-pum-pum. Our little drummer DJ gradually rum-pa-pum-pumped up the tempo while we labored to his rhythm, faster and faster, until it no longer felt like work. Soon we were moving and grooving to his hip-hop beats, striving to reach those one-percent treats.

In truth, however, it already felt like we'd completed a marathon when we were barely at three percent. Some of the elves started to recover from their megatoe hangnails and were able to function well enough to help move the completed toys to the delivery area. I put Tinsel to work in gift wrapping, his specialty, with Vixen assisting him.

Three-and-a-half-percent complete. The Workshop hummed, and still it seemed we were getting nowhere. My friends Crystal and Holly and Starry Knight slaved away in electronic toys. Ginger and Sundae and Marsha Mellow handled books and movies and other media products. Their boyfriends Clarence, Gimbel, and Douglas Fir took care of sporting goods. The butcher, the baker, the candlestick maker—all were giving one hundred and ten percent.

But one soul in town was not helping out, for he had been given the order to pack all his belongings. And that was precisely what Dr. Tutti was doing at a time when Rudy and I needed all the help we could get.

I wouldn't say we were running a sweatshop, but it was getting pretty hot fudge in there. At the four-percent T-C break, I wiped the stickiness off my brow with the back of my hand, then bunched my hair up in a pony tail. We allowed ourselves only a minute to scarf down Chefy's peanut-butter-and-jelly-bean panini melts, then went right back to work.

Rudy rode himself like a sled dog, loading boxes onto pallets for Sparkle the Elf to forklift over to receiving. He stripped down to his T-shirt and I felt a little woozy at the sight of his rugged physique. He saw me staring at him. I must have looked like a stalker. He immediately looked away and found some other work to busy himself with.

I wanted to follow him, to try to explain why I'd stopped believing in him. But I didn't have a good explanation. Daddy had tricked me. Maybe part of me had wanted to believe those lies. Maybe I blew it and the best I could hope for was that we could at least be friends after this fiasco was over. So I wanted to tell him that, to walk up to him and make him listen to me, make him not hate me forever, when someone tapped me on the shoulder.

Rudy's father. He'd just arrived, his cheeks still pink from the blistering cold outside. He wore a long black overcoat with a tweed hat held in place by a pair of gray, fur-lined earmuffs and a wool scarf wrapped snugly around his neck. He slid his fingers out of his thick gloves and asked in a mixed tone of regret, defeat, and anxiety, "Will you take me to your father's office?"

He pretended not to register Rudy's plain-as-day presence ten feet away, his son giving back the same conspicuous disregard. Sugar Plum was at Dr. Tutti's side. I almost didn't recognize her—I'd never seen her frown before. She looked at Rudy and shook her head the way she must have seen her boss do a hundred times by now whenever he talked about his disappointing son.

I escorted them up to Daddy's office. The tall back of his big leather chair faced us through the open door, angled so that I could make out the corner of his elbow on the armrest and a small silver picture frame in his hand. I knew exactly which picture was in that frame. The same one I had on my dresser: a happier little Candycane in her daddy's lap.

Mom tended to the Snow Angel, applying grape shaved ice to the disabled fairy's injuries as she lay motionless across Daddy's plush plum-colored couch.

"Is she going to be okay?" I asked.

My father spun around in his chair. For a second, I saw a flash of the normal Daddy, happy to see his little princess, half-rising to his feet. But he caught himself when he saw who I'd brought with me. He humped back onto his cushiony seat with a glower.

"She'll be as good as new," my mother answered. "Some day. The next time she's needed, that is. Her spells for this visit are over, I'm afraid."

Dr. Tutti cleared his throat and removed his hat as if he were addressing a judge. "Mr. Claus? Before you say anything, I take full responsibility for whatever trouble my son has caused."

After a measured silence, Daddy spoke. "I think that I shall never see one boy more destructive than Rudy Tutti."

Sugar Plum looked as though she'd swallowed a thought that was dying to bust out of her. I gave her a nudge and she cracked wide open. "It's like this, Santa. I've gotten to know this man and he's a good, kind, decent man and he does his best to raise his child to be the same and it's not easy as you well know…" She screeched and derailed as Daddy stood and folded his arms. "Uh, what if we started one of those foreign exchange programs at the high school? We could unload Rudy on the South Pole and Dr. Tutti could stay here. I'm sure there's a nice penguin down below that Chefy would like to see again. Who knows? Maybe there could be a Mrs. Chefy one day. Ooh, and think of the feast we'll have! Mouthwatering coconut pheasant covered in roasted jujubes and calling-bird soup with rice pudding and—"

"Oh, good heavens," my mother said. "Whatever would we want to send Rudy away for, my dear Miss Sugar Plum? Rudy is a sweet, sweet boy. No, the reason I summoned the two of you here is to see if you can do something about my husband's incessant toothache."

"*What?*" Daddy's face turned as red as his suit. He'd been blindsided. His anger caused him to grind his teeth, which made him scream in agony.

I bit my lip to suppress my amusement. I could have left then, since they weren't arguing about banishing Rudy anymore. But this would be too much fun to miss.

Relief dripped from Dr. Tutti's pores. "A toothache? Let's have a look."

Daddy clenched his lips tight as the dentist approached. "Get away!" he murmured like a bratty child.

"Come on, Santa, be a good little boy," Sugar Plum said.

Mom snuck up behind him. She yanked on his whiskers, prying open his mouth long enough for Dr. Tutti to squint inside and see whatever he needed to see.

"A-ha! It's his wisdom teeth," he deduced. "Mandibular seventeen needs to come out right away."

"No, *you* need to get out right away!" Daddy shouted.

"Stop being a baby," Mom chastised him. "If the doctor says the tooth has to come out, it's coming out."

"Are you out of your mind? With Christmas hanging over our heads the way it is?"

"You don't even care about Christmas anymore!" I yelled at him. "*Rudy's* doing all the work." His glare made me blanch. I ducked, afraid he might leap over his desk and strangle me.

"It really should come out now, darlin'," Sugar Plum advised. "Otherwise it'll decay and rot and fester and pretty soon you won't even be able to talk out of that side of your mouth anymore and you'll be all…" She sucked in one cheek and spoke all mumbly, "'Huh-huh-huh, liddle baw, whadoyou wan for Rismas hiss year?'" She popped her cheek back out and continued, "Dr. Tutti's done this a million times. I've seen him do it. He's really good. You have nothing to be afraid of. And…" She trailed off, bracing for another jolly outburst.

"Too bad, Sugar Plum. You see, the doctor doesn't have time for this now—because he's been *banished*. Or haven't you heard? Perhaps you'd like to be banished with him? Is that what you're saying. Because I can certainly arrange that! Now both of yo—oowwwww!" He grabbed his cheek like it was falling off.

Poor Daddy. LOL.

"Now will be fine," my mother said, pushing him back in his chair. "I always say, there's no time like the present—like a Christmas present!"

Dr. Tutti approached the desk. "Mr. Claus, I promise, you won't feel a thing."

Daddy's inhuman yowl a minute later caused a hush in the constant din of cooperation two floors below us. The hammering of mass toy assembly started up again just as quickly, the villagers too wrapped up in the dire circumstances of their task—or just plain too afraid—to appease their curiosity and run up to check on the well-being of Santa Claus.

Daddy never would have lived it down if they had. The dentist hadn't touched him yet. He didn't even have his tools with him. Sugar Plum went to fetch a black bag from the car while Dr. Tutti reassured Daddy the procedure would be no more painful than getting a haircut.

Right.

Dr. T took off his coat and went to the bathroom to scrub up. When he came back and snapped on his rubber gloves, Mom had to literally put Daddy in a headlock to keep him from running away.

"Open wide, Santa," Dr. Tutti said while Daddy squirmed and fidgeted like a puffin about to get his wings clipped. The doctor dug into his mouth and bantered, "So the bicuspid said to the wisdom tooth, 'What's the molar?'" And by the time he started to laugh at his own stupid pun, he had extracted Daddy's oral enemy like a magician pulling a coin from a child's ear. Just like that. Then he presented the tooth-shaped quarter to his patient and said, "There you go, Mr. Claus. Good as new. How does it feel?"

"That was it?"

"Told you."

Sugar Plum held up a candied apple she happened to have in her purse. "Go ahead, test it out."

Daddy took a cautious bite. The sweetness hit him first. Then he started to chew. We watched as if we had X-ray eyes that could follow the juicy apple bits shifting slowly to the other side of his mouth. He applied the smallest amount of pressure at first. Then before he knew it, he was chewing like normal. Soon a smile blossomed, like he hadn't smiled in a year, like he just remembered how.

"I can chew again!" he said, elated, after he swallowed. "On both sides!" He took another bite of the delicious candy-coated apple as if it had been delivered from heaven. "I don't know how you did that."

"It's what I do." Dr. Tutti's cheeks rose as he rolled off his rubber gloves. "You think the North Pole cornered the market in magic? I've spent years honing my own brand. Dental magic."

"You need to trust me more," Mom said. "Why do you think I hand-picked Dr. Tutti, out of all the dentists in the world, to come here? Did you think I just posted an ad on Craigslist?"

Mom never took enough credit for being the brains behind Daddy's work, for keeping the whole operation going year after year, so it was easy for Daddy to forget. Maybe he wouldn't remember next time, but I sure would. My mom *rocks!*

"Look, I know you've got a lot of work to do here," Dr. Tutti said. "I'll get out of your hair."

"We could use your help downstairs, sir," I said.

He looked at Sugar Plum. They both nodded, eagerly putting themselves at my disposal.

"Hey, Tutti." Daddy stopped us just as we reached the door, the weight of a thousand reindeer off his chest. "About your kid…" That the banishment was canceled need not be spoken.

"I really am sorry," Rudy's father apologized again. "I'll let him have it this time. You'll see. He'll be a changed kid."

I almost went off on them all about how Rudy wasn't the one who needed to change, when my dad said, "Just promise me one thing, Doc. Go easy on him."

The two dads grinned, a slight nod of respect passing between them, filling my heart with a warm cup of brown sugar and thick, lathery egg cream.

I took Dr. Tutti and his hygienist downstairs and put them

to work in stuffed animals. I couldn't wait to tell Rudy about his father's incredible magic trick. But he was working so hard, so determined to save Christmas, I didn't have the heart to stop him. We couldn't afford even the smallest time suck. With more than a billion toys left to make, we weren't out of the snickerdoodle yet.

forty

The Days-Until-Christmas gauge flashed a proud and gaudy numeral *1* that triggered a motor that rotated a drum that struck a row of pins against a comb that set off the chimes that played the melody that went with the familiar line that started, *"On the first day of Christmas, my true love gave to me…"*

One whole day down, one whole day left. I dared a glance at the Toys-Completed gauge. Forty-eight percent. Just short of halfway there. No time to pat ourselves on the back for our amazing achievement. At that rate we were destined to fall shy of our goal. Already slowing down, sneaking catnaps, needing to switch jobs every few hours to keep from going out of our minds from the rote drudgery of making the same toy over and over, it seemed highly unlikely we'd be able to keep up the first day's pace for another day.

The Last-Day bell brought Daddy out of his cave for the first time since Project Rednose—as we had dubbed it in honor of our fearless leader—had begun. Daddy walked the floor handing out compliments and Merry Christmases as if he somehow had something to do with our success.

But he hadn't crawled out of hiding to steal credit from Rudy. He came looking for me. "Looks like we might actually make it," he said. "Thanks to you and your—" he had trouble getting the word out "—*boyfriend*."

"Yeah, well, you got your other wish, too, Daddy. I don't think he wants to be my boyfriend anymore. Happy?"

The forklift tooted "Merrily We Roll Along" to nudge us out of its path. Happy the Elf sat behind the wheel now, having taken over from Presto the Elf, who'd started when Sparkle's shift had ended.

Daddy led me to a quiet area out of everyone's way, over by the double doors that opened out to the rest of the Workshop. Frostbite whizzed by us, making room for more finished toys by helping Flip and Flop usher their useless puffin friends outside as they began to awaken.

"I wanted to show you something," Daddy said. "Hold out your hand." He pressed a small object into my palm. One of those little candy hearts, the kind you get on Valentine's Day that have little messages written on them. This one was green. "Read it," he said.

I had to flip it over with my fingernail. Red lettering, in all capitals, read: CHECK RUDY TWICE.

"This isn't a good time, Dad." I whipped the lump of colored sugar and high-fructose corn syrup at his flabby chest, refusing to take any more of his anti-Rudy poison. "We're kind of in the middle of saving Christmas for you."

"Sweetheart, wait."

I tried to keep walking, a tear streaming down my face, but a pounding in my head made me turn back and call him out once and for all. "You lied to me, Daddy. Your List said he lied to his *parents*—plural—when he was eleven. His mother died when he was ten. How do you explain that? Huh? And guess what else, Dad. I saw the Christmas present you gave him that year. How did that happen if he was *born* on the Naughty List?"

"Let me explain." Daddy bent down to pick up the little green heart off the floor—not an easy task, considering his girth. He had to lean on me to pull himself back up. "This was in my jelly beans. In the den at home. When I got back from the mall tour. I almost chipped a tooth on it. Who mixes Valentine's candy with Christmas candy? Disgusting..." His jealous rant over that other holiday-of-love trailed off when he saw me fold my arms impatiently. "The point is, somebody wanted me to find this."

I crinkled my eyes. What was he getting at? Maybe I was too sleep-deprived to think straight.

"Goody, they found it!" Flip said as he and Flop flipped by.

"What a clever game," said Flop.

Frostbite shushed them both.

"Frostbite, do you know something about this?" Daddy said.

Frostbite stared at his boots again. His face turned white. Just when he thought he'd gotten away with his ill-conceived plan to speed up the elves, we had stumbled upon another of his secretive, mischievous deeds.

Flip and Flop encouraged him to come clean.

"Tell them, Frostbite."

"Go on, Frostbite. You did it right. Just like you were told."

I took the piece of candy from my father's open paw and thrust it in my little brother's face. "Frostbite, who gave you this heart?"

"Nobody," he said.

"No, that wasn't his name," said Flip.

"It was Tinker," guessed Flop.

"No, it was Tonka."

"No, it was that funny-looking fellow. That half-elf."

"You mean Tinsel?" I said, pointing out my dastardly ex behind a pile of wrapped presents he was juggling across the floor.

Flip and Flop bounced up and down and cheered, "That's it! That's him! I recognize those bells!"

The boxes crashed. Tinsel stared back at the five of us like a reindeer caught in the headlights of a 747. "What's everybody looking at?"

As we loomed toward him, a clearer picture of his deviousness took focus in my mind's eye. "You hacked into Daddy's computer. You knew I'd have to dump Rudy if he was N-Listed, so you put him there yourself."

"That's preposterous. Implausible. Impracticable. Unprovable." He squirmed. He sweated. He backpedaled. His green blood rushed to his nose, flushed his cheeks, and made the points of his ears twitch uncontrollably. He gave Frostbite the evil eye. "That little twerp is lying."

"I am not," Frostbite said. "I did what you told me to do. And that elfnip you sold me was 'toe!"

Everyone within earshot stopped working. Gasps and whispers spread throughout the enormous warehouse like a tsunami.

Tinsel had been behind breaking me and Rudy up *and* nearly ruining Christmas? You just never knew about some people. Simply by showing up in my life, Rudy had saved me from the lousiest boyfriend ever—as heroically as he had saved me from falling into the frozen water at the ice fields and being eaten by the Abominable Snowman.

The more I thought about it, the more I remembered thinking I'd caught a glimpse of Tinsel out of the corner of my eye, lurking at the drive-in that night. I suddenly visualized his grungy ticklers flicking Dasher's ears, spooking her into taking off, dragging the rest of the unsuspecting doe—and me and Rudy in the sleigh—behind her.

I felt so stupid and angry and humiliated and cheated and used. I wanted to scream. I wanted to make *him* scream.

So did Daddy. He went off again, grabbing the first elf who had the misfortune of wandering too close at the wrong moment. "You are responsible for this!" he shouted at Tinsel, shaking poor Winter the Elf high over his head, about to heave her at the frightened, shivering elfman.

Ready...

Tinsel tried to stutter his way out of the serious chocolate he was in. "I d-d-didn't know what the kid was up to. N-n-now let's not l-l-lose our heads over this."

Aim...

Winter covered her eyes. "For the love of stocking stuffers, Santa, *listen to him!*"

"Sweet jelly beans!" Chefy waddled in front of Daddy. "Haven't these elves been through enough?"

Winter nodded like a hopeful jackhammer. Daddy took a mental time-out to visit a happy place, then lowered the greatly relieved elf into Chefy's outstretched flippers, still glowering contemptuously at the larger guilty one.

"We'll take care of this," Flip volunteered. He and Flop whistled for their friends and a thick wave of puffins flew into the building like a swirling tornado of black and white feathers and fiery orange beaks.

Flop pointed at Tinsel and shouted, "Get him, boys!"

They swarmed the condemned elfman. Thousands of them. He screamed and pleaded for clemency, but had no way out. The flock carried him away, far, far away, and if the rumors are true, I wish I could have been there when they chained him up inside Yeti's glacier like Fay Wray, subjecting him to the longest, most abominable tickle torture ever imagined.

At least he got to laugh. The rest of us had to go right back to work. Eradicating the bad seed had driven everyone that much harder, a renewed determination to right the wrongs that rotten old Tinsel had foisted upon the innocent holiday season. The T-C gauge hit fifty percent. Step by step we were making progress.

Daddy stood as an anchor in the midst of a stormy sea of toymaking. I wanted to bring him a chair so I could bounce on his knee and tell him what I wanted for Christmas: a great big hug. Instead I grinned awkwardly at him until Happy the Elf crashed the fully loaded forklift into a stack of beautiful but fragile toy carousels.

Forty-nine point ninety-nine percent.

I rushed over to assess the damage. When I looked back, Daddy had disappeared.

The next few hours were a complete blur. The T-C gauge shot up to seventy percent, faster than I imagined possible. Everyone was tired and sweaty and hungry and overworked, but more and more of the elves were waking up now. They'd rub their eyes and stretch their tiny arms and legs, then jump right into whatever their normal jobs were.

The Snow Angel came to. Still a little groggy, she dragged herself downstairs holding onto my mother's arm for support. As she entered the work area, she yawned and shook herself, spraying the snow and ice off her wings.

I finally found Daddy in the transpo room—helping Rudy, if you can believe it. Daddy had gone to Rudy himself, fully acknowledging Rudy's leadership in Project Rednose. Rudy would tell him where his help was needed most and he'd do whatever the boy in charge said. That explained the sharp rise in productivity. My dad knows his stuff, and Rudy utilized him expertly.

At this point, they were loading an overstuffed, elephant-sized sack of presents onto the Shetland-pony-sized sleigh. Daddy barked out directions as they struggled to balance the toys just right. Rudy pushed his end too hard and Daddy fell off the other side, landing square on his butt. The two of them working together reminded me of Laurel and Hardy. I ran over to help Rudy hold the heavy bundle over his head before the weight of it crushed him to death.

The Snow Angel hovered over to Daddy to see if he was all right; fortunately he had plenty of natural padding where he'd fallen. "Do you wish me to take over?" the Snow Angel volunteered.

"I think I can handle it." Daddy picked himself up and dusted himself off. "How did you get here anyway?"

The Snow Angel rubbed the lump on her head, having trouble remembering. Daddy sent a puzzled look to my mother.

"Don't look at me," Mom answered with a raised eyebrow. "It's been some time since you and I have hit the snow."

He looked away, embarrassed. I imagined his cheeks flushing beneath all those white whiskers.

The Snow Angel recited with a giggle what had just come back to her, and what my father had already known once upon a time. "There is but one way I can be summoned. By a Claus in love."

A race began next to see which of the men in my life would be the slowest to comprehend the preeminent matters of my heart. Daddy got his first hint when he noticed my mother's wide grin as she gazed lovingly at me and Rudy huddled under that massive weight of toys. Our reflection in her spectacles practically had comic-strip hearts encircling our heads. Daddy turned his gaze our way and it seemed like an unbearable struggle for him to picture his precious little daughter frolicking in the snow with a boy the way he and Mom used to when they first fell in love. It probably didn't hit him until that very moment just how much Rudy meant to me. What did he think, that I'd caused all this trouble over a silly schoolgirl crush?

I felt the toys settle above my head as Rudy shifted his weight. A tad slower than Papa Claus, Rudy took his cue from my father's reaction the same way Daddy had required my mother's look to fully catch on. His beautiful blue eyes penetrated my soul, making time stand still as he interpreted the meaning of the Snow Angel's existence. "Love?" he finally said.

"Duh."

No wonder he was so dense, when 'duh' was the most romantic comeback I could think of. But now that it was out there, was he going to say it? That he loved me? Or should I say it first? I waited with literally the weight of the world on my shoulders.

"Candy," my father interrupted.

"Kinda busy here, Dad."

Daddy heaved the load of packages off our aching arms and up onto the sleigh's center of gravity, where it stayed perfectly still. "Can I talk to you for a minute?"

Oh, no. The cookies again. "Right now? In front of Rudy and everything?"

"This concerns him too." He pressed a warm hand against the back of my neck. "You once said you wanted the chance to make your own mistakes. Well, when you do, you'll also want the chance to fix them, if you can. Rudy being on the N-List, that was my mistake. I would very much like the chance to fix it."

"It's okay, Dad. We're good. It was Tinsel's doing. You had no way of knowing."

"No. But I was quick to believe what I wanted to believe."

I hung my head, recognizing my own rush to judgment in this possibly genetic flaw my father had just admitted to.

"I always check the List twice," he said. "I would have known if Rudy was on it."

"So you got bamboozled," Rudy said, collecting a fallen present. "Can we get back to work?"

"Not so fast, son. See, the funny thing is, you haven't been on the Naughty List *or* the Nice List in six years. And I know why."

"Drop it, night rider. I outgrew this stuff. That's all."

"Is that why you spent the last thirty-six hours rallying the whole town to help keep this 'stuff' going?"

"I don't need to listen to this." Rudy tossed aside the silver-bowed yellow box and started to walk away.

"*Rudy*," my father called him back in a sharp tone that acted like a magnet. "What you asked me for that Christmas was impossible."

"Thanks for the news flash, Grandpa." He balled his fists at his sides, itching to run anywhere where he didn't have to face what my father was saying. "You think I don't know that? I'm not still ten."

"A toy train was a lousy trade. I get it. There's only so much a man can do. Even Santa Claus. But I want to make it up to you now." He brushed his fingers lovingly through my hair and said, "Candycane is the most precious gift I have. She loves you. Take her to the Snow Ball. With my blessing."

I didn't know whether to jump or cry or sing. In all the commotion, I had actually forgotten about the Snow Ball. Most of us probably had. I wiggled in place so much it must have looked like I needed to pee.

Rudy was somewhat less enthused. The Snow Angel had to give him a little nudge—well, okay, it was more like a shove—toward me. He grimaced at her, then said to me, "I guess I'm not gonna get out of this now. So, do you wanna?"

I squealed and threw my arms around him and jumped up and down. I felt like I could fly to the Snow Ball on my own power, without the aid of a fairy or an angel or a reindeer or whatever.

I ran to my dad and leaped into his arms, wrapping him in the biggest hug I'd given him since the time I was five and he let me wear his hat for the very first time and it went all the way down to my chest. "You're the greatest dad in the whole wide world!"

"Ho-ho-ho. Now get out of here, and take your friends with you."

Daddy was right. If we hurried, we'd have just enough time to clean up and get dressed for the festivities. I couldn't wait to spread the word amongst the rest of the kids in the Workshop. I wanted to grab Rudy's hand and run with him all the way home. I gave my mom a big hug first.

"You kids have a good time," she said through tears of happiness—the best kind of tears there are.

"Aren't we forgetting something?" Rudy said.

Well, you know where *my* mind was. I planted my lips on his so hard I thought we might burst into flames. I loved him, and I didn't have to be afraid to show it anymore, not even in front of my parents. Nor did I have to care that it made Daddy cringe. He'd better get used to it. I intended to kiss Rudy a lot more.

"I meant…" Rudy said breathlessly when I let him pry himself away. He pointed to the meters on the wall to finish his thought.

Oh, yeah. What about Christmas?

The Snow Angel danced over to the sleigh and waved her wand in the air. "I am still in your service, Santa Claus."

Daddy plucked the wand from her fingers and told her, "You need to rest. The elves are back on their feet. We've been doing this for centuries. A few hundred million more toys in the next ten hours? I like the challenge. This job was starting to get dull."

"Are you sure?" She waited for Daddy to wave her off, then soared out the window with an echoey "Ta-ta!" dropping a trail of stardust behind that shrank the bag of toys to make room in the sleigh for the next load.

"I could have done that," Daddy bragged to the heavens.

"We'd better get going too," I said to Rudy.

"Just a minute. I still have something I want to get off my chest." He stepped up to my dad.

"Don't push your luck, kid," Daddy said.

For a full minute Rudy took in his twinkling eyes, his cherried nose, his rosy, dimpled cheeks, his droll little mouth turned up like a bow, and the beard on his chin as white as the snow. The whole legendary package right in front of him. And he smiled up at him and said, "Merry Christmas, Santa Claus!"

My father embraced him. Rudy let himself sink into the pillowy fur of his suit and I wouldn't have been surprised to have found a tear stain or two when he let go. Daddy patted him tenderly on the back and said, "Merry Christmas, Rudy. Merry Christmas, my son."

acknowledgments

There are so many people I must thank for their help with this book, from Miss Pandabaker, my ninth-grade English teacher, who read many drafts and provided invaluable notes, to Kindle the Elf, who worked overtime formatting the electronic versions.

I am, of course, indebted to my amazing family and my more amazing boyfriend, Rudy. They have selflessly put up with my many nights in front of the computer and were super supportive in allowing me to expose their stories in order to tell mine. I love them all sooo much. The same goes for Snowflake and all my friends at North Pole High.

I thank the truly awesome North Pole Police Department and the owners of the North Pole Drive-In for their leniency against my careless transgressions, and especially for dropping all charges against the always innocent Rudolph "Rudy" Tutti.

I can't say enough about how grateful I am to have Chefy to boost my morale whenever I need it, not to mention feeding me the tastiest dishes anywhere on earth. He's a penguin who will always be more than a lifelong friend to me.

Every Snow Ball is an event to treasure. In my freshman and sophomore years, my trees took home prizes for which I have since foolishly disqualified myself due to my impetuous behavior. There's no way to tell what my senior year Snow Ball has in store for me. But as far as I'm concerned, no moment in my life will ever be as perfect as the Snow Ball of my junior year.

I wore a floor-length white chiffon gown with delicate

pink candy-cane stripes. Snowflake went with a strapless mini in Christmas-tree green with snowflake patterns exquisitely embroidered onto the fabric. Delicious donned a heavenly chocolate-colored halter dress with mouthwatering banana ruffles down the middle. Sugarcookie was draped in a beautiful beaded, form-fitting, buttery-yellow satin-and-lace number designed to catch the blue and red spectra of all the stars in the sky to create a dazzling, ever-changing color-shifting effect.

The boys wore their usual tuxedos in black and silver and olive and mauve and peach and violet and lemon and cream, their greensleeves peeking out at the cuffs. Rudy wouldn't tell me where he got his and it still kills me not knowing how he pulled it off. It looked custom made but I don't know when he had the time, considering he had no intention of attending the ball until a scant few hours before it commenced.

He sported a tuxedo jacket and pants, both of deep crimson, with white fur lapels softer than any polar bear I'd ever met, and a thick black cummerbund. Shiny black leather boots adorned his feet and a candy-striped Santa hat covered his head. Silentnight made a few Oedipal jokes, but I thought Rudy looked smart and handsome. He'd found his Christmas Spirit and who could blame him wanting to show it off to the world? After all, it had been missing for quite some time.

The event was held, as it was every year, in the Tannenbaum Bowl, a natural outdoor amphitheater that resembled an inverted igloo. Even in the heart of our always-nighttime winters, the arena needed no artificial light, being sufficiently illuminated, moon or no moon, by the brilliant canopy of stars above and the natural lightbuds of the fir trees that ringed the perimeter of this tranquil gathering place.

Everyone had arrived well before the joyful caroling of the midnight bells rang out, when Silent pointed and shouted,

"Look, up in the sky!"

Rudy put his arm around me as the jingling sleighbells echoed through the night. He warmed me so, I wouldn't have known I was still in the North Pole if we hadn't been watching eight tiny reindeer in all their glory pulling Daddy through the wondrous Northern Lights. He seemed so far away already, yet we could hear him distinctly.

"Now, Dasher! Now, Dancer! Now, Prancer and Vixen! On, Comet! On, Cupid! On, Donner and Blitzen! To the top of the porch! To the top of the wall! Now dash away! Dash away! Dash away all! Ho! Ho! Ho!"

With Daddy officially out of the Circle, DJ Kanye North got the party started.

The Christmas tree projects from every grade in the North Pole School District had been transported to the festival for display and judging. Delicious and Snowflake had created a tree of sugar-coated snowflakes with all sorts of yummy, edible ornaments. Cookiejar and Silentnight turned in a tree made of dark chocolate chips and rainbow sprinkles with flickering lights in patterns of Orion, Andromeda, the Big Dipper, and other recognizable constellations. The tree that Sugarcookie and Johnny Toboggan had collaborated on spun and danced and beamed lasers onto its branches and ornaments and into the sky in wild, outrageous patterns. They were all incredible, as usual.

Rudy's candy-cane-train tree was there amongst them, but you could hardly see it. The others were all twenty footers; Rudy's barely reached above my waist. But I didn't care. It was still my favorite, and I gave him a big kiss for building it.

We weren't the only pair seen locking lips that night. While Mr. Polar Bear, Miss Pandabaker, and Queero the Flamboyantly Gay Polar Bear judged the trees from the senior class, Sugar

Plum dropped a couple foots of megatoe into Dr. Tutti's coffee. A few minutes later, the two chaperons were rolling in the snow like a couple of teenagers, unable to keep their hands off each other.

Just before the judges reached Rudy's tree, I rushed over to stick the Snow Angel's star on top of it for luck. I blew it a kiss and stood back as it magically blossomed to fifty feet tall.

I must point out, lest I be accused of cheating, that neither I nor Rudy benefited from this circumstance. Technically I had no tree at all entered in the pageant this year, having destroyed the one I made with Rudy and demolished the one I made with Tinsel. Mr. Polar Bear had already graded the second one, so I didn't flunk out, in case you were wondering. Rudy, on the other hand, had unofficially dropped out—he'd missed enough classes that he'd have to make up the year in summer school. So although he did build the most wonderful tree in the history of trees, his name could not officially be attached.

It did win first place. The blue ribbon went to Walter, his partner of record. Knowing he didn't have all that much to do with its design, Walter didn't feel right claiming a prize. Instead of an acceptance speech, he recited a poem he had composed that told the story of how this particular Christmas tree had been conceived.

So last, but not least, I thank Walter the Asthmatic Walrus for graciously allowing me to reprint in its entirety his North Pole High junior-year Christmas tree first-place acceptance speech. And so, without further ado...

A Rebel Without A Claus

'Twas the end of the school year
when, wouldn't you know,
They expelled Rudy Tutti.
He was caught selling 'toe.

His father was angry.
He paced back and forth.
"No school will take you.
We're moving up North!"

They packed their belongings
and moved right away.
They arrived at the Pole
on a one-horse open sleigh.

The most popular girl
at North Pole High
Was Candycane Claus,
and Tinsel's her guy.

"You study with Rudy,"
Mr. Polar Bear said,
To which Candy replied,
"I would rather be dead."

Then Candy and Tinsel
went off seeking thrills.
In their Snow Pods, they raced
across Butterscotch Hills.

O'er in Eggnog Alley,
at an ice bar called "Rocks,"
Tinsel challenged his rival,
whom he could not outfox.

Rudy beat him so badly,
Candy finally saw it:
"Tinsel's yesterday's news;
Rudy's so hot chocolate!"

Now her friends, they all praised
Candy Claus for her pick.
Not so, with her daddy,
the grumpy Saint Nick.

Santa fumed as he vowed
to protect his young lass,
"If he touches my daughter,
I will kick Rudy's tush."

He grounded poor Candy.
She put up a fight.
When no one was looking,
she snuck out one night.

With Dasher and Dancer
and all of the others,
She took to the sky
and picked up her lover.

Her joyride with Rudy
did not go as planned;

They flew by the glacier
of the Abominable Snowman!

The monster awakened
and stomped through the town.
Then Rudy took over
and knocked Yeti down!

The hero was treated
to tasty delights:
Snow angels with Candy
under bright Northern Lights!

Then something magical happened.
'Twas nothing to fear,
When Candy and Rudy
became lighter than air.

The Angel they carved
in the snow and the ice
Lifted off with the children
as it came to life!

They flew on her wings
as she soared like a dove,
For this only happens
when a Claus finds true love.

Still Santa objected.
He fretted. He frowned.
He schemed to keep Candy
away from that hound.

As he plotted to part them,
his elves felt neglected.
Christmas Spirit was low.
Santa's lunacy wrecked it.

The toys were all broken.
They could not be fixed.
Christmas this year, it seemed,
would have to be nixed.

Disappointing the kids
of the world would be tragic.
Only one thing could help:
True Love's Angel's magic.

So Candy kissed Rudy
to summon the fairy,
Who flew through the workshop
and made the toys merry.

"Your boyfriend saved Christmas!"
Santa cried with delight.
"It seems I misjudged him.
Rudy Tutti's all right."

He gave them his blessing
to go out and have fun.
"Merry Christmas, my children.
Have her home by one."

ABOUT THE AUTHOR

Candace Jane Kringle is a junior at North Pole High. She likes candy canes, unicorn races, and making snow angels. Her father is the most well-known and beloved toymaker and distributor in the world. Her memoir, *North Pole High: A Rebel Without a Claus*, is her first book. After high school, she plans to enroll at North Pole University and write more books.

WWW.NORTHPOLEHIGH.COM

Made in the USA
San Bernardino, CA
16 September 2016